OUTSTANDING PRAISE
FOR CASEY SHERMAN

SEARCH FOR THE STRANGLER
(Originally published as *A Rose for Mary*)

"A Passionate, intimate look (at the Boston Strangler case) ... Dramatic."
—*The Boston Herald*

"Rich in detail ... compelling ... chillingly realistic. Exhaustively researched, this is a must-read for true crime aficionados."
—*Booklist*

"Substantial.... Valuable."
—*Kirkus Reviews*

"Nobel Prize-winning writer and erstwhile law student Gabriel Garcia Marquez once wrote, "Justice limps along, but it gets there all the same." In the case of the Boston Strangler, justice took forty years to arrive. That it's here at all, we can part thank Casey Sherman, whose fascinating *A Rose for Mary* recounts his ten-year odyssey to find his aunt's true killer."
—*Northeastern University Magazine*

"The author makes a compelling argument for reopening the case."
—*The Improper Bostonian*

"Casey Sherman has written a penetrating, incisive book that manages to avoid the mawkish sentimentality one would expect from such a personal perspective of so mammoth a tragedy. It is also a model of investigative reporting, raising deeply unsettling questions about the true identity of the Boston Strangler, questions, ultimately, that turned my blood to ice."

—*Dennis Lehane,* author of *Mystic River*

"A compelling contribution. Sherman's book fits right into another important journalistic tradition—that of looking back at a long accepted version of an event and digging for the deeper truth. He debunks the myth surrounding (Albert) DeSalvo and the popular version of the Boston Strangler and, in so doing, has made a valuable contribution in correcting a city's understanding of its past. This is no small feat."

—*Dick Lehr,* author of *Black Mass*

"This is a chilling book, and not for the fainthearted! We will welcome more books by this very talented writer."

—*Ann Rule,* author of *The Stranger Beside Me*

BLACK
IRISH

BLACK IRISH

A NOVEL

CASEY SHERMAN

iUniverse, Inc.
New York Lincoln Shanghai

BLACK IRISH

Copyright © 2007 by Casey Sherman

iUniverse books may be ordered through booksellers or by contacting:

iUniverse
2021 Pine Lake Road, Suite 100
Lincoln, NE 68512
www.iuniverse.com
1-800-Authors (1-800-288-4677)

This is a work of fiction. All of the characters, names, incidents, organizations, and dialogue in this novel are either the products of the author's imagination or are used fictitiously.

ISBN-13: 978-0-595-43080-2 (pbk)
ISBN-13: 978-0-595-87421-7 (ebk)
ISBN-10: 0-595-43080-5 (pbk)
ISBN-10: 0-595-87421-5 (ebk)

Printed in the United States of America

Come all you young rebels and list while I sing,
For the love of one's country is a terrible thing. It banishes fear with the spread of a
flame, and makes us all part of the Patriot Game.

—Dominic Behan

For Laura, Bella & Mia

CHAPTER 1

LONDON, ENGLAND

She let out a giggle as her lover stumbled in the darkness. He was trying to remove his Italian leather shoes but four tall glasses of Scotch had turned this simple chore into a comedy of errors. He pushed and pulled and tripped over himself as she continued her high pitched laughter on the bed.

"Bloody hell," he chuckled as he shimmied the heal of the calf leather Roberto Cavalli off his left foot. The shoe felt as tight as a ski boot and his throbbing toes were begging for mercy. He pulled hard with both hands and finally achieved success. The right shoe came off next with the same level of difficulty. Italian leather shoes were designed for slender male models; not strapping men like him. Once he finally managed to get both shoes off, he kicked them across the room and lifted his arms like some conquering hero.

She clapped her hands and cheered. "Bravo, bravo!"

His black pleated pants and boxer shorts came off next. This time, he had no problems. He noticed her supple breasts glowing in the moonlight and was focused now on the task at hand.

He stood before her completely naked with his hands on his hips. He saw the hunger in her eyes and could hardly blame her. He was fifty-five years old and graying at the temples, but thanks to rigorous exercise, Charles Geoffrey still felt like the twenty-eight-year old SAS commando he had once been. His young lover certainly approved. She got up on her hands and knees and crawled around the large brass bed like a tiger circling its prey. She tempted him with a soft purr, but he just stood there waiting for his erection to take hold. She had told him many times not to be embarrassed about his condition and he wasn't. He only reminded her that all good things came to those who waited. *Any time now Captain,* he thought. *Captain* was a nickname he had given his penis. It was an organ that had served him well in the past, but it was times like this that he thought seriously of demoting the selfish prick. Soon, the *Captain* began to show some signs of life as she continued to bait him. "I want you so badly darling," she panted. Her luscious red hair spilled over her shoulders and her creamy skin made his mouth water. He felt like a starving man getting his first look at a steaming hot meal.

Theirs was a forbidden romance built largely around interludes like this one. She was the wife of a prominent barrister; he was an aging adventurer who now spent his days arguing with other aging white men in the great halls of the British Parliament. They both had come from a black tie affair at the Royal Opera House. It was the London premiere of the Broadway smash hit *The Lion King* and both had gone to the show alone. She was a patron of the arts. Her workaholic husband encouraged the hobby. It kept her in the society columns and out of his thinning hair. Her husband had not attended the night's performance. He was locked away in his legal office poring over briefs pertaining to his latest high profile case. His young wife liked it better that way. The slender red head was completely captivated by the distinguished rogue standing in front of her. Charles Geoffrey was a born again bachelor after having suffered through three rather expensive divorces. He was a bad boy and she liked bad boys.

"Come taste me, Charles," she purred.

He walked slowly toward her, his rigid penis leading the way like a divining rod in search of water. He lay down beside her, his naked body cooled by the touch of the white satin sheets. His strong hands traced the soft curves of her skin, his lips soon covering hers. They could feel the wetness as their tongues explored. She moaned as he kissed his way down her neck toward her breasts, rubbing them, sucking on them hungrily getting her pink nipples firm to the touch. He then slid his tongue across her stomach toward her navel. Charles Geoffrey could feel the heat building from deep within her. He moved down her body and between her legs where he began to lick small circles around her inner thighs. The feel of his tongue made her squeal with delight. He could smell her but now he must taste her. He lowered his tongue onto her mound, wetness permeating his mouth. She lifted her hips to meet his face as he pushed deeper inside her. Her fingers ran through thick locks of his salt and pepper hair as he continued to fuck her with his tongue.

An intruder watched the love making from a few feet away, a silent witness to the seduction. He had been hiding in the closet for the past two hours waiting for the right moment to make his presence known. Michael Logan had hoped to confront Geoffrey alone, but fortunately he prepared himself for this very situation. He had killed many times before but this one would be like no other. Beads of sweat began to form under his mask in the deep creases of his forehead. As he stood and watched this heated dance between two hungry lovers, Logan felt waves of excitement and anxiety wash over him. He was not sexually aroused, although he could not help but notice the woman's beauty. He was nervous because he had been planning this night in his mind for decades. He just never thought it would be this simple. Geoffrey's security system had been surprisingly easy to breach and the man's backup alarm, a chocolate Labrador named Rufus was lying in his doggie bed still sleeping off the effects of a chunk of hamburger laced with Valium.

Logan opened the closet door slowly. A slight creak could not be heard over the woman's passionate moaning. Geoffrey was now on top of her, his bare buttocks thrusting up and down in rhythmic motion. The sound of the man's balls could be heard slapping against his lover's ass as he continued to pound her flesh. Logan opened the closet door a little wider and waited again. After several minutes, Geoffrey arched his back on the verge of climax. It was the moment both men had been waiting for. Seeing there was now enough separation between the Charles Geoffrey and his young lover, Logan extended his right arm and locked it at the elbow. He squeezed down on the trigger of his Walther P99 and fired. The silenced pistol made a slight hissing noise as the bullet struck Geoffrey behind his left ear.

"Fuck me, Charles! Fuck me!" his lover screamed oblivious to the attack. She dug her manicured fingernails into his buttocks.

"I'm coming, don't stop," she cried.

Suddenly, the thrusting halted and the redhead felt a warm liquid flowing down her right arm. "Charles?"

He did not answer.

She brought her hand up to her face. It looked pale in the moon glow except for the dark stream that extended from the tip of her wedding finger to her elbow. "Blood!" she screamed as she struggled to push his lifeless body off her own. "What's happening?"

"I'm sorry it had to be this way," said a voice in the darkness.

Her terrified eyes moved in the direction of the sound. She saw him standing in the moonlight dressed in black; a mask was covering his face.

Geoffrey's lover wanted to move but couldn't. She wanted to scream again but this time she was paralyzed by fear. *I'm going to die.* She closed her eyes as he approached her side of the bed. Suddenly she felt a sharp pain in her left arm and soon after the room began to spin. Seconds later, she saw only darkness.

"No innocent victims," Logan whispered to himself as he took the plunger out of her arm. He then retrieved a small photograph from inside the breast pocket of his black jacket. He pulled the mask off his head freeing his untamed black hair. He stared at the picture briefly while rubbing the whiskers on his weathered face. The black and white photo showed three young soldiers standing proudly in front of a large armored assault vehicle. The men were scowling through faces covered by dark grease paint. Someone had written *West Belfast, 1981* on the back of the picture. Logan flipped the photograph into the air and watched it fall onto the dead man's back. "And so it begins," he muttered as he opened the bedroom window and disappeared into the night.

CHAPTER 2

WEST BELFAST NORTHERN IRELAND—1981

"How long do we have to stand in this shite?" Eamon Logan asked still fighting an overpowering urge to vomit. The smell of raw sewage burned his nostrils and made him gag.

"We could be here an hour, we could be here a fucking week. It all depends on when the Brits bugger off," his companion whispered back.

Logan knew that he could not last much longer hunched over in the dark, dank sewer under Falls Road. He was freezing now and he was up to his waist in human waste. The young man began to shiver uncontrollably; his older companion could hear teeth chattering in the darkness.

"Keep it together boyo," the man whispered. "I know it's your first time down in the hole, but you done good today my son. The leadership will be proud."

Fuck the bloody leadership, Logan thought to himself. In his mind's eye he could still see the British soldiers they had just killed. Only minutes ago, the young man had been standing guard when his older partner lobbed a pipe bomb through the door of Darcy's Pub tearing the oak bar to shreds. The blast shattered the windows and knocked Logan to the ground. As he stumbled to his feet, he peered through the burning embers of wood and saw the scorched flesh of the military officers who had stopped at the pub for a late day pint. He could feel his companion tugging on his arm. "Let's get the fuck out of here," the man screamed. But instead of fleeing the scene, Logan walked forward pushing his way past wounded patrons as they ran out of the bar. He had to see for himself the hell he had just wrought.

One British soldier was killed on impact. He was the lucky one. His comrade lay semi-conscious under the splintered, smoking wood. His hands were frantically searching for legs that were no longer there.

"Oh God, what have I done?" Logan thought.

His more seasoned companion followed him into the pub and dragged him out by his collar and away from the blast. One block away, Logan could hear the sirens wail as the older man lifted a manhole cover and pushed him down into the bowels of the city.

"We'll be safe here," the man promised. The West Belfast sewer system was a convenient escape route for IRA men on the run. No one knew the shitter trail better than Logan's companion. It took them nearly two hours to make their way away from the bomb scene. The sloshing of their feet mixed with the sounds of scurrying rats and other creatures that Logan dared not think about. The older man led the way as the beam from his flashlight followed directions scrawled along the dank sewer walls. The IRA men who had come before had left the sewer system well marked with white chalk. The pair finally reached a cast iron ladder and began to climb. "I think it's okay now," the older man whispered. "I'll go out first. You wait five minutes and come out after me. We'll meet at Donovan's at eight o'clock."

Logan had already thrown up three times since entering the sewer and another five minutes felt like an eternity. *I could really use a smoke,* he thought. His companion read his face in the darkness. "Just wait here, and whatever you do don't light a match. There's enough methane gas down here to blow Belfast to kingdom fucking come," he warned.

Logan tried to be patient. He closed his green eyes and hummed a little ditty his mother, Evelyn used to sing around the tiny kitchen of their Belfast flat. "In Dublin's fair city, where the girls are so pretty I first set my eyes on sweet Molly Malone." He stopped before getting to the second verse of Cockles & Mussels.

His singing had attracted a gang of rodents that were quickly moving toward the sound. Only two minutes had passed since his companion had gone, but Logan could wait no more. He climbed out of the outfall pipe and reached the surface under Queen's Bridge. He looked to his right and then to his left and found himself completely alone. Logan paused for a moment as he let the clean air invade his lungs before tearing off his filthy clothes. He stripped down to his boxer shorts and felt the frigid February air bite at his bare skin.

He peeled off a plastic bag that had been taped around his waist and tore it open with his teeth. The package held a clean cotton shirt, jeans and sneakers. He made the quick change then slowly climbed his way up a hill and onto the street. It took him a few moments to get his bearings as to exactly where he was standing. Logan noticed two fair haired boys kicking a football hard against a brick wall. The wall was spray painted with the orange, white and green colors of the Irish Republic. Above the makeshift mural, someone had written, *Like the Patriots that have come before us, we will never give in.* The message was scrawled in blood red.

Logan recognized the mural and knew he was now just east of Queen's Bridge on Crumlin Road and only three blocks away from his brother's grocery store. To his left was the so-called Peace Line, a six-meter high wall that divided Catholics from the Protestants. The wall had been put up as a temporary measure in 1970. Built with corrugated steel and concrete, the Peace Line was covered with republican mottoes written in the ancient Celtic language. 'Tiocfaidh Ar La' *Our Day Will Come* and 'Caisc 1916' *Easter Rising 1916* provided Catholic residents daily reminders of their long struggle and fueled a deeper hatred of the British. Logan continued east to Sevastopol Street where he passed the modest headquarters of Sinn Fein, the political arm of the IRA. He then took a left onto Falls Road and continued walking.

Eamon Logan moved along confidently in his fresh set of clothes but there was no disguising the odor. He kept his distance from the other pedestrians, but feared they could still smell the shit that was now soaked into his pores. Lucky for him, no one walking on this stretch of road noticed it. Folks in this neighborhood only washed once a week anyway.

"Hold them like this," Patrick Logan advised. "Please don't drop them again," he pleaded with his young son, Michael who was struggling to carry a heavy crate of fresh lettuce and cabbage back inside the family's small grocery store.

"Why can't Vincent help," the boy nodded over at his twin brother.

"Because he needs to study for his entrance exams," his father reminded him. "The test to get into St. Mark's is just a week away."

Michael shot an angry glance at Vincent who was sitting at a small table in the back corner of the store. Their mother Ann was busy helping him with a complicated math problem. Vincent looked up from his notebook and stuck his tongue out when she wasn't looking.

"Why can't I go to St. Mark's too?" Michael asked his father.

"We've discussed this son," he replied. "St. Mark's is a seminary school. One priest in the family is enough. I thought you wanted to be a football star."

Michael shrugged and looked down at the heavy crate. "Then I should be out playing ball with the other lads instead of hauling cabbage in here."

Patrick Logan bent down and whispered in the boy's ear. "Michael, you're already the best player in the neighborhood. You've got the skills, but you'll need the strength if you want to go toe to toe with the real players."

"I don't understand, Da."

His father ran his hands down the boy's arms. "I promise you Michael, A few weeks of crate lifting and these arms are gonna be rock hard. It's all part of your training boy. You've got the makings of another Tommy Gemmel," Patrick said referring to the Celtic star that propelled his team to the European Cup in 1967.

"Have you seen my wheel kick lately? I can do it just like Pele," Michael boasted.

He glanced over to his left bicep and then to his right. "I betcha I'll be tearing open this shirt like the *Incredible Hulk*," he said loud enough for all to hear.

His mother waved a strand of gold hair away from her face and rolled her eyes.

"Patrick, what did I tell you about letting the boys read comic books?" she lectured her husband. "You know they just fill their heads with fanciful nonsense."

Patrick let out a hearty laugh. "My boy will be as strong as the *Hulk* and as fast as the *Flash.*"

"What about me, Da?" Vincent asked lifting his pencil.

"I don't remember reading about a hero called, *Super Priest,*" Michael teased him.

His father gave him a playful slap on the back of the head. "Be quiet you," he said before walking in Vincent's direction. The man reached down and lifted the boy off his chair and carried him around the room like *Superman*. The twins were 13 years old now, but their tall and muscular father could still pick them up like they were toddlers. Vincent giggled as his father whisked him across the room. Michael and their mother were soon laughing also.

"Vincent, from now on you'll be known as *Super Brain ... able to solve tough math problems in a single bound,*" his father predicted with dramatic flair.

"Put the boy down now Patrick," Ann called out as she rubbed her swollen belly. "You've got me laughing so hard, I may have the baby right here in the store."

Patrick set his son gently on his feet. "You're mother's right, there'll be no birthing of babies on the floor of my store. I'm a shop keeper not a doctor."

"You're the finest shop keeper in Belfast," Ann reminded him.

Her words were comforting but Patrick Logan knew that kind words were not enough to pay the bills. Business had been exceedingly slow since Bobby Sands and his men had gone on the blanket a month prior. Sands and the other IRA soldiers held at Long Kesh Prison had refused to wear the standard inmate's uniform arguing that they were not criminals at all, but prisoners of war. Instead of wearing a prisoner's uniform, they wrapped their bodies in woolen bed blankets. The prisoners were also refusing to leave their cells for anything, even a bathroom break. Instead, they defecated on the floor and then smeared their own feces along the concrete walls of their cells. If they were going to be treated like animals, the prisoners felt they should live that way. There was also a rumor among the prisoners' families that IRA Commander Bobby Sands was organizing a hunger strike. *What madness!* Patrick Logan thought. *How can a man raise a family in the midst of this chaos?*

"What do ya say we go to McNeill's for a bite of custard?" Patrick asked his family as he desperately tried to push the dark thoughts out of his mind. The question drew loud cheers from Michael and Vincent.

"I think the baby will want some too," Ann said with a grin.

"What'll it be mom?" Vincent asked with great curiosity.

"Well, it's not much of a kicker that's for sure," she told him. "Only the Lord truly knows but I have a feeling it'll be a girl."

Michael snickered. "Aw, Vincent was hoping for a boy so that he'd have someone *he* can push around."

Vincent ran over and punched his twin playfully on the shoulder and soon the two were wrestling on the floor. Michael had his brother pinned down when his father broke up the match.

"Fetch your coats, while I lock the cash register," he ordered.

The boys did as they were told. A loud rap at the front door startled the family.

"We're closed for God sake," Ann sighed as she made her way slowly to the door. She was nine months pregnant now and her doctor had urged her to get more bed rest. "It's probably Mrs. O'Sullivan," she told her husband. "I'll wager she's run out of her favorite tea."

Ann lifted the curtain and saw her brother-in-law staring back at her. His hair was wet and his eyes were wild.

"Eamon!" she gasped as she worked the locks quickly and ushered him inside.

"Jesus, Mary and Joseph! You smell awful! Where in God's name have you been?" she asked.

Eamon did not answer right away, he couldn't. He had been running for two blocks and needed a few seconds to catch his breath. He bent down and placed both hands on his knees. "Ann, Patrick, I'm sorry to bother you but I had no where else to go."

Ann rubbed Eamon's narrow shoulders but Patrick looked at his younger brother with growing suspicion. "You weren't involved in that business at Darcy's Pub? The bombing that I've been hearing about on the radio?" Patrick asked, yet confident that he already knew the answer.

"Oh Patrick, how could you even think such a thing?" Ann said while fetching a clean wool sweater out of the closet.

Whenever the two brothers had quarreled in the past, Ann would always defend her brother-in-law because she knew too well how stubborn her husband could be. At this moment, Eamon felt a deep pain in his heart. "Honestly, I didn't know it was going to happen," he explained. "I fell in with a group at university. We hated what the RUC boys were doing to lads our age, shooting at us with rubber bullets or even worse. So we decided to level the playing field. I was told that we were going to steal a truck load of guns, but the mission was changed at the last minute."

Patrick, the taller of the two brothers put his hands on his hips and said nothing. He looked into his wife's eyes and shook his head.

"Out! Out you go Eamon! You didn't join up with any civil rights group; you've sold your soul to the bloody IRA. How could you bring this violence into my store … into my family?"

Eamon looked at his pregnant sister-in-law and the twins and knew his older brother had been right, again.

"I'm sorry Paddy, I really didn't know that we were going to hurt those two men," he said with slumped shoulders turning to the door.

A loud bang on the door stopped him in his tracks.

"Open up, it's the police," came a commanding voice from the outside. "Open this door, or we'll break it the fuck down!"

Patrick froze, but his wife was quick thinking. "Let's get Eamon down stairs to the cooler. Now, let's go!" Ann Logan grabbed her brother-in-law by the arm and hurried to the cellar door, down the steps and into the dark basement.

Patrick Logan had to think and he had to think quickly.

"Da, they're trying to break down the door," Michael screamed to his father.

Wood was beginning to split along the doorframe with each thrust from the intruders outside. Patrick ran his trembling fingers along his bald head.

"State your business, my store is closed," he shouted marching swiftly to the door.

It was too late; in the next moment, another powerful thrust exploded the front door off its hinges. Vincent and Michael screamed in unison as three large men rushed into the store carrying Heckler & Koch MP5 submachine guns. They were dressed in black parachute pants and black sweaters. Each was wearing a dark hood to cover their menacing scowls.

"I demand to know the meaning of this!" Patrick yelled as he tried to block the men from entering his store. "I am a business owner and I do have rights. I demand to see some identification."

The three men did not acknowledge Patrick's presence. "Check the basement," One intruder barked from under his hood.

The second man pushed Patrick Logan aside and strode toward the cellar door. Young Michael Logan saw what was happening and dove at the man's legs with a loud roar coming from his lungs.

"No, Michael!" his father screamed.

The man picked the boy up by the collar of his cotton rugby shirt and flung him atop a candy rack, toppling it. A row of chocolate bars spilled out across the floor. Michael was sprawled out next to the scattered candy, his eyes were closed and a small trickle of blood began to drip from his pale forehead.

"You bastards," Patrick Logan screamed as he tried to claw at the man who had just hurt his son. But his strength was no match for the other two men who held him tightly by the arms. Vincent, now panicked with fear found a hiding spot under the checkout counter just below the cash register. He could not see what was happening in the store, but he could surely hear it. Ann Logan also heard the commotion and ran up the stairs. Her gaze spanned from the intruders to her bleeding child. She frantically moved her pregnant body over to the unconscious boy.

"Have you no mercy? He's just a boy," Ann cried.

She took out her kerchief and tried to stop the flow of blood which was now pouring from a deep gash on Michael's forehead. Meanwhile, the man who had thrown the boy was now making his way to the cellar steps.

"Alright, I'll come out. No more violence please," a voice pleaded from the darkness. Eamon Logan walked out of the cold storage room with his arms held high.

The intruder descended the steps casually and threw his automatic weapon over his shoulder. Seeing this, Eamon let out a sigh of relief.

No more running, he thought.

The hooded man smiled under his mask. He pulled a Browning High-Power 9mm semi-automatic pistol out of his side holster and shot Eamon Logan once in the forehead. His body crumbled to the floor. The man in black lowered his weapon and pulled the trigger once more exploding the back of Logan's skull like a melon. The spray of blood and pink brain matter turned the cellar floor into a macabre version of a Jackson Pollack painting. The killer took a moment to admire his work and then marched back up the stairs where he was met by an enraged pregnant woman screaming and pounding at his chest. With lightning reflexes, the man grabbed Ann Logan tightly by the wrists and jerked to the right sending her careening down the flight of stairs. The man in black walked over to Patrick Logan, still being held by his two comrades. The store owner was in hysterics now.

"I'll kill you, I'll fucking kill you," he cried out.

With one outstretched hand, Patrick lunged at the killer's head and tore off his dark hood. The man in black stepped back; raised his pistol once again and fired. Patrick Logan's screams ended with dead silence. The two men holding Logan's arms dropped him gently on the floor and ran for the door.

The man in black was in no hurry though. He stood calmly taking in the carnage he had wrought. The killer bent down in front of the dead man and was transfixed by the small hole in his skull and he didn't notice that young Michael Logan was coming to. The boy's brown eyes locked on the man kneeling before him. He was not wearing a hood now. Michael could see that the man had blond hair and a deep tan. The killer finally noticed the injured boy staring at him and slowly walked over. Michael Logan held his breath and closed his eyes, awaiting the inevitable.

"Look at me boy!" The man in black commanded as he knelt over the child. Michael's eyes opened slightly. "Get a good look at me boy, because I am *Hell* and *Hell* will come back for you one day!"

With that, the killer got up, stepped over Michael's dead father and walked breezily out the front door. Michael glanced over at his father's lifeless body but could not move. Suddenly he heard a faint whimper coming from behind the counter. He slowly made his way over and found his brother Vincent, curled up underneath the register. Vincent had wet himself. Michael bent down; hugged his twin and both began to cry.

CHAPTER 3

The Land Rover motored slowly toward the century old farmhouse thirty miles southeast of Londonderry in a tiny village called Lifford on the River Deele. The driver parked the vehicle beneath a row of large pine trees that were tucked behind thick brush. It would make the Land Rover impossible to spot from the road. The men in black exited the vehicle and crept toward the small farmhouse with weapons drawn. Faint crunching noises could be heard under their black combat boots as they walked over an inch of crusted snow. They could smell the burning peat from a plume of black smoke drifting upward from the chimney of the thatched roof cottage. *My informant was right,* the blond haired commando thought to himself. *This isn't an abandoned farm house after all.* Inside the cottage, three leaders from the IRA's West Belfast Brigade huddled around the warm fire taking stock of the day. "The attack at Darcy's Pub should put the fear of God in the Brits," Tommy McGee said before taking a hearty pull from his mug of Guinness. The frothy top soaked the heavy set man's wild red mustache.

The other two men nodded in agreement.

"It's a crying shame what they did to that family though," one added.

The trio paused as each made the sign of the cross.

McGee reflected for a moment and then continued. "It's a tragedy that's true," he said. "But it could also be a blessing. It will show the people what savages the British are. They should know that they'll never be safe while living on Irish soil." McGee shouted as he balled his beefy right hand into a tight fist.

The others nodded in agreement and raised their glasses.

"To the glorious cause," they cheered in unison.

The celebration was interrupted by a violent kick through the front door. McGee and his men immediately dropped their glasses and grabbed for their rifles. They were not quick enough. The blond assassin fired his Browning twice, hitting one of McGee's men in the throat, the other man above the left eye. The assassin's gun was now trained on McGee. The large IRA man raised his rifle, but the assassin intercepted the motion. He fired a single shot that tore through McGee's right shoulder. The IRA man screamed in pain and dropped his weapon.

"Don't fret princess," The blond assassin said with a smile. "I won't shoot you again." He pulled a large knife from a sheath that was tied around his waist. The assassin then walked over to the fire and ran the long steel blade back and forth over the flames. He stared into the hearth and began to speak. "We are the Knights of the Round Table. You will not be joining your fellow scum at Long Kesh Prison, and you will receive no pardon tonight princess. Look into my eyes. I am your executioner."

The assassin turned to Tommy McGee whose green eyes were wide with horror.

The two other commandos closed the cottage door and let their comrade go about his business. They had seen him flay a man once, and even these trained killers could not watch it again. The men stood guard in the cold night as Tommy McGee's screams echoed through the dark valley.

"What an awful, bloody tragedy. And the boys witnessed it all," Bridie O'Sullivan said as she pulled a picture of the Logan family from her mantel. The photo had been taken when the twins were just toddlers. The picture showed the smiling young parents with Michael and Vincent straddling their laps. Another tear began to stream down O'Sullivan's puffy cheek. She was a heavy-set woman with a pleasant face and wooly hair that she routinely turned up in a bun. O'Sullivan had lived next to the Logan family since the birth of their boys. The old woman had lost her husband in a car accident and had no children of her own. She acted as a surrogate grandmother to the twins. O'Sullivan had opened her two story flat for the throng of mourners following Patrick Logan's funeral. This gathering lacked any of the singing and dancing that usually accompanied an Irish wake. How could one celebrate Patrick Logan's life, with the knowledge of how he died? There had been enough excitement at his brother's funeral.

High-ranking members of the IRA had collected their comrade's body at St. Matthew's Church and continued in a mighty procession through the streets of

West Belfast toward Milltown Cemetery. Hundreds of mourners marched behind Eamon Logan's casket as they pushed past a heavily fortified police barracks at the gate of the graveyard. As was the custom, each pallbearer wore green fatigues and a dark mask, the un-official uniform of the Irish Republican Army. Logan's casket was draped with the green, white and orange colors of the Republic. His body would lie among several generations of fallen republicans. The first Fenians to be buried here had found themselves on the wrong end of a bullet during the Irish civil war of the 1920's. The Milltown Cemetery is exclusively Catholic, while the nearby City Cemetery is predominantly Protestant. Hundreds of Catholics are buried at City Cemetery, but they are kept separate from Protestant burial plots by an underground wall. In Northern Ireland, sectarianism follows you from one life to the next.

Although Eamon Logan only participated in one attack on the British crown, he was eulogized as a martyr and hero to the city's demoralized Catholics. After the priest finished his sermon, six masked gunmen fired a volley of shots over the casket. Many in the large crowd flinched at the loud noise. With the sound of gunshots still echoing through the cemetery, a tall skinny mourner with thick black hair broke from the crowd. Gerry Adams was a commander in the Londonderry Brigade. The bespectacled young man pulled a bullhorn from under his green fatigue jacket began to speak.

"We come here today to bury another brother. Eamon Logan lies next to Tommy McGee, Jackie Nolan and Finn Barry. These men were outspoken in their belief of a united Ireland, and they did so in a peaceful way."

Adams shifted the crowd's attention to the cemetery gates, where thirty heavily armed members of the Royal Ulster Constabulary force stood watching.

"Those men are the men of violence," Adams shouted as he pointed his finger toward the police. "Each has the blood of a republican on his hands. Let us not forget what happened to Pat and Ann Logan. Who will pay for that heinous crime?" Adams asked the mourners all of whom were now seething.

Constable John Somers watched as Gerry Adams continued to ignite the crowd. Somers was new to the job and he was scared. The twenty-three year old baby faced rookie had already endured a barrage of jokes that day about finally getting his "cherry popped." It was his first time standing out on the line. He looked down the row at his older battle tested comrades. To a man they advised him to show no mercy if the gathering dissolved into a riot. "You want to give those pogues something to remember for the next time," his RUC. commander had told him. *Just plant the bugger in the ground and go home peacefully,* Somers prayed. The rookie was equally disgusted by the attacks on Patrick and Ann Logan. There were rumors that it had been carried out by The Knights of the Round Table. This mysterious hit squad had been credited or blamed for several attacks on IRA soldiers and sympathizers. Many still thought the Knights were just a myth, created to scare the Catholics. But in truth, Protestants were also frightened by the squad's brutality.

Adams was still speaking when someone tossed a bottle from the crowd. The glass came down and shattered across the thick plastic shield covering Somers' face. Dazed, he stumbled backward from the line. Somers was struggling to stay on his feet while trying to clear his head when the first shots rang out. The constables opened fire on the mourners, spraying rubber bullets into the terrified crowd. Mothers clutched their screaming children as the bullets zipped past their heads. Men and women in black mourning attire pushed and pulled to get away from the line of fire.

Eamon Logan's pallbearers left his casket and took up position behind six Celtic gravestones. One by one, the IRA men fired back at police. The thirty R.U.C. officers were now joined by twenty more of their comrades. The constables charged through the cemetery gates, swinging their black metal shields at anyone foolish enough to get in the way. *Show no mercy.* John Somers watched in horror as a heavy-set constable swung his baton at a teenaged girl less than half his size. The girl fell to the ground after getting struck on the head, her face covered with her brown hair and blood. *This is insanity;* Somers wanted to scream out. As hundreds of funeral goers fled the scene, one mourner accidentally knocked over Eamon Logan's casket, which still had not been lowered into the ground. Logan's pale corpse spilled out of the pine box and onto the green grass of Milltown Cemetery.

CHAPTER 4

Bridie O'Sullivan praised God that she had had the foresight not to allow the boys to attend their uncle's funeral. Their father's service was much quieter.

O'Sullivan opened her home to Patrick's regular customers and friends from the neighborhood. The couple did not have an extended family. Both Patrick and Ann's parents were dead. This posed a major problem for the twins.

"Bridie, you're too old to care for the lads. What are you going to do?" Father O'Bannon asked. O'Bannon was the parish priest for St. Matthew's Church and had given Patrick Logan's funeral mass.

"Father, I can manage til their mother gets out of the hospital," Bridie promised with a hopeful tone in her voice.

"Ann Logan is lying in a coma," O'Bannon replied. "She lost her baby in the fall. The doctors say she may never come back to us."

"So much for the power of prayer," the old woman shot back.

The twins sat together on the staircase in the foyer of O'Sullivan's apartment. They were sharing sweets and listening intently to the conversation between the old woman and the priest.

"You see Vincent, Ma isn't coming for us. We're on our own," Michael whispered. He had suffered a concussion in the attack that left him with a two-inch scar on his forehead. At least there was now a way to tell the twins apart.

"Where will we go? I don't want to leave the neighborhood," Vincent said with worry in his young voice.

"Listen brother, as long as we're together, we'll be alright. I'll never let anything happen to you," Michael replied draping his arm around his twin. The boy was boasting to be sure. Inside, Michael did not know what would happen to either of them.

The food was gone, the coffee was cold and the mourners began filing out of O'Sullivan's apartment. The men patted the boys on the head, the women planted kisses on their cheeks as they said goodbye. Father O'Bannon stayed behind. He wanted to talk to the twins alone.

"Boys, come sit on the couch. I need to have a word," the priest ordered.

The Logan boys did as they were told.

"Mrs. O'Sullivan and I have been talking. We both think it's best that the two of you get out of Belfast and get your minds off of what happened to your parents. There is a school about an hour's drive east of here in a town called Greyabbey that will suit your needs."

The priest looked Vincent in the eyes, then Michael. "It's called Saint Christian's School for Boys. The school has a tremendous teaching staff and I also hear it's got a great football team." Father O'Bannon knew where the twins' passions lay.

Michael and Vincent nodded to the priest and then looked up at Mrs. O'Sullivan who immediately looked away. She was caught off guard by O'Bannon's comments. Bridie had not yet made up her mind to send the twins away, but she was a good Catholic and reluctantly agreed with her parish priest.

"It's for the best boys," she said staring out her living room window at the falling rain tapping against the glass pane. "At least until your mum is feeling better."

The Logan twins knew they would never see Mrs. O'Sullivan again.

That night, the boys slept in their bedroom for one last time. Michael clutched his pillow and gazed up at the ceiling of the room. "I wonder what Da's doing right now?" he whispered in the darkness.

Vincent could not hear the question over Mrs. O'Sullivan's loud snoring coming from the living room. "What'cha say?"

Michael repeated the question. Vincent sat up on his bed and shook his head. "Da's in heaven right now watching over us," he replied matter of fact.

"What if he's not Vincent? What if he's just lying in the ground? It could be like that lamp there," Michael theorized as he pointed to their dresser. "What if Da's light went out and there's just nothing left after that?" The boy could not get over the touch of his father's cold hands folded over his chest in the coffin. The hands that once gave hugs and playful slaps were now no more alive than a block of wood, they were unfeeling. There was nothing there.

"Of course there's a heaven," Vincent frowned.

"How do you know?" his brother pressed him.

"Because the priests and the nuns tell us it's so," Vincent replied weakly.

Michael clutched his pillow tighter in his fists. "What kind of God would take a man like Da away from his family?"

Vincent had no reply. The twins contemplated the question in silence until both fell asleep.

Father O'Bannon brought a car around the next morning. The boys crammed everything they could into the small suitcases their parents had owned. The brothers were trying desperately to hang onto the lives they once knew. Included in Vincent's luggage were his mother's tiny porcelain figurines of Joseph, Mary and the baby Jesus. Michael had packed his father's apron from their grocery store. Father O'Bannon pulled his tan station wagon up to Mrs. O'Sullivan's flat and grew agitated once he saw the suitcases.

"This won't do boys. I'm sorry, but you're gonna have to pack lighter than that," the priest said. "Just take one change of clothes, because you'll be issued uniforms at Saint Christian's."

Vincent began to unpack his suitcase but Michael did not move.

"I'm sorry Father, but I'm not leaving my parents things behind. If I have to go to this place, this suitcase comes with me," Michael said defiantly.

Father O'Bannon stood six-foot-two and was solidly built. He was not used to being spoken to this way, especially by a child. He wanted to scold the boy, but inside, O'Bannon admired young Michael Logan. The priest felt that the boy and his brother already had enough crosses to bear. "Alright son, take your bags and place them in the back. It's getting late and we should be shoving off."

O'Bannon opened the car door and slipped into the driver's seat. The twins placed their luggage in the back of the hatch and then filed into the backseat of the station wagon. Any other time and this would have been cause for some excitement. The Logan boys could count on their fingers how many times they had gotten to ride in an automobile. But they were now leaving their West Belfast neighborhood and everything they had ever known. The priest pulled the station wagon out onto Falls Road while the brothers sat silently in the back seat, staring out the windows.

They passed Porter's Pub, where their father had taught them to play darts and snooker. It was the one secret Da made them keep from their mother. The tan station wagon then rolled past Logan's Grocery where yellow crime scene tape was still draped over the front door. Michael and Vincent looked at each other, but neither said a word. Father O'Bannon casually glanced into his rear view mirror.

I can only imagine what must be going through their minds, the priest thought as he took a right turn onto Highway A20.

The road out of Belfast provided a whole new world for the Logan twins. Soon, the thick layer of city smoke was replaced by blue sky and the littered side walks gave way to rolling green hills. Living in West Belfast had been like living in a black and white film. Harsh weather and chimney smoke had dulled the colors of the city. Michael cracked his window and breathed in the cold, fresh air. About fifteen kilometers outside Belfast, Father O'Bannon pulled off at the front gate of a large estate.

"What do you say, we stretch our legs boys," he said as he opened the back-door of the station wagon.

"Where are we Father?" the inquisitive Vincent asked.

"Well son, this is the Mount Stewart House and Gardens," the priest replied staring up at the stately mansion. "She was built in the 18th century, but it's the gardens that make this place so special. Would you like to take a walk with me boys?"

"I would indeed," Vincent answered gleefully.

"I think I'd rather stay in the car," Michael replied kicking up a few inches of gravel from the parking lot.

"Alright then, Michael. I won't force you to come along. Vincent shall we go inside?"

The pair walked off through the garden gate. "Lady Edith Londonderry built these grand gardens," O'Bannon told Vincent as they both gazed at the elegant shrubbery. "They cover eighty five acres, if you can believe that. You'll see flowers and plants here that you've never seen before. Lady Edith had them imported from as far away as Australia."

Vincent nodded his head while trying to soak in the scenery. The boy stared at the Shamrock Garden, shaped like three clovers. Lady Edith had also created a Red Hand of Ulster from a collection of begonias and a topiary Irish harp. Even in this beautiful setting, there was a constant reminder that the northern counties of Ireland maintained separate identities. As they walked, the priest placed his hand on the boy's shoulder. "Son, what was done to your parents can never be undone," he told him. "The doctors say your mother, god bless her will never be well. That's why you should leave and never come back to West Belfast. Get your education and get as far away as you can. This tragedy has given you an opportunity to make something of yourself," Father O'Bannon pleaded, hoping his words would sink in. "You're a smart lad, Vincent. I have faith that you'll do the right thing. It's your brother that is troubling this priest's soul. He's got hate in his eyes. That hatred will only lead to his demise." Father O'Bannon bent down and put both arms on Vincent's shoulders. "Protect your brother," the priest ordered. "He's the tough one, but you Vincent are the smart one." The boy nodded his head but said nothing. O'Bannon mussed up Vincent's black hair and smiled. The blue skies were now covered by dark clouds and the rain began to fall. "Let's get back to the car, we've got a little ways to go yet," the older man said as he ushered the boy out of the garden.

CHAPTER 5

The three arrived a half hour later in Greyabbey, a small village named after the Cistercian Abbey that was founded there in 1193. Father O'Bannon took a slow drive down Main Street, which was lined with quaint, brightly painted antique shops huddled close together. The boys had only traveled 35 kilometers, but they were already light years away from West Belfast. Father O'Bannon stopped the station wagon in front of a small Tudor style restaurant called the Wildfowler Inn. "We still have about an hour to kill before the Franciscans will expect you at St. Christian's. What do you say we grab some lunch?" asked the priest. The twins nodded eagerly.

O'Bannon led them into the pub, which was filled to capacity with the noon-time crowd. The tall priest was forced to hunch over due to the wood beams that hung low from the ceiling. Copper jugs and ceramic tankards lined the walls of the Wildfowler. A young fiddle player sat in the corner and plucked his chords to the tune of *The Wild Colonial Boy*. Father O'Bannon called for the barmaid who was able to secure a snug in the back of the pub. They sat along the benches inside the snug and the priest inquired about menus. The young waitress pointed to a large chalkboard that hung over the bar.

"Order up boys, it's on me," O'Bannon said. "This old priest has managed to save a few schillings in his day," he added trying to lighten the mood.

The twins settled on dishes of bangers and mash and the priest ordered grilled salmon.

"Why do they hate us?" Michael asked while chewing on a bite of sausage.

The question startled O'Bannon because he had not heard the boy speak for more than an hour.

"I take it you're talking about the Protestants?" the priest replied with an arched eyebrow.

Michael shook his head yes.

"Well, there's enough hate on both sides. I can assure you of that. We've been throwing sticks and stones at one another for hundreds of years. First, King Henry II invaded and conquered Ireland back in the year 1171. Out manned and out financed, the Gaelic tribes continued to fight for generations to follow. The violence came to a head in 1690 when William of Orange defeated Catholic King James II at the Battle of the Boyne." O'Bannon explained.

Vincent was enthralled by the history lesson, since his own parents had rarely mentioned the Catholics' long struggle at home. Michael stared blankly at O'Bannon. He clearly was not interested in the past.

"Son, I guess I do not have a real answer for you," the priest confessed. "But I can tell you that your Da had no hate in his heart. In fact, he had several Protestant friends who lived across the Peace Line over on Shankill Road."

"Why is it then that my uncle is being treated like a hero? Michael asked. "Kids in the neighborhood say my Da should have done something more to protect us, that he should have had a gun in the store or something."

"You listen here young man!" the priest shouted while slamming his large fists on the wooden table. His loud voice caused heads to turn inside the smoky pub. O'Bannon lowered his voice to a whisper as he looked around the pub.

"Michael, your uncle Eamon Logan was no hero. He was a coward. His actions made orphans out of the children of two British soldiers. Your father did everything he could to steer you away from all that violence. Now he was a real hero."

The three of them sat silently for a few moments. They picked at their plates until finally Vincent spoke.

"Promise us you'll look after Mum," he pleaded to the priest.

"That's a promise," O'Bannon replied cutting into his salmon. "We should be able to sell the store and use that money to make sure your mother receives the best possible care."

Michael turned his head and stared blankly at the other patrons of the pub. "What was it?" he asked.

"I'm sorry?" the priest was confused.

Michael turned his head to Father O'Bannon. "What was it? Did my mum have a boy or a girl?"

"Does it really matter now?" the priest asked.

"It does to me," the boy replied.

O'Bannon lowered his head. "It was a girl," he muttered softly.

Silence hung over the snug. The boys didn't say a thing. Michael wiped a small tear from the corner of his eye as the anger built inside him.

The trio finished their lunch without a word and piled back into the station wagon and continued on to the school. St. Christian's is located on the northern part of town and was built in the shadow of the Grey Abbey ruins. The Cistercian Abbey was one of the oldest in Ireland. According to legend, the abbey was founded by a knight's wife to give thanks for a safe landing after a treacherous storm at sea. The church remained in use until the 18ᵗʰ century when generations of bad weather finally took their toll on the roof of the abbey. Franciscan monks, who also ran St. Christian's school, now cared for the site. Father O'Bannon drove the boys north of the village center to the site of the Grey Abbey ruins. Vincent and Michael both marveled at the view from the backseat of the station wagon.

"Oh, you'll get to know the abbey soon enough," the priest promised. "But right now, let's get the both of you checked into school."

Father O'Bannon parked the station wagon; walked to the back and popped the hatch. Michael and Vincent both climbed out of the automobile and stared up at their new home. The St. Christian's School for Boys comprised of three two-story buildings and a small parish. Unlike the Grey Abbey ruins, there was nothing beautiful about St. Christian's. With its brick and concrete facade, it looked more like a prison than an academic institution. O'Bannon noticed the solemn expressions on the faces of both brothers.

"There's a splendid football field around the back of the building," O'Bannon pointed out. "Plus, I hear it's got one heck of a science lab."

The priest ushered the boys inside the main building. About a dozen students dressed in white collared shirts and gray trousers filed past the twins on their way to class. "I think I'm seeing double," snickered one youth to a friend. "Yah, they look like a couple of circus freaks," the other replied.

"No talking in the halls!" bellowed a short, stout man in a robe. "Do not be late for your next class," he added with a wave of his pudgy finger. The friar's mood changed when he recognized Father O'Bannon.

"Father, it's good to see you again," Brother Mark said extending his hand.

"Praise be all here," O'Bannon replied with a firm handshake. "I'm here to drop off your two newest students. Boys, shake hands with brother Mark."

The twins offered their hands in a lukewarm gesture. "Welcome to St. Christian's," Brother Mark told them. "I've read your transcripts and I believe you will both fit in well here. You'll find this school both challenging and rewarding," he beamed with pride. Young Michael had seen enough salesmen sweet-talk his Da at the grocery store. He recognized a sales pitch when he saw it. *Relax, Brother Mark. We've got no other place to go,* he thought.

"I'll give the boys a tour of the grounds and then let them check into their dorm. They can begin their studies tomorrow," the monk told Father O'Bannon.

The priest looked at his watch. "I should be heading back to Belfast. I'm scheduled to give mass at five."

Before leaving, the priest huddled with the twins. With one long arm draped on each shoulder, Father O'Bannon looked into their eyes.

"Now remember what I told you. This school is offering you a chance that most boys from West Belfast will never receive. Please take advantage of it."

With that, the priest nodded to Brother Mark and strolled out the door. O'Bannon climbed into the station wagon and began the journey back to Belfast, back to the war zone. He watched the Grey Abbey ruins get smaller and smaller in his rear view mirror.

"God help me if I ever have to bury another Logan," O'Bannon muttered to himself as drove out of the village.

CHAPTER 6

Brother Mark led the boys down a wide hall; its walls were lined with oil paintings of the apostles.

"Father O'Bannon told me that you might be interested in the science lab, Vincent."

The friar turned right and opened the sturdy oak doors leading to the lab. There was a class in progress so Brother Mark spoke quietly.

"Through many donations, some even coming from America, we've been able to upgrade the lab with all the latest equipment."

Six large tables filled the room. At each table sat four students with their own beaker and microscope. Another friar was scribbling furiously at a stand-alone chalkboard.

"Sorry to disturb you, Brother Tobias. But may you explain what you're working on today?" Brother Mark asked.

The tall teacher had his back toward Brother Mark. He responded without taking his eyes off the chalkboard.

"Today, we are learning the science of dissection," Brother Tobias explained. "I am drawing a rudimentary diagram of a frog's anatomy. I do apologize to you and your guests Brother Mark, but my students need to focus on the task at hand. So if you'd be so kind." Brother Tobias turned and pointed his stick of chalk toward the door.

"Yes, yes … carry on then," Brother Mark replied as he ushered the twins out of the laboratory.

The friar looked sheepishly at Michael and Vincent. "Brother Tobias is an excellent teacher," Brother Mark informed the twins. "We are very lucky to have him. He's been with us for only two months, but he's already made quite a team of our football players," he added.

The twins looked at each other. Each knew what the other was thinking. *We're both going to have to deal with Brother Tobias.*

Brother Mark returned to his office and grabbed his wooden cane.

"Would you like to see the ruins?" he asked with a smile.

The boys nodded their heads and the friar led them out of the school building and across the street and up the grassy hill toward the historic site.

"The Latin name for this abbey is *Iugum Dei,* which means the Yoke of God," Brother Mark noted as he tried to catch his breath.

He was about forty pounds overweight and the walk up the rugged hill took its toll on his short frame. The friar continuously side stepped large rocks as he battled back a long strand of brown hair that kept falling over his forehead. Brother Mark did not consider himself a vain man, but he did take great pains in combing the side of his hair over the gaping bald spot on top of his head. The friar was a physical wreck but the abbey he stood before was a glorious work of art. Although it was built 800 years ago, the stone work was nearly perfect, as were its five lancet windows. The boys walked around to the south side of the ruins and came across two stone effigies. The carvings were of a man and woman lying on what appeared to be their deathbed.

"No one knows for sure, but the statues you are looking at are believed to be that of Affreca and John De Courcy," the friar pointed out. "De Courcy led the Anglo-Norman invasion of East Ulster back in 1177 and he built this abbey 16 years later. His wife, Affreca was the daughter of the King of Man,"

Vincent was fascinated by the history, which surrounded him, but Michael felt nothing but a cold chill running through his body. He could not explain why, but he did not like this place. Brother Mark continued the archeological tour for another half-hour before returning the boys to St. Christian's. He walked Michael and Vincent to the front door of their dormitory building.

"Now lads, this is your new home. You'll be sharing a floor with twelve other students. Many have gone through similar tragedies as your own. We have Catholic children from all six counties here in Ulster. Your beds have already been assigned to you, and Brother Tobias will make sure you receive the proper uniform."

With that, the stocky friar made the sign of the cross and waddled back to the main building.

The twins had been assigned to St. Paul's dormitory. The other dorm named after St. Peter was located directly across the dirt covered courtyard. Michael and Vincent walked into the front hall. Directly ahead was a large staircase; to the right was a small sitting area which was decorated with a coffee table surrounded by two worn leather couches. The couches sat just a few feet away from a large fireplace. Several bricks of peat were being roasted to heat the building. Off the sitting area was a door with a small sign nailed to its wooden exterior. It read, *Brother Tobias Shepard. Dorm Master.* Michael walked forward and knocked on the door. There was no answer. The boy turned and began walking away when suddenly the door flew open. Standing in the entranceway was Brother Tobias. The tall friar had his hands on his waist. He had steely blue eyes and muscles that bulged from under his brown robe. His crew cut was so thin that one could not tell the true color of his hair. Brother Tobias looked down at the boys but said nothing.

"Excuse me sir, I'm Michael Logan and this is my brother Vincent. Can you point us to our quarters?"

Without word, Brother Tobias turned and walked to the staircase. He looked back at the twins. "Well, are you coming?" he asked.

The boys followed the friar to the second floor. Rows of bunk beds were lined up along each side of the large room.

"Find your suitcases, and you'll find your bed," Brother Tobias told them. "Dinner is served in one hour inside the main building."

Brother Tobias turned on his heal and walked back to his quarters.

"Well here we are," Michael said staring at the large cold space. "It's not exactly home is it?"

Vincent nodded in agreement as they walked down the line of beds until they found their own. Michael's luggage was placed on the top bunk; Vincent's was on the bottom. Michael hoisted himself up to his bed and popped the hatches of his small suitcase. Once opened, a familiar odor filled his nostrils. The smell of the grocery store still clung to his father's apron. The boy took the apron with both hands and brought it up to his nose. The odor was an odd blend of cabbage and cherry pipe tobacco. Anyone else would have been repelled by the smell. Michael breathed deeply for a moment, his mind lost in the past. The boys shared a small nightstand where Vincent placed his mother's porcelain nativity figurines. Their school uniforms hung from a wire hanger on the post of their bed.

"We'd better get into these monkey suits and shove off to supper," Michael suggested.

He then wrapped his father's apron into a tight ball and stuffed it into his pillowcase. The twins dressed into their uniforms, which hung off their lean bodies.

"I guess we'll have time to grow into these," Vincent joked.

"Bollocks," Michael replied. "I don't see why I can't wear my football jersey. We both look like bloody fools."

"Shh! Brother Tobias might hear you," Vincent warned with his brown eyes focused on the stairs.

The boys wrapped black ties around the collars of their white shirts and headed toward the dining hall.

CHAPTER 7

The line for dinner was already deep with hungry boys fresh off the football field. There was some playful pushing and shoving as the students jockeyed for position with their tin dinner trays. A tall brown haired teen eyed the twins as they fell into line.

"Over here lads," the young man called. "It's okay, they'll let you cut," he said pointing to the six other students standing ahead in line. "Its fish stew night and none of us are in a rush to sit and eat."

Michael and Vincent walked over with their trays.

"I'm Gerry Devlin, glad to meet you," the freckle-faced teen extended his hand and smiled through two broken front teeth.

Vincent stared at the shattered smile and then quickly looked away.

"Ah, I wouldn't say that I have much use for a toothbrush," Devlin joked.

"I came face to face with a football last month. Brother Mark took me to a dentist in town who said he could give me caps. I said, no bloody way. I like the way I look.

I reckon I'll be the scariest bugger in my neighborhood when I go back."

The three boys were served their stew out of steaming pots. "I hope it tastes better than it smells," Vincent sighed holding his nose. They grabbed a few slices of black bread and butter and sat down.

"So you're the Logan boys," Devlin said. "The lads here have heard a little about ya. Tough break what happened with your Ma and Da, but your uncle seemed like a 'right' lad."

The twins were startled to find out their situation had already been bandied about by the students at St. Christian's.

"How long have you been here?" Michael asked Devlin.

"I'm in my second year. You'll find the boys here are fairly pleasant to be around.

There are no rivalries among us, and usually no fights. We figure it's us against them," Devlin whispered nodding to the friars' table.

"Brother Mark said many of the students came here after being terrorized by the Brits. So what's your story?" Vincent asked.

"Ah, well you boys in West Belfast think you have it tough. I was lucky enough to be brought up in the Short Strand," Devlin answered facetiously.

The Short Strand is a Belfast neighborhood on the other side of the Peace Line where a Protestant majority surrounds small enclaves of Catholic households.

"My Da had a job working the docks over at the Harland and Wolff shipyard. That's where the Titanic was built," Devlin pointed out. "Well one night after work Da gets invited for a pint at a pub near the docks. He's in there with the lads from work no doubt entertaining the whole lot of them." He paused and took a sip of powdered milk. "My Da was quite the storyteller. And from what my Ma tells me, he had a thirst that could cast a shadow. It was about ten o'clock when a group of hooded men raided the pub."

The term 'hooded men' made the hair on the back of Michael's neck rise. Devlin continued his story.

"These buggers divided the bar between Catholics and Protestants. My Da thought he noticed a tattoo of King Billy on the arm of one of the men."

"King Billy" is the term Catholics used when referring to William of Orange.

William was the Dutchman who led an army of 36,000 Protestant soldiers in the Battle of the Boyne massacre.

"Well when they asked Da if he was a Prod or Catholic, he lied and said he was Protestant." Gerry Devlin took a deep breath and finished his story. "Da lined up with a half dozen Prods against the wall of the bar. I bet he was a little scared but he thought he was in the clear. That's when the gunmen opened fire. The Proddys were torn down one by one. My Da was the last one in line. I guess he tried to tell the killers he was really Catholic, but the buggers didn't believe him. They shot him like a dog in the street. The IRA gunned down my father. It's funny but I don't blame them though; they were there to avenge the rape of a Catholic girl inside the bar two weeks before."

Michael and Vincent sat at the table speechless. The pain of their own tragedy was still fresh in their minds, but they were at a loss for words for their new friend.

The boys did not get much sleep on their first night in the dorm. It would take time before they grew accustomed to sharing the room with twelve other students. Their first class was at seven thirty the next morning. Michael and Vincent jumped out of their beds; dressed quickly into their uniforms and joined the other students for breakfast. The twins and their new friend, Gerry Devlin kept the conversation light as they devoured their powdered eggs. The three finished their meals and marched out of the dining hall and into Brother Mark's class.

The stubby friar was already busy scribbling something on the chalkboard.

Michael and Vincent could not make out the words.

"How many of you understand this?" Brother Mark asked pointing back to the chalkboard. There was a moment of silence and no one raised his hand.

"Ah, such a pity that young Irishmen cannot even recognize their native tongue," The friar observed with arms folded. "Dia duit," Brother Mark bellowed. "It's Irish for God be with you." He pointed at another odd grouping of letters. "Dia is Muire duit," he recited for the class. "This means, God and Mary be with you."

The friar stared back at the blank faces of his students. "Boys this Gaelic language, your language, has faded into oblivion in the last generation. It's our job to make sure that it does not become extinct. The Irish language is part of who we are."

Brother Mark wrote a few more Gaelic phrases on the board and recited them with the students. Class was suddenly interrupted by a knock on the door. In walked Brother Tobias who moved at a quick pace down the aisle toward the front of the classroom. Without acknowledging the class, Brother Tobias whispered something into his colleague's ear. Brother Mark's eyes went wide and he shook his head slowly. Tobias patted Mark on the shoulder and left the room as quickly as he entered. The stocky friar took his wire-framed eyeglasses off and pinched the bridge of his nose. "It's a sad day for all here," he announced. "The prisoners have made good on their threat. The hunger strike has begun."

CHAPTER 8

Todd Forrest stepped out of a cab about a block away from Long Kesh Prison. He padded his jacket frantically before realizing that he had left his note pad in the back seat of the car. Forrest waved his arms and tried to get the attention of the driver who took a quick turn and sped off. He had nothing to write on, he was out of cigarettes, and he now had to play catch up on a story he knew very little about. The day was not going well for the young reporter. Forrest had been sent over from London by the Associated Press and it was a last minute assignment for the 24 year-old American expatriate. The reporter that normally covered Northern Ireland had suffered a bad fall on the steps of his flat that morning. Forrest routinely covered the British financial market for the wire service, but had jumped at the chance for this assignment. He found the financial market as exciting as dry toast and yearned for something important to write about, something that would spark an emotional debate. There had already been a number of failed hunger strikes at the prison. The prisoners would eventually give up, wouldn't they? This was the thinking of Forrest's editor when he tossed the kid the assignment.

It was Sunday, March 1st and dusk had fallen over Belfast. The air was raw and Forrest stuck both hands in his pockets as he made his way north toward the prison. His walk was illuminated by a trail of flickering candles held by about sixty supporters who had gathered for a vigil at the prison gate. A silence hung over the crowd. Forrest made his way slowly to a middle-aged woman holding a candle with one hand while clutching rosary beads with the other.

"Who is leading the prisoners in this hunger strike?" he whispered.

"Bobby Sands is the organizer here," she replied in a thick Belfast brogue.

"What kind of man is this Sands?" Forrest inquired.

The woman made the sign of the cross and kissed her rosary beads. "Bobby Sands, is a saint. A living saint," she told him.

There's no way that I'm gonna get an unbiased view of the hunger strikers from this crowd, he thought. As if he was reading Forrest's mind, an older gentleman in a tweed coat walked up to him and gently grabbed him under the arm of his tan trench coat. "I can tell you all about Bobby Sands," the man told Forrest.

"Who are you?"

"I'm his Da," the older man replied with a trace of sadness in his voice.

The men walked away from the crowd to a small coffee shop across the street.

The owner recognized John Sands and quickly offered him a table and two chairs.

Within seconds, two hot cups of coffee were placed on the table between them. The reporter patted down his coat once more and was relieved to find a pen hidden in the breast pocket. He grabbed a stack of paper napkins and spread them out on the table. John Sands looked on curiously.

"I left my note pad in the cab," Forrest admitted sheepishly. "I guess the first question I have is; can you tell me why your son is willing to give up his life?" The older man nodded his head and paused for a moment in deep thought. "Let me start at the beginning," Sands said as he folded his wrinkled hands and rested them on the table. "We raised Bobby in North Belfast in a place called, Rathcoole. It's a Protestant neighborhood and we didn't advertise the fact that we were Catholic. But the people around us found out quickly anyway. They made our lives a living hell. Our next door neighbor tried to drive my wife Rosaleen insane. She'd pound on our walls with her pots and pans at all hours of the night. The evil woman also brought Protestant couples by our house to see if they'd like to buy it once we were driven out."

Todd Forrest had already filled two napkins with notes. John Sands waited until the reporter had finished writing a sentence before continuing his story.

"Protestant gangs would also stand outside our house yelling, *Taigs Out!* Poor Bobby turned into one hell of a cross-country star because he was always trying to outrun the Prod bullies. He tried to steer clear of the violence and found a job building trolleys. But the Prods wouldn't leave him alone. One co-worker pulled a gun on him; another left a note in his lunch box telling my boy to get out! That's why he joined the IRA, Mister Forrest."

They continued the conversation while their cups of coffee cooled. John Sands told Forrest that his son was in prison for a bombing attack on the Balmoral Furniture Company in Dunmurry. Bobby Sands was pulled over near the scene. Police found a revolver in his car.

"Was he involved in the bombing?"

"I honestly do not know," Sands replied shrugging his shoulders.

The older man also educated the reporter about the history of Long Kesh. The prison had been built on the site of a World War Two aerodrome and prisoners were divided by allegiance to their paramilitary organization. Long Kesh operated much like a prisoner of war camp. IRA prisoners had even been allowed to drill with wooden rifles, which were supplied by the prison. This all changed by 1976, when the British government vowed to break the IRA's back once and for all. Irish nationalists were no longer considered prisoners of war. They were now treated like common criminals.

Under this directive, Long Kesh was split into two separate prisons. Prisoners arrested before the 1976 cut-off date were still given special quasi-military status.

Those inmates, dwindling in numbers were housed in the Maze section of the prison.

Bobby Sands and the men arrested after the cut-off date were locked away in new prison sections called the H-Blocks. Guards in the new wing had been given orders to brutalize IRA prisoners whenever the opportunity arose. The *Screws* as they were called handed out severe beatings to inmates considered the most dangerous by prison officials. At first, the IRA fought back from outside the prison walls. Members carried out a bloody campaign of selective assassination. In all, 18 guards were murdered, including one female. But the killings just made life harder for IRA members jailed inside the H-Blocks. First, the prisoners conducted *the blanket protest*, and when prison officials showed no movement, the inmates employed an ancient Irish strategy, the hunger strike. The Gaelic tribes called it, *Cealachan* (winning justice by starvation). Irish prisoners used this strategy in 1916, following the ill-fated Easter Rising insurrection, and again in 1917 after Republican Thomas Ashe had been arrested for sedition following a speech he had made against the British. Ashe and his fellow prisoners had refused to wear the standard prison uniform. He started his hunger strike on September 20, 1917. Thomas Ashe died five days later after he was force fed by prison guards. His funeral was one of the biggest Ireland had ever seen. Nearly 40,000 people marched in back of his casket. Irish nationalists fired several rounds over the body of their fallen comrade. Republican hero Michael Collins stood tall before the masses and said: "The volley you have just heard fired is the only speech, which it is proper to make over the grave of a dead Fenian." The figures in this current hunger strike would soon become as revered as those legends from the past.

Todd Forrest rubbed his head and looked down at his Timex watch. It was now 11:30 PM. The reporter had been chatting with John Sands for nearly five hours.

He would have to get back to his hotel soon, or he would miss his deadline. That would incur a fate worse than death, the reporter imagined. He shook the old man's hand and gathered up his notes, which now filled twenty napkins. Forrest rushed out the door and hailed a cab back the Europa Hotel. Before leaving for Long Kesh that afternoon, he had asked for a typewriter to be brought up to his room. Forrest let out a sigh of relief when he found the machine waiting for him when he arrived. The reporter sat down on his firm bed, loosened his tie and began to write.

Somewhere in the darkened bowels of the H-Blocks, another man was also writing about the day's events. Bobby Sands kept a secret diary in his cell. The prisoner sat in the corner of his rancid cell and released these thoughts from his mind.

I am a political prisoner. I am a political prisoner because I am a casualty of a perennial war that is being fought between the oppressed Irish people and an alien, oppressive, unwanted regime that refuses to withdraw from our land.

I believe I am but another of those wretched Irishmen born of a risen generation with a deeply rooted and unquenchable desire for freedom. I am dying not just to attempt to end the barbarity of H-Block, or to gain the rightful recognition of a political prisoner, but primarily what is lost in here is lost for the Republic and those wretched oppressed whom I am deeply proud to know as the 'risen people'.

CHAPTER 9

Brother Tobias held a whistle between his teeth but could not hide his smile. *This is the one I've been looking for,* he thought to himself as he watched the boy from West Belfast dribble the ball past two defenders and shoot it into the upper right corner of the net.

"Nice work young mister Logan," the friar shouted from across the field.

He looked down at his watch as the players jogged back to the center of the field.

"That's it for today," he told his team. "Hit the showers, grab some supper and get plenty of rest. We've got a big match tomorrow."

As Michael Logan trotted off the field, Brother Tobias grabbed him gently by the arm. "I want to speak to you son."

"What is it Brother?" Michael asked as he watched his teammates disappear into the locker room.

The friar ran his fingers through the boy's thick black hair and smiled.

"I like the way you play Michael. You're the youngest player on the team but it's clear to me that you're also the best. I'm going to put you into the starting lineup for tomorrow's match. How do you feel about that?"

Michael pumped his fist in the air and smiled. Brother Tobias pulled the boy closer and gave him a warm hug. "You're a very special boy," he proclaimed.

Michael was truly happy for the first time since the attacks on his parents. *Maybe it'll be alright here after all,* he thought to himself.

Michael went to bed thinking about the following day's football match. But soon after the boy fell asleep, his dreams were invaded once again by the man who murdered his father.

A gloved hand turned the doorknob slowly and entered the dormitory building. The blond haired assassin moved quietly past Brother Tobias' room. The door was closed and the friar was fast asleep. The killer found the oak staircase and began climbing the steps to the boys' sleeping quarters. The man reached the second floor where he stood atop the staircase observing the students as they slept. He pulled off his black mask and his golden locks fell to his shoulders. The killer then reached into the back of his black fatigue pants for his long flaying knife. He stared at its razor sharp tip momentarily before making his way down the long line of beds. Michael lay there on his top bunk watching the man make his silent approach. The boy wanted scream, he wanted to run, but he was frozen with fear. The only parts of his body that seemed to be working were his eyes and ears. He kept his brown eyes locked on the dark figure as it moved closer to his bunk.

"I am Hell," the man whispered in the darkness.

The blond assassin arrived at Michael's bunk. He held up the knife, which glistened in the moonlight. The killer brought the blade down to the boy's neck. Michael closed his eyes and waited for the inevitable.

"No!" Michael screamed as he shot upright in his bed. His eyes darted across the room, but there was no one there. The boy was panting heavily and dripping with sweat. The commotion stirred Vincent from his sound sleep.

"Michael, what's the matter? Are you alright?" he asked from the bottom bunk.

"I'm … I'm okay Vincent. Go back to sleep."

Vincent rolled over and closed his eyes once again. Michael was afraid to do the same. He had been having these awful dreams every night since the attack on his parents. However, he never discussed his nightmare with his brother. Michael feared that the blond haired assassin would begin to invade Vincent's dreams as well. His mouth was dry and the boy yearned for a glass of water. The water bubbler was located on the first floor of the dormitory. He slid down the post of his bunk bed and crept past his sleeping floor mates to the staircase.

He descended the staircase slowly, the wood floor cold under his bare feet.

Brother Tobias' door was open a crack and a light shined from within. Michael tiptoed to the water bubbler and quenched his thirst. He swallowed as much cold water as his small stomach would allow. He wiped the water off his chin and turned back toward the corridor. The boy was startled by a tall, dark figure standing in his way. *It wasn't a dream, he really is coming to kill me,* Michael thought.

"Michael, what are you doing out of your bed?" Brother Tobias asked.

"Ah, ah … I was thirsty sir," the boy replied with relief in his voice.

"You know the rules, son. Lights out is at nine o'clock. That means you have to stay in bed, unless there's an emergency."

The friar placed his powerful arm on Michael's shoulder and guided the boy back toward the staircase. Suddenly, Brother Tobias had another thought.

"Michael, you look like you've seen a ghost. Come into my room and tell me what it was that frightened you so badly."

Michael entered Brother Tobias' room. The Franciscan's living quarters were sparse. There was a small reading lamp sitting atop a wooden desk, two folding chairs and a twin bed. Michael told the priest about the attacks on his parents and the nightmares that followed. The man tried to comfort the boy by rubbing his shoulders.

"Son, your shirt is full of sweat. Why don't you take it off before you freeze to death."

Michael did as he was told.

Brother Tobias then reached into the bottom drawer of his desk and pulled out a brown bottle.

"It seems you need a little something stronger than water to get over that heinous nightmare," the priest said. He held the bottle of Midleton Whiskey up to the light of his reading lamp.

"We Irish call this *Uisce Beatha.* It means, water of life. This, my boy is the rarest, richest whiskey in all of Ireland. You know Michael, only 600 bottles are sold each year. Look here, it even comes with its own serial number."

Michael read the small print on the back of the bottle. The boy had often sneaked a sip of his Da's Guinness. *I think I can handle a man's drink now.*

Brother Tobias twisted off the cap, put the bottle to his lips and took a small sip. The priest then passed the whiskey to his thirteen year-old companion.

"Go ahead, my boy," he urged.

Michael lifted the bottle with both hands and took a hearty pull. The liquor felt like lava pouring down his throat. Michael gagged and immediately coughed up the rare Irish whiskey. Brother Tobias sat back in his chair and laughed. Michael tried to wipe the tears from his eyes.

"Let me show you," the priest said as he inched his chair closer.

The man held the bottle with one hand and massaged the boy's neck with the other.

"You have to treat the whiskey with respect," he told Michael. The friar placed the bottle back to the boy's lips and urged him to drink.

"Just sip it, Michael."

The boy took one small sip, and then another. Soon, Michael and the priest were passing the bottle back and forth until it was empty. Michael's eyes were growing heavy and although he did not realize it, he was slipping in and out of consciousness.

Brother Tobias cradled the boy in his arms and placed him on the bed. Michael watched through glassy eyes as the priest unfastened his robe. The man pulled it over his broad shoulders and let the robe drop to the floor. The priest stood naked before the boy.

"I like you Michael, I really like you," he said softly as he moved closer toward his prey.

CHAPTER 10

When Michael awoke, he was back in his bed. *It must have been another night-mare.*

He was lying flat and tried to roll his legs over so that he could lie on his side. That is when the first traces of pain shot through his lower body. His thighs had cramped and his buttocks felt sore. The memories were coming back to him now. The friar's hands on his shoulders, his lips on his neck.… Michael lay on his bed and started to cry. *Why me God, why me?*

"What's wrong brother?" Vincent asked frantically from the lower bunk.

"I need your help Vincent. I can't move my legs."

Vincent grabbed a chair and climbed up to the top bunk. He looked into his twin's eyes and saw nothing but fear.

"What happened to you?"

Michael did not know what to say. He did know that he could not tell his brother the truth.

"Too much football," he replied.

"I've never seen you seize up like that," Vincent said as he scanned Michael's quivering body.

Vincent offered his hand, which Michael grabbed and hoisted himself up to a sitting position. The injured boy screamed in pain.

"What's all the ruckus?" Gerry Devlin inquired as he made his way over to the boys' bunk.

"I got clipped at yesterday's practice," Michael lied. "It didn't feel half as bad as it does now."

Devlin helped Vincent pull his brother from the top bunk. The two boys dressed Michael in his white collared shirt and gray trousers. Using their shoulders as crutches, Michael slowly limped his way toward the dining hall. He knew the sight of food would make him physically sick, but he desperately wanted to get the stale taste of whiskey out of his mouth. Michael saw Brother Tobias sitting at the teacher's table and immediately stopped hanging on his two friends for support.

The boy's legs were burning, but he stood upright and marched past his molester.

He would never give the priest the satisfaction of seeing him victimized. Brother Tobias did not even look up at the boy. He was too busy laughing at a joke told from across the table by Brother Mark.

"Will you be well enough to play in today's game?" Devlin asked.

"You won't be taking my place as striker, if that's what you're asking."

"You have to see the nurse, you can't play like this," Vincent added.

"I'll be there," Michael winced. "They'd have to kill me to keep me off that field."

Michael Logan was true to his word. He gritted his way through a full day of classes and limped toward the locker room. After gingerly putting on his green shorts and shirt, the boy trotted toward the field. He could feel his legs loosening up with each stride. Michael would take his pain out on his opponents.

There was nothing graceful about Michael's play on this day. He pushed the ball past each defender with sheer force, throwing his whole body into his game. In the first period, Michael took St. Augustin's top player out of the game with a vicious hip check. The play drew loud cheers from Vincent and two dozen other St. Christian's students sitting in the stands. On the following play, Michael intercepted a kick and dribbled up field. He outran two defenders and had a clear shot at the goal. Just as he had done in practice, Michael blasted the ball over the goalkeeper's head and into the upper corner of the net. Gerry Devlin ran to hug his teammate but backed off when he saw that Michael was still in agony. The boys jogged off the field at the end of the period. Players trotted past Brother Tobias, who playfully patted them on their backside. Michael wanted to stay as far away from the priest as possible. He left the field about twenty yards away from his tormenter. St. Christian's ended up winning the game on Logan's first period goal. The players were laughing and celebrating in the showers when their coach walked in unannounced.

"Good job to you all," Brother Tobias said enthusiastically. "And good job to Michael Logan. As the player who scored the winning goal, you get the honor of ringing the abbey bell tonight."

Michael's body went numb when he heard his name. *Oh God no.*

"I'll fetch you at the dorm before supper," the priest said gleefully as he walked out of the locker room.

Logan's mind raced as he tried to find some way to get out of it. *Do I tell Brother Mark? But I'm just a kid. How can I accuse a priest? Who would believe me? It would be his word against mine.* Michael decided his only option was to fake an illness and avoid Brother Tobias as much as possible. He returned to the dorm where the other boys were getting ready for dinner. Instead of changing back into his school uniform, Michael climbed back into bed and hugged the covers around him.

"Aren't you coming to dinner?" Vincent asked his brother. "After the game you played, you must be starving."

"I'm not feeling too good, but if you can swipe some bread from the dining hall, I may get hungry later."

Suddenly, Michael heard Brother Tobias' heavy footsteps climbing the stairs. The boy hid his face in his pillow and pretended to be asleep. The priest walked toward Michael's bunk where Vincent and Devlin stood knotting their ties.

"The conquering hero gets a special honor tonight," the friar reminded the boys.

"I … I'm not feeling well. I'm sick to my stomach," Michael announced with a raspy voice.

The priest easily saw through Michael's charade. "That's unfortunate my son. Ringing the bell is a great honor here at St. Christian's. Perhaps your brother would like to go instead?"

Vincent's eyes lit up at the opportunity. "I'd love to go."

Before Michael could voice protest, the priest placed his arm over Vincent's shoulder and led him to the staircase.

"They call the bell Old Gomery," Brother Tobias told Vincent as the pair walked down stairs. "She's one of several bells given to the village by Viscount Montgomery in the 17th century. Old Gomery is the only one that survives to this day."

It was an unusually warm evening. Fog was beginning to roll in from the nearby Lough. The predator priest led Vincent across the road and up the hill toward the historic ruins. The bell tower was the only part of the ancient structure that had been rebuilt over time. Vincent had to watch his step as he climbed the hill. There were dozens of rocks scattered across the landscape and hidden by tall grass. The rolling fog made it even more difficult to see. Vincent stumbled on a stone and leaned on the older man to catch himself from falling. A wave of excitement shot through the priest's body. The bell tower was only a few yards ahead of them.

Michael was stricken with panic as he watched Brother Tobias lure his twin away.

He jumped out of bed and rushed to put his football cleats back on. He ran down the stairs and out into the night. Frightening images were being replayed in Michael's mind. *Why didn't I just go with him myself? Please don't hurt my brother.*

Brother Tobias slowly led Vincent up the winding stone steps of the bell tower. The priest held his large hand on the small of the boy's back as they navigated the awkward twists and turns of the ancient stairwell. The bell tower stood five stories high and both were gasping for breath when they reached the top.

"Let's rest a second before we ring this magnificent bell," Brother Tobias suggested.

Vincent turned his attention to Old Gomery. The cast iron bell weighed two tons. Its ring could be heard throughout the village. The priest noticed the boy marveling at the giant figure.

"It's beautiful Vincent, just like you."

Michael ran as fast as his young legs could take him. The boy caught a stone under the toe of his cleat and fell hard to the ground. He felt blood trickling from his kneecap but could not see it in the thick fog. The pain was incredible but Michael suppressed his scream. Instead, he picked up the heavy stone and kept moving toward the bell tower.

The priest stared at his prey and smiled. Vincent felt uneasy when he saw the hungry look on the man's face. "I'd like to go back the dorm," he told the priest. "I feel sick. I guess I'm afraid of heights."

Vincent turned to the stairwell and was jerked back around by Brother Tobias' strong arm. "I won't hurt you Vincent," the priest promised. A crazed smile formed on his rigid face. "I think you're beautiful," he stated again. "Even more beautiful than your brother."

There was little room to maneuver in the bell tower. Old Gomery hung to Vincent's left. There was an open window to the right. The boy stepped back and hugged his body against the cold stone wall. He could only watch as Brother

Tobias pulled his Franciscan robe over his head. The man stood before him in his white briefs and socks.

"Now it's your turn to get undressed," he said softly.

Vincent did not move.

"Take your fucking clothes off you little shite!"

Tears streamed down the boy's face while he did as he was told. Vincent was soon naked. The quivering boy used his hands to cover his private parts.

"Don't cry Vincent," Brother Tobias said his voice now calm. "I'll make you feel better."

The priest took two steps toward Vincent and dropped to his knees.

Michael finally reached the entrance to the bell tower. He was still holding the large rock in his hands. He could faintly hear Brother Tobias' voice coming from above. Michael darted up the stone staircase taking two steps at a time. He reached the top step and saw the horrifying image of his naked twin pinned against the wall. Brother Tobias' large hands were on the boy's hips. The priest was about to lower his mouth onto his victim's organ. Michael ran up with the rock held high over his head and brought it crashing down on the priest's skull. Brother Tobias crumbled to the floor and rolled over. Michael looked to Vincent who was still crying against the wall.

"Get out of here," he shouted.

The priest got up on one knee and tried to shake his blurred vision. He swung his right hand at Michael but missed. The boy yelled and ran at the wounded priest.

Michael struck his tormentor again, this time behind his left ear. Brother Tobias let out a mighty scream of his own as his body twisted and fell near the open window. The child molester was bleeding severely and completely incapacitated now.

"I think you've killed him Michael. Let's get outta here," Vincent pleaded frantically.

Michael looked his twin in the eye and turned back toward the priest. He calmly walked over to Brother Tobias and lifted his body up to the open window. The man weighed over two hundred pounds, and Michael used every muscle in his body to accomplish this feat. Brother Tobias' upper body was now hanging out the window five stories above ground. Finally aware of his predicament, the molester looked back up at Michael with total fear in his pale blue eyes. Michael stared back at him but did not say a word. Instead, he pushed the man's legs upward and out the window. At that very moment, Vincent reached over and rang Old Gomery. The priest's screams were muffled by the deafening sound of the church bell.

Michael helped his twin put his clothes back on. They walked back down the stone steps of the bell tower in silence.

"I've got to run away," Michael said finally.

His brother understood.

"Let me come with you."

"No. I killed Brother Tobias, not you. It's easier to run alone."

The twins hugged each other and started to cry.

"I'll always be with you," Michael said swallowing his tears. "You are my twin. You are a part of me."

The Logan brothers shared one final hug before Michael disappeared in the thick fog.

C H A P T E R   1 1

It was the fourth day of May 1981, but still unusually warm for this time of year. Todd Forrest sat inside the coffee shop across from Long Kesh prison. He stared out the window and was amazed by the masses of people who were now standing outside the prison supporting Bobby Sands' cause. The reporter had been meeting with John Sands every night since his son's hunger strike began in March.

Bobby Sands could die at any time now. His frail father quietly entered the coffee shop and spotted his new friend sitting at their corner table. The temperature was sixty-eight degrees, but the old man still wore his Donegal Tweed coat. He sat down across from the reporter and slowly removed his cap. John Sands looked like he had aged ten years in the past two months.

"I want to thank you for all you've done," he told Forrest. "Just look outside. We began with a few dozen supporters. Now there are thousands out there including journalists from all over the globe. You were the first one to bring my son's story to the world. You are responsible for all of this."

Todd Forrest felt a little uncomfortable by the praise. He was by no means a cheerleader for the IRA. He felt the outlawed group had plenty of blood on its hands. But he also believed it was a war brought to Irish soil by the British government. Forrest only wrote what he saw. It was up to the reader to decide which side he or she was on.

Bobby Sands was now lying in the prison hospital. Much had happened since he stopped eating in March. Following the sudden death of Parliament member Frank Maguire, the people of Fermanagh and South Tyrone nominated Sands to take his place. But Bobby knew there would be only one ending to his story.

"I'd like you to come with me," John Sands told the reporter. "Bobby said that he wants to see you."

Todd Forrest tried to maintain his composure. But inside, the young journalist wondered if he was ready for what he was about to witness. The two men left the coffee shop and cut a winding path through the sea of protesters blocking the gate to Long Kesh prison. Many people recognized John Sands and immediately stepped aside to let the men through. James Higgins, the Assistant Warden of the prison met the men at the front gate. His presence set off a loud chorus of boos from Sands supporters.

"Killer! Killer!" protesters shouted at Higgins, who refused to look in their direction.

From their perches atop the prison watchtowers, heavily armed guards kept their riflescopes trained on the crowd below. Privately, James Higgins was torn. He had grown to admire Bobby Sands. That is why he granted Sands' wish to meet the American journalist. But as a prison official, Higgins felt he also had to maintain order inside the walls of Long Kesh. Two dozen policemen dressed in riot gear formed a wall in front of the protesters as the large iron gate opened to let the two men inside.

Todd Forrest carried three notepads and a small tape recorder. The napkin incident had taught him a valuable lesson.

"Sorry Mister Forrest, but you'll have to leave your equipment with the prison guards. It is not allowed inside the infirmary," Higgins declared.

The reporter was about to protest, but decided to keep his mouth shut. He realized what an incredible opportunity he had been given. Higgins walked the men into the prison hospital. Forrest took mental notes of the layout. It did not appear much different from any other hospital ward. There was an anti-septic odor in the air and several nurses and doctors were walking about carrying various charts and medications. The only stark difference from what Forrest had seen before were the patients themselves. These were the men who were sacrificing their own bodies for the cause they believed in. Forrest and John Sands walked slowly past each hospital bed. The men lying there were wasting away before their eyes. They once had been fierce IRA soldiers. *Now they look like small boys,* the reporter thought to himself. Their skin stretched tightly over their pale faces. Their glassy eyes bulged from the sockets. John Sands led Forrest down the hospital ward.

Bobby Sands lay on the last bed on the left. A small wooden cross was bolted into the hospital wall above his head. Todd Forrest had only known Sands from a photograph. That picture showed a vibrant young man with a winning smile. The reporter could not recognize the man now lying in the bed before him. Bobby Sands' long red hair was now cut short to the scalp. His fleshy cheeks had sunken into hollow pools. An intravenous drip worked in vain to pump saline into Sands skeletal body. The inmate's eyes were closed as the men approached.

"Did you bring him?" Bobby Sands asked in a reed thin voice.

"He's here my son," the father replied.

"Bring him closer," Sands pleaded. "I cannot see that well."

Todd Forrest took another step forward and stood over the hospital bed.

"Ah, there you are Mister Forrest."

There was a long pause before Sands continued.

"Do you think my death will change anything?"

The reporter thought of the legion of supporters gathered outside.

"It already has Bobby."

Sands lifted his right arm slowly; his bony hand was open. Todd Forrest took the hand into his own and held it for several seconds. Bobby Sands then closed his eyes once again and faded back into unconsciousness.

At 1:17 a.m. on Tuesday, May 5th, Bobby Sands went into kidney failure and died.

He had completed sixty-five days on hunger strike. John Sands and Todd Forrest were at the Republican's bedside. Forrest hugged the old man, who wept quietly on his shoulder. The dazed reporter was escorted to the prison gates where supporters had just received the news. Protesters wailed openly and the tears spilled in front of Long Kesh prison that morning could have filled the Shannon River. Forrest did not feel the need to get reaction from the mourners on Sands' death. The reporter knew that he already had his story. It was a story like no other. He continued to walk the crowded streets of Belfast and arrived back at the Europa Hotel just before dawn. Forrest dialed up the Associated Press office in London and filed his report over the phone. Afterwards, he poured himself a Scotch and raised the tall glass to the ceiling. "Cheers Bobby."

Todd Forrest took a long gulp and collapsed onto the bed.

CHAPTER 12

LONDON, ENGLAND
PRESENT DAY

"Any messages for me?" asked the man in mirrored sunglasses.

"Your secretary in Barcelona called. She would like you contact her right away, Senor Tomba," the concierge replied with a smile.

"Si. Gracias Senor."

"How was your visit to The Guards Museum, Senor?"

"The Wellington Barracks is truly an impressive sight. We have nothing quite like it in Spain. Thank you for the recommendation Mister Oglethorpe."

"Anything to make your stay here at the Savoy as pleasurable as possible, Senor."

Raymond Oglethorpe fit the public image of his five star hotel. The tall, thin concierge had a pedicure to match his perfect posture. The man's blue striped suit hung so well on his body; it was as if the tailors at Saville Row had stitched him into it.

Michael Logan tipped his tan fedora hat toward the concierge and walked across the large art-deco lobby toward the elevator. He passed a newsstand and casually scanned the headlines of the London newspapers. *Tory Leader Slain: Politico in Sex Romp with Barrister's Wife* shouted the bold print headline of the *Daily Mail.* A black and white photo of Geoffrey Ferguson accompanied the front-page story. The report was filled with few facts and much speculation. The reporter wrote that sources close to the investigation said suspicion had fallen on the husband of socialite Camille Archibald. Archibald and her husband, Dexter were now reportedly in seclusion at their Surrey estate. Logan waited until he was safely inside the elevator before cracking a slight smile.

He exited on the 15th floor and took a right out of the elevator door. The corridor was empty. Logan walked to room 227; the Ambassador Suite. He retrieved the electronic key from the breast pocket of his beige sport coat. Before sliding the key into the lock, Logan examined the door from top to bottom. There were no signs of forced entry. He then scanned the doorknob and spotted a tiny piece of white thread hanging on the shiny brass handle. It was right where Logan had left it that morning. Satisfied he slid the key into the lock and watched as the light turned from red to green. He entered the suite and took off his jacket. The Savoy clearly spared no expenses in the suite's decoration. A large crystal chandelier graced the marble tiled entryway. Two antique vases filled with fresh cut flowers sat on a Waterford glass cocktail table in the center of the room. The living room was also equipped with a lavish home entertainment center that featured a state of the art sound system. Logan grabbed the remote control and hit *Play* on the C-D player. The generous space was immediately filled with the deafening noise of techno-music. Logan increased the volume until it was almost unbearable. Senor Tomba liked his music loud. He then walked through the living area and into the bedroom. A king-sized bed lay on a frame of dark mahogany in the middle of the room. Logan knelt down and fished for an aluminum suitcase he had hidden under the bed. The bulletproof case had a digital pass code that could only be opened by a ten-digit combination. He placed the case on top of the bed and punched in the numbers. The case slowly opened to reveal a small laptop computer stored inside. To the naked eye, it looked like any other laptop, but in fact it was one of the most powerful computers in the world. A twenty four-year-old student from MIT had designed the super computer, which he sold to the National Security Agency two years before. The NSA now used it to keep close tabs on the nuclear programs of Iran and North Korea. The Asian-American student believed he had been pressured to sell his design to the U.S. government for below market cost. He then sold three of his computers on the black market and made a killing. The computer whiz was now MIA from MIT and was believed to be living somewhere in South America. Logan had purchased one of the computers from a Chilean arms dealer for $500,000 three months before.

He fetched a disc from inside the suitcase and slid it into the computer. The small computer quickly proved it was worth the small fortune that Logan had paid for it.

It was designed with a digital worm that could penetrate even the most secure computer system. With a few keystrokes, Logan managed to hack his way into the MI-5 internal database. It was now time for the worm to go to work. It took about twenty minutes for the worm to successfully penetrate the program's firewalls. The MI-5 internal database kept records of all former intelligence personnel and soldiers who had served the Royal Crown. Logan typed a name into the search engine and hit *Enter*. It took only seconds before a small photo appeared on the screen. Michael Logan took a good look at his next victim.

Malcolm Rogers was a sixty-three-year old Scottish Laird who lived in a 12th century castle in the rugged Scottish Highlands. He was also one of the two surviving members of The Knights of the Round Table. The computer flashed a question on the top of the screen. *Download information now—Y/N?* Logan hit *Enter* and then got up and walked into the spacious bathroom. He flicked the light on and rested his strong hands on the opulent marble sink. He stared at himself in the mirror. The super computer was gathering valuable information to help him learn who Malcolm Rogers was. But who was Michael Logan?

For the past two months Logan had been immersed in the role of Senor Roberto Tomba, successful businessman from Barcelona. He had flown to Spain via Mexico City and had spent several weeks establishing his new identity. While staying in Barcelona, he had met a dark skinned beauty in the early morning hours at a discothèque. After taking her to bed, he coaxed her into playing the role of his secretary. He gave the woman an untraceable satellite phone and a list of phone numbers. Logan also handed her 10,000 euros and promised even more for a job well done. Her assistance would be vital in maintaining his new identity. Logan now had a new name, but his physical appearance had not changed much. He was still strikingly handsome. Logan's jet-black hair now fell around his meaty shoulders. His once clean face was now hidden behind a neatly trimmed beard. The only cause for concern thus far had been the flight from Spain to Heathrow Airport. Michael Logan was still on a terrorist watch-list. He had spent ten years as the IRA's most dangerous assassin before vanishing without a trace. He now found himself back on enemy soil.

How did this enemy of the Crown manage to slip through tight security at Heathrow Airport? Logan relied on advice he had once received while training under a colonel of the KGB in the late 1980's. He blended into the crowd by sticking out. In the guise of Senor Roberto Tomba, Logan acted so obnoxious that people were too annoyed to give him a serious look. Senor Tomba was a pain in the ass to everyone he came across. With a thick Spanish accent, he complained loudly after learning he could not smoke in customs. He argued with the baggage handler after noticing scuff marks on his leather suitcase. Personnel who were eager to make Senor Tomba some one else's problem processed him quickly through the airport.

The Spanish businessman was no more gracious to employees and his fellow guests at the Savoy. He played loud music at all hours of the day and brought home a different woman each night. He dined at the elegant Savoy Grill and made a habit of sending every meal back to the kitchen, much to the chef's dismay. The hotel was known for catering to its most eccentric guests, especially those who paid well for the privilege. The Savoy staff once even provided use of the hotel pool to opera singer Luisa Tetrazzini's crocodile. But the new concierge privately prayed Senor Tomba's vacation would end soon.

The London phase of Logan's mission was nearly complete. He went back to the super computer and began memorizing the intimate details of Malcolm Roger's life.

As the only son of Laird Alan Rogers, he had taken over stewardship of Claymore Castle upon the death of his father in 1995. Built in the shadow of a rocky crag at the foot of the Cairngorm Mountains, Claymore Castle had been home to the Rogers Clan for 700 years. Because the castle was listed on the National Trust, its design specifications were part of the public domain. This information would be most valuable when Logan finally paid Malcolm Rogers a visit. The man's file also stated that he was a member of a special military unit that had operated in the Falkland Islands, the Middle East, and Northern Ireland in the 1980's. Logan stared at the computer and right clicked onto *Northern Ireland.* He waited for data to fill the screen. Nothing happened. Logan repeated the keystroke but still nothing happened.

Their missions were so sensitive that even the lads at MI-5 don't have high enough clearance, he thought.

Logan also knew that he would need more than a silenced pistol to take down Malcolm Rogers. He had traveled to England unarmed. The weapon he used to assassinate Geoffrey Ferguson was taken from a small locker in the cavernous London Metro Station. Logan had left it hidden in a duffle bag years before.

Options Comrade Logan! You must always give yourself plenty of options.

Logan could still hear the KGB colonel's raspy voice echoing in his mind.

He had planted the gun inside the locker in case he was ever in need of a weapon while operating in London. But he was startled to find it still there ten years later.

Logan was now in need of more firepower and he had another back up plan in mind.

CHAPTER 13

Senor Tomba stood in line with the black Nikon camera wrapped loosely around his neck. He was just one of a dozen tourists taking in the city's newest and most popular attraction. While he waited to purchase his ticket, he gazed up at the towering London Eye and marveled at the architecture. The Eye, also known as the Millennium Wheel was one hundred and thirty five meters high. It took six years to build and was designed as an entry in London's millennium landmark competition. The observation wheel was fitted with passenger capsules that offered visitors a 360-degree panoramic view of the majestic city on the Thames River.

Senor Tomba handed the cashier twenty euros for his ticket and followed a group of Asian tourists as they stepped inside one of the capsules. A raven-haired young woman called their attention to the front of the large pod.

"Welcome to the British Airways London Eye. My name is Corly and I'll be your guide on this one of a kind tour of London," she said with a smile.

The observation wheel began moving slowly on its circular mounted rings. Tomba and the other visitors snapped pictures as the young woman continued her presentation.

"The Eye is the sixth tallest structure in the city of London. The Eye weighs more than seventeen hundred tons. That's the equivalent of two hundred and fifty of our double decker buses," she informed the Japanese tourists who smiled and nodded in unison. The capsule continued to rise giving way to an incredible view west of the city.

"To your right is Trafalgar Square. It's London's main venue for public meetings and rallies," Corly pointed out. "The tall monument you see in the middle there is called Nelson's Column. It was constructed in the 1830's and stands fifty meters high. The monument commemorates Admiral Lord Nelson's heroic death fighting the French at the Battle of Trafalgar."

For the next twenty minutes, the tour guide continued to highlight various points of interest as the Eye made its leisurely turn back to the passenger dock. Once the pod was firmly on the ground, she thanked the tourists and ushered them all to the exit door. Logan hid behind his mirrored sunglasses in the back of the crowd. He approached the tour guide slowly, looking for any hint of recognition in her soft violet eyes.

"Thank you sir, and please come again," she said extending her hand.

"Gracias Senorita," he replied. Logan then lowered his glasses to reveal his intense brown eyes and whispered in her ear. His Spanish accent was now replaced by an Irish brogue. "Corly Cunningham, my haven't you grown into a beauty of a woman."

His words clearly startled the woman who pulled her hand back from his.

"Relax child. It's me, It's Michael Logan."

They were now alone in the Passenger Pod.

"Your Da always said you'd reach the top," he said with a smile.

"I ... I can't believe it. I'm looking a ghost."

"Well this ghost is made of flesh and blood, despite the rumors you've heard."

"We can't talk here," she said nervously.

"Calm down girl. Meet me across the street at Bunratty's Pub. I'll be waiting for you when you get off work."

The young woman's nerves started to settle. "A date with Michael Logan; now that's something I've dreamed about since I was a wee child," she smiled.

Logan was sitting alone at the bar when she walked in. Corly was blessed with a petite, yet curvaceous figure. Her short black hair hugged her high cheekbones. She looked nothing like the chubby freckle-faced child Logan once knew. He stood up from his stool and took her by the hand. For a moment, Corly thought he was going to kiss the back of her hand. She tried to hide the excitement. Instead, he guided her to a tall booth in the corner of the pub. Logan glanced over to the barkeeper whose eyes were glued to an overhead television set. He appeared pre-occupied with a football match between Manchester United and Liverpool. Logan sat Corly down and spoke in hushed tones.

"Does your father still own that farm outside the city?" he inquired.

"What, no fore-play? Just right to the subject at hand huh," she joked.

Logan's intense expression quickly gave way to a smile.

"Please forgive me, Corly. I've never been that good around women."

The young woman rolled her beautiful violet eyes. "This from the man who had every girl in Belfast wrapped around his trigger finger."

Her playful banter was now becoming dangerous.

"Watch your words," he warned her. "I need to drop by the farm to check on the crops."

Corly Cunningham understood what Logan was asking for. "It's been a good season," she told him. "I've got tomorrow off. I'm studying for exams. Why don't you stop by in the afternoon?"

Logan nodded. "I'm glad to see you've kept up with your education Corly. Your father really would be proud."

He leaned over and kissed her on the forehead. Corly had her eyes closed and was still smiling when he slipped through the front door of the pub.

Logan returned to The Savoy and was greeted by a smiling William Oglethorpe.

"How was your day, Senor Tomba?" asked the concierge.

"Splendid," Logan replied. "I traveled over to White Chapel and retraced the steps of your Jack the Ripper."

"Oh, that's one of London's most popular attractions. But I must say; it's even better when you go at night."

"Senor Oglethorpe, That would be much too scary for me," Logan replied as he scratched his hairy neck and eyed the brochures placed on the counter.

"Senor Oglethorpe," he asked. "Could you secure me a vehicle tomorrow?"

The concierge nodded his head. "We have a Rolls Royce set aside for our very special guests. We also provide a driver who can take you anywhere you want to go."

Logan shook his head no. "I need a rugged vehicle. I need a Land Rover. And I always drive myself."

"Consider it done, Senor. May I ask what you need it for?"

Logan lifted the camera from his neck. "I plan on doing some shooting in the country," he said with a smile. He returned to the Ambassador Suite where he observed his usual security ritual. Once satisfied that no one had entered the room, he walked in, kicked off his tan loafers and fell asleep on the couch. Logan lay there unconscious for the next seven hours. It was the soundest sleep he had had in weeks. The former IRA hit man would need all the rest he could get for the next phase of his mission.

The next morning, he had a pitcher of fresh squeezed orange juice and a hearty English breakfast delivered to his room. Logan devoured the sausages and bacon.

His eggs were served over-easy and this time he did not return them to the hotel kitchen. After breakfast and a hot shower, he dressed in a cardigan sweater and blue jeans, packed a small overnight bag and retrieved his computer case from under the bed. Logan had paid in advance for four weeks in the Ambassador Suite.

He still had a week left on his stay, so he did not bother to pack the rest of his things.

Michael Logan tucked his pistol in the waistband of his jeans and walked out of the grand hotel room never to return.

He received a set of keys at the front desk and was escorted to the carport where a white Land Rover awaited him. Logan threw his bag and computer case in the back seat and drove away. He continued one block east before pulling into an alleyway. Logan got out of the Land Rover and took out an instrument that resembled a laser pointer from the pocket of his leather jacket. It was another item that he had paid the Chilean arms dealer handsomely for. He ran the instrument down the hood of the automobile and proceeded around the back of the vehicle. The laser's red beam would flash if the instrument detected any type of tracking device or microphone. The small laser found nothing. He got back in the SUV and sped off.

Logan arrived in the village of Lower Slaughter just after noon. Cunningham Farm was tucked away in the heart of the Cotswolds, a range of limestone hills spanning roughly fifty miles. The region's thin soils are nearly impossible to plough, but the area is ideal for grazing sheep. There were currently two hundred head of sheep on Cunningham Farm. Logan drove the Land Rover down a winding dirt path, the sun was now breaking through the clouds and the sheep were milling about the rolling hills outside the farm house. He saw two barns, one he knew was for livestock, and the other he knew was for something else. Logan had visited the farm several times in his former life. The owner, Devin Cunningham was also a successful arms dealer with a soft spot in his heart for the men of the IRA. Logan pulled up to the manor house at the end of the long driveway and stepped out of the vehicle. He nodded to two farm hands as they ate their lunches on a wooden bench. The young men nodded in return and continued to consume their sandwiches. The two-story manor house had a steeply pitched roof that added to its rich character. Craftsmen using the ancient technique of dry stonewalling built the manor in the 17th century. Each stone in the home was held in place without mortar. During his days in the IRA, Logan often dreamed he would retire to a farm like this. Retirement was no longer an option. He walked to the front door, which was open.

"Hello, Corly," He shouted. "Is anyone home?"

"I'm just getting out of the shower," she hollered back. "Come in and make yourself at home."

Logan walked through a small entryway into the kitchen. He stood next to a large wooden butcher block and waited for Corly to come down the stairs. He looked around and noticed the interior design had changed greatly since his last visit. Gone were the framed pictures of Devin Cunningham's favorite hunting dogs. Picasso lithographs and candle filled sconces now hung in their place. The manor house truly had a woman's touch.

"I like what you've done to the place," Logan said with a smile as she strolled down the stairs. Her black hair was still wet and her skin smelled of jasmine. She was wearing a low cut top and a short black skirt. Corly Cunningham was not your typical farmer's daughter.

"I felt that I needed to make a few changes after Dad died. I've also watched a lot of Martha Stewart on the telly," she laughed.

She motioned Logan to the kitchen table and then fished two cups out of the cupboard.

"Care for some tea, Michael?"

"Ah, aren't you the proper English woman," he joked. "You wouldn't have any strong coffee would you?"

Corly poured water in the kettle and placed it on top of the cooking stove.

"It looks like you're running quite a farm here," Logan observed.

"To be honest, I spend most of my time in London," she sighed. "The money I make working at the Eye gives me a declarable income in case the government gets curious. The income generated here at the farm goes back into keeping this old place operational. Besides, I'm more of a city girl at heart. The workers here do fine without me," she said running her delicate fingers through her short hair.

"Your old man taught you well."

The young woman smiled back. Logan heard footsteps and sat upright in his chair.

"Relax, Michael it's just one of my workers. He's probably going to use the toilet."

You're among friends here. You're being too paranoid, he thought.

Logan sat back and took a long sip of his strong black coffee. He closed his eyes and let the hot liquid course down his throat.

"So Michael, where have you been for all this time? It looks like you've been hiding out in the sun."

He smiled. "Let's just say that I've been a citizen of the world for the past few years."

"Why have you come back? You're looking for weapons. It's what's brought you here. Are you fighting for the glorious cause again?"

He shook his head no. "I'm fighting for a cause of my own and let's just leave it at that."

"Ah, a case of the Irish Alzheimer's is it?" she asked with a laugh.

Logan couldn't see the humor. "What is that?"

"You only remember the grudges."

He let out a polite chuckle as she moved closer toward him; her eyes were locked on his. "I had the biggest crush on you when I was younger," she purred.

Logan replied with an uncomfortable laugh.

"I haven't been able to get you out of my head since seeing you at the Eye yesterday," she continued. "I've been thinking about what I'd do to you when I got you alone."

He sunk lower in his chair. Corly squeezed her small breasts together and offered them to him. He fought to resist, but the smell of jasmine was overpowering. Logan set down the coffee cup and closed his eyes. His defenses were lowered now. If she truly wanted him, she could have him. Logan's thoughts then drifted to the woman he'd left behind for this mission. *I can't do this,* he told himself. "Let's not do something we'll both regret," he said as he sat up straight. "You don't want to do this, trust me," he protested. He heard a familiar clicking sound and his eyes zeroed in on Corly, who stared back at him with a coy smile as she moved quickly away. He looked to his right and saw one of the farm hands aiming a loaded shotgun in his direction.

"Get up slowly Mister Logan and place your hands on the back of your head," the man ordered in a thick cockney accent.

"Corly, I guess the bounty on my head was too tempting for you."

"Oh, don't blame me Michael. I'm just a poor Irish girl trying to make her way in a harsh, unforgiving world," she replied with an accentuated brogue.

Logan could hear another man approaching from the back.

"Now you just stand there while my brother checks for any weapons," said the man with the shotgun. "We know how dangerous you can be, Dorcha."

Logan had not been called by that name in nearly ten years. His IRA commander had given him the nickname, Dorcha or "The Dark" because of his complexion. Logan was *Black Irish*. His fair skinned mother often joked that her twins had been left on her doorstep by gypsies. The IRA assassin known as Dorcha once had the ability to make blood run cold in anyone he encountered. But these men had no fear in their eyes. The brother ran his calloused hands down the sides of Logan's leather jacket and felt a bulge around the waistline.

"What do we have here?" he asked while pulling Logan's pistol out from the back of his pants.

"IRA legend; what bollocks," the brother said as he tossed the pistol to Corly.

"Look at him, he doesn't look so special to me," he continued.

The man was right; Logan was not physically intimidating. He was shy of six feet tall and weighed one hundred and eighty pounds. What the men did not know was that every muscle in his body was coiled to attack. And like a cobra, his strike would be felt before it was seen. Logan continued to stand motionless with his fingers folded around the back of his head.

"I tell you what boys. I'll let you walk out of here and I'll forget this ugly incident ever happened. It's an offer I only make once," Logan said with confidence.

"Shut the fuck up!" Corly screamed back. "Take him out to the barn and do him there."

"My, what a right bitch you've grown into. What would your father say if he could see you now?"

"Oh he'd be disappointed," she laughed. "He hoped he'd live long enough to get the reward for you himself."

The farm hand walked over to Logan and jammed the barrel of the shotgun into his back. "We're going to have a nice little walk, Mister Logan. My brother Chester will lead you out. Don't get brave or I'll scatter your brains all over this kitchen."

Logan let out a loud laugh.

"What the hell's so funny?" the man with the shotgun asked.

"Ah Boyo, I've been dead for years," he replied with a smile.

The three men walked slowly out into the sunlight.

"So what did the girl tell you?"

"She said her friends in the IRA would pay a king's ransom for your head," Chester replied.

Logan quickly sized up his captors in his mind. They were bigger than he was. Each man stood over six feet and weighed about 230 pounds, he guessed. But

Logan also deduced the men were slow and he smelled traces of whisky on their hot breath.

The former IRA hit man waited until they were near the barn before he made his move. With blinding speed Logan spun around and grabbed the stem of the shotgun with his right arm. The weapon fired, tearing a small hole in the side of the barn. Logan threw a punch with his left hand catching the gunman with a crushing blow to the temple. Logan seized the shotgun and trained it on the man's brother who was now rushing forward in full fury. Quickly realizing the weapon was now out of bullets; Logan held the gun like a cricket bat and swung it at his attacker. The wooden arm of the shotgun connected with Chester's chin and he fell to the muddy ground. Logan hit him once more on the head for good measure. The other farm hand was slowly coming to. Through glazed eyes, he saw Logan beating his brother unconscious. He tried to get up but it was too late. Logan ran toward him as if he were setting up for a penalty kick. He threw his leg back and kicked the man in the face with tremendous force. The farm hand saw Logan's boot coming down and then only darkness.

What's taking those idiots so long? Corly asked herself. *I knew they couldn't go through with it.*

She grabbed Logan's pistol and marched outside. Logan found two shells in the farm hand's pocket and quickly reloaded the weapon.

"Drop it, girl," he said with the shotgun trained on her chest.

"It always takes a woman to do a man's job," she shouted back while raising the pistol in Logan's direction.

Please don't, he thought.

A loud gunshot rang out. Frenzied sheep ran for the security of the barn as a wave of birds launched themselves off the branches of a nearby tree. Down below Michael Logan walked slowly over to the woman's body and dropped to his knees. Corly Cunningham's violet eyes were closed and she was no longer breathing. He cradled her head in his arms as tears formed at the corners of his eyes. "Oh dear girl. I'm so sorry," he whispered. He hugged her lifeless body for several minutes. Finally he dragged the young woman and her two co-conspirators into the barn. He lay the Corly's body down on a soft bed of hay and tied the two men together with cord. Logan climbed a tall wooden ladder into the loft and ran his hands through the piles of hay. In a few moments, he found what he had come for. He grabbed a rifle, a long range scope and three cartons of bullets. He carried the cache down the ladder and placed it in the trunk of the Land Rover. Michael Logan made the sign of the cross with his sore hands and drove away.

CHAPTER 14

CLAYMORE CASTLE, SCOTLAND

Laird Malcolm Rogers sat in a large leather chair. His feet rested on a small otto-man while his eyes watched the dancing flames of a roaring fire. The cherry-pan-eled library off his master bedroom suite was Rogers' favorite room in the castle. No one could bother him here. No one could disturb his darkest thoughts. Rogers had just finished reading the obituary of his former comrade Geoffrey Fergu-son. The newspaper article was now just a pile of ashes on the stone floor of the massive fireplace. Rogers had often thought that his friend's womanizing would eventually catch up to him. *But this just isn't right* he thought.

After their numerous brushes with death, it did not make sense that a Knight of the Round Table would perish at the hands of a jealous husband. The husband had not been formally charged with Ferguson's murder, but the newspaper report implied that it was only a matter of time. Rogers first met Ferguson and the blond haired man in 1972 in the Black Mountains of Wales. All three were hun-gry recruits challenging for membership in Britain's most elite fighting force, The Special Air Service. The unit was created by another Scottish Laird named David Stirling during World War Two. Its purpose was to wreak havoc behind enemy lines in areas controlled by the Axis Alliance. In one particular operation code-named, *Houndsmith,* nearly 150 SAS men parachuted into Dijon, France with jeeps and supplies. They were successful in cutting more than a hundred rail lines and inflicting heavy casualties on German soldiers. After the war, the SAS was used to hunt down Gestapo agents and bring them before the War Crimes Tribunal. Some Germans were captured; others were executed on the spot. The SAS had a need for men willing to kill with no questions asked.

Rogers and his two mates completed their SAS training, also known as *Selection* after a grueling 60-kilometer march through some of the world's hardest terrain. Called, *the Long Drag*, recruits had to complete the hike carrying fifty-five pounds of equipment. It took most soldiers twenty-four hours to conquer the rugged course. Rogers and his comrades finished in just under seventeen hours. Fitted with the coveted tan beret and winged dagger patch, the trio was first sent to Oman to quell a disturbance at a British owned oil refinery. Rogers, Ferguson and David Stirling's nephew Robert took to the task with a level of violence rarely seen, even in the Arab world. Attacks on the refinery came to a halt within days after Robert Stirling executed the Bedouin ringleader by cutting off his testicles and stuffing them into his mouth. Stirling then took out his long knife and severed the leader's head. He took the skull to the Bedouin's camp later that night and tossed it onto the fire as dozen-armed tribesmen watched in horror. Rogers could never forget what the blond haired man said to the tribe.

"We are the Knights of the Round Table. Any attack on British Sovereignty will be met with castration followed by decapitation. The rule applies to you, your women and your children. Who will be next?"

Not one brave warrior stepped forward to answer the challenge. Rogers immediately recognized that Robert Stirling had no sense of fear. He also knew the blond haired commando was totally insane.

"We were all a little crazy back then," Rogers said aloud as he took another sip of Cognac.

His mind was now filled with memories of their missions in Ulster. He vividly remembered the evening spent raping a fourteen-year-old girl as her Catholic father, bound and gagged, was forced to watch. Both bodies were still buried in a deep marsh outside Londonderry. Rogers rubbed his growing erection through his silk pajamas. He lifted his tall glass toward the ceiling.

"To the Knights of the Round Table," he shouted before he finished the glass with one great gulp. He then cocked his arm and threw the crystal into the stone fireplace.

Michael Logan arrived in Cairngorm, Scotland just after midnight. Claymore Castle loomed large over the tiny village. The drive from London took twelve hours.

The trip would have taken ten had it not been for the ambush at Cunningham Farm. Logan still could not get the image of a dying Corly out of his mind. He had killed many times before but he felt that each victim had done something to justify the death sentence. Corly Cunningham was just a screwed up kid who had acquired a taste for easy money. Logan rubbed his tired brown eyes. It was now too late in the evening to find lodging. He planned on spending a few days in the area and did not want to arouse any suspicion. He pulled the Land Rover off the main road and parked behind a row of tall trees. Logan reclined his leather car seat back and prayed that sleep would come easy that night.

I am Hell and I have returned for you. Michael Logan was back on the streets of West Belfast. He was thirteen years old and he was running. He could hear the footsteps of the blond haired assassin and could feel the killer's hot breath on his neck. The killer was getting closer. The boy finally reached the front door of his parent's store. He pulled at the door handle but it would not open. He could see his parents in the store-front windows. His mother was holding a baby in her arms. What was it? He asked Father O'Bannon. It was a girl, he replied. His parents stared back with blank expressions. It's me, Michael! He screamed. They did not respond. Logan's parents stepped back into the shadows of the darkened store. Logan looked farther down the street and saw Vincent waving back at him from the bell tower of Old Gomery. Suddenly a man appeared at Vincent's side. Brother Tobias was also smiling and waving. The priest put his arm around Vincent and led him slowly away. Michael Logan screamed for his twin. A hand reached out for his shoulder. The boy turned expecting to see the blond haired assassin. Instead he saw the white face of Corly Cunningham. She stood before him in her blood soaked top. Why Dorcha? Why? She asked. I am not the Dorcha! I am just a boy, he cried.

Logan awoke in a cold sweat. He looked straight ahead, and then to his right and his left. "Where the bloody hell am I?" he asked himself. After a brief moment of panic, Logan remembered his surroundings. He pressed the palms of his hands over his eyes, but still could not stop the pain. The bells of Old Gomery continued to chime loudly in his head. He reached into the pocket of his jacket and fished out a small bottle of aspirin. He popped the plastic top and dug through a layer of cotton for three tablets. He placed the pills in his mouth and swallowed hard. His mouth was dry and the pills felt like small stones traveling down his throat. Logan closed his eyes and waited for the pounding to stop. He caught himself drifting back to sleep and opened his eyes wide. He looked down at his wristwatch. It was now 5 a.m. Logan stepped out of the Land Rover and stretched his legs. He was alert now. The early morning chill was better than a cup of coffee. *I have to complete this mission. It does not matter if I live or die. Either way, the nightmares must end.*

CHAPTER 15

Logan turned on the radio as he drove into town. The female BBC announcer made no mention of a murder in the Cotswolds. Logan figured as much. If those two drunken farm hands were also aiding Corly with weapons sales, they would not want homicide detectives nosing around Cunningham Farm. Logan thought the brothers might bury the girl's body and then wait a week to report her missing.

She spent most of her time in London and anything could have happened to her there. *Poor girl.* He continued to drive one kilometer north toward the center of the Scottish village where he discovered a small inn. The twelve-bedroom hotel catered mostly to hikers and mountain bikers daring enough to challenge the treacherous Cairngorm Mountains. Logan entered the inn with his Nikon camera draped noticibly around his neck.

"Would you be interested in a room sir?" asked the white haired innkeeper.

"I would indeed," Logan replied reverting back to the thick Spanish accent of Roberto Tomba.

The elderly man with a kind face offered Logan a pen and asked him to fill out a registration form. Unlike the concierge back at the Savoy, there were no traces of arrogance in the innkeeper's voice.

"Are you here to hike sir?"

"Ah no, too dangerous for me," Logan grinned. "I'm actually working on a book about Scottish castles. My editor told me that I just had to include Claymore."

The inn keeper nodded his head and pointed his pipe in Logan's direction. "Well, you'll be doing yourself a favor there sir. Claymore is one of the finest castles in the Highlands. Will you be interviewing Laird Rogers?"

"I hope so, but I hear he's a tough man to track down."

"Oh he is," the man leaned forward and whispered. "He just stays up there in that castle all the time. His father, now there was a fine man. Always came down to the village for the Spring Festival."

"So you rarely see Laird Rogers?" Logan pressed.

"Yes, why would he come down here? He's fancies himself as quite the hunter and I hear he's got a splendid reserve of pheasants and foxes."

Logan paid the innkeeper in cash and walked up the creaky wooden staircase to his room. He opened the door to find a twin bed, dresser and small window. The bed room had been converted from attic space, with a slanted ceiling that made it impossible for a tall person to stand up straight. Logan's head was about an inch away from the ceiling. It was not the Ambassador Suite at the Savoy, but Logan had seen worse, much worse. He placed his bags on the bed and stared out the window at the castle which stood roughly a kilometer away. Even at this distance, it was a truly impressive sight. The medieval fortress was surrounded by four tall spires that disappeared in the cloud cover.

Where is Malcolm Rogers vulnerable?

He locked the door, opened his briefcase and spread the diagrams across the bed. Claymore Castle was a classic Scottish 'Tower House'. The large manor house was built up vertically with square turrets designed to cover any approaching enemy. Two giant Yew trees stood at the gateway of the castle. Those trees once provided the Rogers clan wood for bows and arrows. The grounds of Claymore were now fitted with hi-definition surveillance cameras and laser guided motion detectors.

There would be no storming this castle.

Malcolm Rogers had to suck in his stomach in order to button his wool trousers.

He stood before a full-length mirror and could hardly recognize himself. "What happened to you?" he asked the stranger in the mirror. As a young man, Rogers was a physical specimen. He could bench-press three hundred pounds and run for miles without losing his breath. That seemed like a lifetime ago, before his back injury and before nobility fattened his wallet and dulled his senses. Now Malcolm Rogers weighed well over three hundred pounds and often used a motorized scooter to travel around castle grounds. Rogers' only physical exercise came during his weekly hunt. "I've got to lose this weight," he said with disgust. The first thing he was going to do was toss out that blasted scooter. *Maybe I'll get a mountain bike like those crazy kids in the village.*

He promised himself that his life would change following the death of his old friend. In an odd way, he felt invigorated by the murder of Geoffrey Ferguson. Rogers could not wait to get out on his reserve. However, he knew his hunting partner would be less than enthused.

"Bonnie, it's almost noon time and I want that boy dressed and ready to go," Rogers snapped at his daughter.

"But dad, he hates hunting. You know that! Yet, you make him go every week," she replied with frustration.

"As long you and your son live under this roof, you will do as I say. Hunting is good for the boy. Someday he will become Laird of Claymore. I won't raise my grandson to be a fag like his father!"

Bonnie hit her father firmly on the shoulder. "Shh, he can hear those awful things that come out of your mouth."

"Tell him to drop that blasted Harry Potter book and meet me on the reserve in ten minutes. Or I promise he'll go straight to military academy."

Ethan Rogers sat and listened as his grandfather's words echoed through the walls of the castle's great hall. The sixteen-year-old was in the middle of J.K. Rowling's latest Hogwarts adventure and he did not want to stop reading for anything; especially for the man he hated most in his life. He and his mother had been staying at Claymore since the divorce six months prior when Dad had come home to their Edinburgh flat and announced that he was in love with a young dancer. The truly stunning news came next. The dancer's name was Stephen. Ethan's mother was devastated, but the teen actually admired his father's courage. His Grandfather was another story. Laird Rogers had threatened to shoot the couple if he ever saw them. Dad was now traveling with his lover's ballet troupe across Europe.

God, I wish I could be with him, Ethan thought.

The teen knew that if he did not go on his weekly hunt with his grandfather, the old bastard would take it out on Ethan's mom. He grudgingly dressed in his hunting garments and walked out to the reserve.

Michael Logan had parked his Land Rover along a deserted road at the southern end of the reserve. He was now resting his lean upper body on the thick branch of a giant pine tree as he watched the castle through a set of high-powered binoculars. The day was supposed to be for surveillance only. But the mission changed when Logan spotted the hefty Scottish Laird waddling toward the hunting reserve. He waited to see if any bodyguards would accompany Malcolm Rogers, but the man appeared to be alone. Logan climbed down the tree and raced back to the Land Rover where he popped the trunk and grabbed the rifle. He fastened the scope onto the centerpiece of the weapon and filled the pockets of his green cargo pants with shells. Logan ran back to the castle and hoped he would get lucky.

"You're late," Malcolm Rogers shouted as he watched his grandson approach.

"Sorry Grandfather," the teen replied meekly.

Rogers handed the boy an Auguste Francotte double barrel hunting rifle. It was a smaller version of the weapon Rogers used.

"Will it be pheasant or foxes today boy?"

Ethan hated being called, boy. In his entire life, he could not remember his grandfather ever calling him by his name.

How about we go hunting for fat old white men? I know where I'm gonna start.

"Whichever you want grandfather."

"Pheasant it is then," Rogers smiled through his thick, ruddy cheeks.

The two started walking in the high grass when Ethan felt the urge to relieve himself.

"I have to go to the bathroom," he told his grandfather. "I'll be right back."

Rogers looked back at his grandson oddly.

"What do you mean, you'll be right back. If you have to piss, do it out here."

"I'll just be a few minutes," Ethan promised. "I meet you up by the crag."

The old man shook his head and kept walking. *He is a fag just like his father.*

Ethan turned and started back to the castle. He could not hide his grin. Sure he could have relieved himself outside, but what satisfaction would there be in that? Ethan would rather play the dainty and get under his grandfather's skin.

Logan crept up to the reserve with his rifle tucked under his right arm. He knew that he had a lot of ground to cover; the reserve itself was spread over three thousand acres. But he also knew that he had to remain patient. *Take the shot only if the opportunity presents itself,* he reminded himself. It was twenty past noon and the fog was just beginning to burn off, still, the Highland mist hugged Logan's legs making it difficult for him to see where he was going. He cut through a barbed wire fence and crouched down in the tall grass. He waited there for several minutes. Logan heard no footsteps so he continued his advance.

Malcolm Rogers kept his eyes focused and his ears open for anything moving in the bush. The pheasants on his reserve were always elusive. That is why Rogers enjoyed the hunt so much. Apparently, others did as well so the Laird was forced to set traps along the border of his reserve to discourage poaching. Rogers wore a crimson hunting jacket and Logan spotted a flash of red appearing through a row of small trees. He placed the scope of the rifle up to his steady eye but the red flash was gone. He took another step forward and heard a loud snap as a set of iron jaws sprung up violently from a pile of leaves. Startled by the trap, Logan fell backward in the weeds.

Rogers heard the commotion to his right and raised his rifle. He was hunting pheasant today, but if a fox were to make itself available, the Laird would oblige the creature. Rogers fired his weapon in the direction of the noise. Logan was still lying in the grass when he heard the bullet zip by his head. He immediately grabbed his rifle and got up on one knee. Logan had the fat man in his scope and returned fire. The bullet shattered a tree branch just above Rogers' shoulder.

"What the hell is this," Rogers screamed as he watched the broken branch fall to the ground. "Is that you boy? Playing games with your old Grandpa? You'll learn to aim better than that when I send your ass to military school!"

Rogers started walking when Logan fired a second shot. The bullet knocked the man's rifle right out of his hands. Rogers let out another scream as the pain reached his fingertips. "That's it you little shit! It's time this old man taught you a lesson."

The Laird shook the sting out of his hands and boldly marched toward the area where the shots were fired.

Logan centered the rifle scope on Rogers' chest. He squeezed the trigger but nothing happened. The gun was jammed. Rogers was now thirty yards away. Because of the tall waving grass, the older man still did not have a clear view of his attacker. Logan jumped to his feet and charged. A sense of disbelief fell over Malcolm Rogers as he witnessed the man running forward. It was not his grandson after all. The Laird froze but his attacker kept coming. Logan leapt in the air with his right leg extended. His boot came down hard on Rogers' beefy chest and both men went tumbling to the ground.

The Laird felt a burning sensation shoot through his upper body. He rolled over in the mud and reached out for the splintered tree branch. Logan twisted his ankle during the fall and was still on the ground when Rogers approached with the branch held high over his head.

"Who the fuck are you?" The large man demanded in short breaths.

Logan remained silent while clutching his badly sprained left ankle.

"I said who the fuck are you?"

"West Belfast," Logan replied through clenched teeth. "The couple in the grocery store, they were my parents."

Before Rogers could answer, Logan kicked up with his right foot catching the man in the groin. The Laird keeled over coughing up blood on his crimson tunic.

Logan pulled a small knife from his boot. Rogers saw the blade and started to run.

Logan limped after him as the hefty man began climbing a rocky hill in the center of the reserve. The crag was over sixty feet high. Rogers was sweating profusely now as he tried to make his way to the top. Logan was gaining ground as he moved his body to avoid the large stones Rogers had tossed in his way. The Laird reached the top of the crag and quickly realized he had no place to go. Years of drinking and bad diet had robbed the man of his instincts and SAS training. Rogers stood up completely out of breath and did the only thing he could do in this situation. He pleaded for his life.

"Is it money you want? As you probably know, I am a very rich man. I can give you as much as you desire," he offered desperately.

Logan limped toward him holding the small knife.

"What kind of price can you put on a murdered father?" Logan shouted back.

Rogers shook his jowls like an overfed Basset hound but remained silent. The Dorcha was in a full rage now. "What would you pay for an invalid mother and her stillborn baby?" he yelled with a trace of spittle accentuating every syllable. "What would you pay for a young boy's innocence?"

Malcolm Rogers still did not answer. Instead he reached forward and tried to tackle the smaller man. Logan swatted Roger's hands away with his iron-like forearms. He took Rogers by the lapel of his muddy hunting jacket and looked into his panicked eyes.

"This is for my family," Logan hissed as he pushed Malcolm Rogers off the crag. Michael stared into the man's bulging eyes as he continued his free fall. For a brief moment, Logan thought back to Brother Tobias and Old Gomery. "Another sent to hell," he whispered as the Laird landed with a thump in the high grass sixty feet below.

Exhausted, Logan limped his way back down the hill. He pulled a black and white photograph from his leather jacket and slowly approached the body of Malcolm Rogers. He tossed the picture in the air and watched it float gently down on top of the dead man's twisted, broken body. It was not the same memento he had left behind at the Ferguson murder. This photo showed a young Irish couple with a twin boy seated on each lap. The family was smiling.

Logan's trance was broken by the sound of cracking twigs. He turned to find a teenaged boy standing just a few feet away. The lad also wore a hunting jacket and had his rifle pointed at Logan's chest. The Dorcha was still holding the small knife in his left hand. Training and instinct told him to throw it at the boy's chest, but instead he dropped it to the ground.

"This man had a debt to pay," Logan told the teenager. "I guess that I too must pay a debt of my own."

He waited for the teen to pull the trigger.

Ethan Rogers brought his rifle down to his side.

"You must get going," he told Logan. "My grandfather had a terrible accident. Nothing more, nothing less."

Logan studied the teenager for a moment. "Thank you Laird Rogers."

Michael Logan bowed to the boy and limped slowly away. He ignored the pain in his ankle and made a hasty retreat to the Land Rover. He was awed by the gesture he had just received. Rogers' grandson had honesty in his eyes and kindness in his heart. Michael Logan had known someone like that once.

CHAPTER 16

DUBLIN, IRELAND
1996

Vincent Logan stumbled down the steps of Long Hall and out to South Great George's Street. He bent down and placed his hands on both knees. Two buddies from the police academy followed him out of the noisy pub.

"I told you he couldn't hold his drink," one friend slurred to the other.

The men laughed while they clung to one another for support. Their knees were buckling. Vincent paid no attention to his friends. He just stared at the ground and prayed that he would not throw up.

"We made it Vincent," the friend said with excitement. "We're officially Garda Siochana."

Blurry eyed, Logan finally looked up at his drinking partners. "I'd say we're all officially shite faced."

The trio had been drinking in the Victorian saloon since receiving their police badges that morning. Logan's wife Fiona gave him a congratulatory kiss after the ceremony at Phoenix Park before sending him off to this fraternal rite of passage. He lost count of how many shots of vodka he put away through the course of the day. It was now 2 a.m. and Vincent hoped Fiona would be as understanding when he found his way back to their small apartment.

"We're gonna catch a cab home, need a lift?" his buddy asked.

Logan waved the men off. "I'll walk back to the flat. It'll give me time to sober up."

The two drunken cadets walked away on wobbly legs singing the chorus to the American television show, *Cops*. "Bad boys, bad boys, What'cha gonna do? What'cha gonna do when we come for you…."

Vincent shook his head and laughed. They certainly had plenty to celebrate. The three recruits had just gutted out twenty two grueling weeks at Garda Siochana College at McCann Barracks in County Tipperary. All had received a National Diploma in police studies. Vincent had graduated at the top of his class.

"Boy, if my instructors could see me now. I can't even walk a straight line," he admitted to himself.

Vincent had a long walk ahead of him. His apartment was ten blocks away.

He shoved both hands in the pockets of his blue windbreaker and made a determined effort to appear at least, partially sober. He began walking when suddenly a white van pulled up to the curb beside him. Vincent glanced over as three hooded men jumped out from the sliding side door. The Guarda recruit tightened his fists and turned to face the men.

"We're going for a ride," one man announced while pulling a sawed off shotgun out from under his black trench coat.

Vincent realized that fighting these men off would be impossible. His reflexes were slowed by hours of drinking, and there was no defense against a shotgun. He put his hands in the air and did not resist while the hooded men led him into the van. He was told to sit on a crate as a kidnapper grabbed another black hood and ordered him to put in on. A thick layer of duct tape covered the eyes of the hood and Vincent was in total darkness. He tried to remain calm. Could the men have mistaken him for his brother? Vincent's college instructor had warned him that something like this might happen. He had his new police badge tucked in the pocket of his pants. That would surely clear up any confusion. But if these men were after his brother, Vincent felt it was better to wait a while before revealing his true identity. That way, Michael would have at least a head start against the men who were chasing him. The van ride lasted a half-hour. Because the driver had taken many turns, they could have traveled twenty miles or only two. Vincent had no way of knowing. Although he could not see, his ears were alert for any familiar sounds.

Are we on a highway? Or are we on a city street?

The sounds were much different. You virtually never heard a car horn on a highway. Vincent had listened to several honking horns since the journey had begun. He figured he had not left the city. The van came to a sudden stop before continuing down a short path.

Are we in a parking garage? He wondered.

The vehicle came to another abrupt stop and Vincent could hear the side door pull open. He was grabbed by the shoulders of his jacket and yanked out of the van. The kidnappers played rough, but so far they had done nothing to harm him.

They must have other plans for Michael.

One kidnapper pushed Vincent up against the wall and ran his hands down over his body.

Why didn't you check for weapons before I got in the van? Vincent wondered.

The man felt the bulge in his front pocket and fished out the police badge.

Wait til they realize whom they've captured. They wouldn't be stupid enough to harm a police officer.

"It's him," the kidnapper announced to his comrades.

They were coming after me?

Vincent felt confused and truly scared for the first time since the ordeal had begun. He could hear a metal door open and he was shoved through. They continued down a long corridor to another door. This one was locked. One of the men wrapped his knuckles on the door three times. He paused for a couple of seconds and knocked twice more. The door opened and Vincent was led inside.

"Good job boys. You can leave us now," a voice ordered from the corner of the room.

Vincent could hear retreating footsteps and then the door slammed shut. He stood at attention with the hood still covering his face. He could feel someone slowly approaching. His body tensed up as a pair of hands pulled at the hood.

"Hello brother."

Vincent opened his eyes and saw his twin standing before him.

He tried to get the words out but could not speak.

"I know Vincent. It's been quite a long time."

Michael stepped back and the twins stared at one another. Vincent had not seen his brother since that fateful night inside the bell tower at Grey Abbey. He looked at Michael and saw a scruffier version of himself. Michael had long wild black hair and a week's growth of beard on his weathered face. The scar on his forehead had shrunken over time. Michael's eyes ran from Vincent's shoes to his shoulders. The police recruit was neatly attired even after a night of heavy drinking. Vincent's brown loafers were polished and his blue slacks were pressed. His olive skin was smoothly shaven. Vincent's black hair was cut much shorter than Michael's.

"You smell like a saloon floor one minute after closing time," Michael laughed. He handed Vincent a cup of hot coffee. "Take this, it will make you feel better."

Vincent hesitated for a moment before reaching out for the cup.

"Why did you have to kidnap me? I would have come on my own."

"I wanted to go to your graduation ceremony this morning. But under the circumstances, I didn't feel it was appropriate."

Vincent's eyes scanned the room. There were several maps spread out on a folding table and a dozen AK-47 rifles lined up in the corner. They were in an IRA safe house of some kind.

"Is this where you plan all of your murders?" he asked.

"Ah, my brother doesn't approve of me," Michael said as he folded his muscular arms and nodded his head. "You're fighting your war Vincent and I'm fighting mine."

"No, you're wrong Michael. This morning I took an oath to protect the innocent, to protect them from people like you."

Michael laughed. "That's right, you're officially a cop now. That's a dangerous line of work. You know they don't allow you to carry a gun, yes?"

"Not until I make detective," Vincent pointed out. "Is that why your goons didn't search me when they grabbed me on the street?"

Michael nodded.

It was a proud tradition of the Garda Siochana that uniformed officers carry only wooden truncheons. "But don't worry," Vincent told his brother. "I'm not the scared kid I once was. I've learned to use my hands."

"You should learn to use your feet and run the hell away from any trouble," Michael advised. This reunion was not going the way he planned. He decided to take a softer approach. "It's been fourteen long years, Vincent. Can we at least try to be civil with one another?"

"You cannot undo what's already been done," Vincent told Michael. "Why must you continue the violence?"

"I see Da's killer in the face of every man I've erased from this God forsaken place," Michael replied coldly.

"What do you mean to accomplish? Do you think a united Ireland is even attainable at this point?"

Michael shook his head. "I'm not fighting for a free Ireland. I just want to close my eyes for once and sleep without the nightmares."

Vincent was confused. "Do you think killing people will make this happen?"

Michael shrugged his broad shoulders. "It's the only thing I know how to do," he said as he motioned Vincent over to a pair of wooden armchairs and the two sat down facing each other. They sat in silence for several minutes hoping the awkwardness would wear off.

"Have you visited our mother recently?" Michael asked.

"I've been at police academy for the past few months," Vincent replied staring at the floor. "I haven't had the chance. What about you?"

"I slip in from time to time when the police aren't watching. It's tough being the most wanted man in Ireland," Michael managed to smile.

Ann Logan was being cared for at St. Mary's Home a few miles outside Belfast where she remained in a vegetative state.

"Sounds to me like you've got the doctors in your pocket," Vincent accused his brother.

Michael shrugged. "I've got doctors and police officers on the payroll."

Vincent stood up as the wooden chair tipped over behind him. "Is that why you brought me here, to buy me off?" His voice was louder now.

"Please sit down Vincent. I'm not offering to buy you off and I'd be pissed if you ever took a bribe. We need good cops on the streets. You see, there's a war being waged within the ranks of the IRA." Michael's voice trailed off.

"What kind of war?"

"I've already said too much here tonight brother. Let's get back to mum," Michael said quickly changing the subject. "You know, she can't express it, but I think she knows I'm there. I hold her hand and she blinks her eyes. I always wonder. Does she know the man I've become?"

Vincent sensed the concern in his brother's voice. "I'm sorry for what happened to you. I really am."

Michael shook his head and pointed his finger toward his twin. "I know you blame yourself Vincent, but don't. I made the decision to kill that bugger in the bell tower, not you. And you know what? It felt good. It felt good because I knew that I not only spared you from getting hurt, but I probably spared dozens of other boys as well. The only problem is … I can't get the sound of those damn bells out of my head. Old Gomery is always there. Sometimes, it's just background noise … other times the sound's so deafening I think my head will explode."

"Have you tried to get help?"

Michael shook his head and laughed. "It's not as if a guy like me can just plop myself down on some shrink's couch."

"How do you deal with it then?" Vincent asked.

"I concentrate on other things."

"So how did you end up here?" Vincent asked nodding toward the stack of AK-47's.

Michael got up and poured himself another cup of black coffee. He sat back down took a small sip and told his story. "Well after Grey Abbey, I made my way to Londonderry where I lived in an abandoned warehouse and begged for food."

Michael paused before continuing. He did not want to remember his past.

"I was sick of begging, so I stole to stay alive. Then one day, this older fella said he'd pay me to stand watch while he and his boys robbed a jewelry store. They were leaving the store when the owner gave chase waving his pistol. No one saw the man but me. I ran up behind him and stuck him in the back with my jack knife. The storeowner bled to death and the boys got away. Turns out, the robbers were IRA. Word spread that there was a kid who didn't hesitate when it came to killing. I was quickly brought into the fold."

Vincent ran through Michael's police file in his head. His instructors at McCann Barracks had given him a private briefing on his twin brother. They wanted to know where Vincent Logan focused his allegiance. The file stated that Michael Logan had committed five murders before turning 18 years of age. So impressed was the IRA governing council that the hierarchy ordered him to Libya and Moscow for training in a number of terrorist camps. Once Logan had returned to Ireland, he allegedly committed seven more murders, including the assassination of the commanding officer of the RUC. Vincent swore to his superiors that he would do everything in his power to bring down his twin brother. Now sitting across from him, he wondered if he could fulfill that promise.

"You saved my life in that bell tower," he told Michael. "Had you arrived a few minutes later, that bastard would have gone through with it. I don't think I could have lived with myself afterwards."

"Yes, you could Vincent," Michael responded looking away. "I've had to."

Vincent sat back in his chair and tears filled his eyes. He had never known that Brother Tobias had also molested Michael. *Maybe I did,* he thought. *But I just blocked it out.* It all made sense to him now. The brothers got up from their chairs and reached for each other. The cop and the killer hugged each other and cried.

CHAPTER 17

Vincent was ushered out of the safe house the same way he went in, with a hood over his head and three IRA goons leading the way. Although Vincent was Michael's brother, he was still a cop and the Dorcha could not take any chances. Vincent was loaded back into the van and driven away. This ride took only half as long as the previous one.

"How are your knees?" asked one of the kidnappers, finally breaking the silence.

"I … I guess they're okay," Vincent replied from under the hood.

"Good."

The driver of the white van shifted his foot from the gas pedal to the break and slowed down from forty miles per hour to about twenty. Vincent could hear the side door pull open.

"At least stop the van so I can get out," he protested.

He was grabbed by the shoulders and thrown out the door of the moving van. Vincent hit the pavement hard and rolled four times before his bruised body came to a stop on the curb. He reached up to pull the mask off and felt a stinging pain in his right elbow. Vincent winced as he pulled the hood off his head. It was morning now and the sun penetrated his eyelids. He lay there on the sidewalk for several minutes as the immediate pain began to wear off. He got up on one knee and rested. Vincent gritted his teeth and forced himself to stand up. His knees were sore but the worst pain came from the elbow. Vincent knew that he had chipped the bone during the rough landing. Luckily, he did not have to walk very far; the gunmen had thrown him out of the van in front of his apartment building.

Vincent limped up the front steps and fished for his keys with his good arm. It took two tries before he successfully inserted the key into the lock. He pushed open the heavy front door and staggered down the hall toward his apartment. He was in too much pain to try another lock so he pounded on the door with his fist instead. He could hear his infant daughter crying from inside the flat.

"Vincent, is that you?" Fiona asked as she scrambled out of the bedroom toward the front door.

"Yes, baby. Please ... let me in," he cried.

Fiona turned the lock and deadbolt and opened the door.

Vincent leaned against the doorframe. His windbreaker was torn and he was bleeding at the knees.

"What happened to you? Oh my god, did you get into a fight?" asked his horrified wife.

"No, I didn't Fi, just help me to the couch," he said through clenched teeth.

He leaned on his wife as she guided him slowly toward the sofa. Their five-month-old daughter Audrey continued to wail from her crib.

"Should I call an ambulance?" she asked frantically.

"No ... Go check on the baby. I'll be alright."

Fiona left her husband and walked into the small nursery. The child soon stopped crying and Vincent could hear the familiar sucking sound coming from her bottle of formula. Fiona then pulled some ice cubes from the freezer and wrapped them in a face cloth. She returned to her husband who was stretched out on the coach.

"What happened darling? Who did this to you?" she asked while placing the cold cloth on his swollen elbow.

"You're not gonna believe this Fi, but I've just come from a meeting with my brother."

Fiona did not respond right away. Vincent had only spoken of his twin twice since meeting his wife.

"Is this some kind of joke? Did you get yourself banged up after drinking?"

Vincent moaned as he tried to sit up on the couch. "Listen to me, I am deadly serious."

He told Fiona about the kidnapping turned family reunion. She nodded back at her husband but could not speak. Her heart was now in her stomach.

"What are you going to do?" she asked finally.

"He saved my life when we were kids honey. He may be the Dorcha to everyone else, but he's still Michael to me. I plan to keep our meeting a secret. I owe him that."

Fiona closed her beautiful hazel eyes and clutched a small cross that hung from a chain around her neck. She was concerned not only for her husband, but also for their baby. Vincent knew what she was thinking.

"Fiona, I promise that I'll never go chasing after my brother. This reunion was a one-time thing. You'll be safe and so will Audrey. Michael's life is too dangerous for me."

Fiona reached down and hugged her battered husband gently.

"Let me rest for a bit, and then if I can manage I'd like to take you both to see my mother," Vincent told her before nodding off on the couch.

"Daddy, Christopher called me a cow!" Elizabeth Forrest cried to her father from the living room of their spacious Dublin apartment. Todd Forrest was in his upstairs bedroom trying desperately to tie a Windsor knot.

"Christopher, apologize to your sister," he ordered.

So far, the morning had not been going well for the veteran reporter. He had already nicked his chin while shaving and was now in the process of strangling himself with his own necktie.

"Relax dear, you're just a little nervous," his wife Katherine said as she approached from behind. The tall blond lifted the starched collar of his white shirt and slowly folded and twisted a tight knot in his red tie.

"Just perfect," he said staring into the mirror. "Do you know how long I've been trying to tie this friggin' thing?"

Katherine giggled and kissed him on the cheek.

"Remember, you're a Pulitzer Prize winning journalist," she told him in a soothing tone. "You have nothing to worry about."

His wife was right. He had nothing more to prove. He had been awarded the most prestigious prize in journalism at the age of twenty-five. Forrest's reports on Bobby Sands and the 1981 Hunger Strike won him fame and financial stability and now the American expatriate was given his choice of assignments anywhere in the world. He chose to stay in Ireland and was now considered one of the world's foremost experts on the IRA. The reporter's critics had called him the media mouthpiece for the outlawed group, but his latest book shattered that perception.

The Green Hand—The Birth of the Irish Mafia was an international best seller. Forrest had spent the past two years writing the blistering expose that showed how the IRA had turned its back on its goal of a united Ireland for the profits and power of organized crime. According to Forrest's book, the IRA was now heavily involved in the narcotics and prostitution trades. The reporter received much of his information from an anonymous source deep within the IRA. The book caused such a stir that he was now invited to address the *Dail Eireann* (Irish Parliament) on the problem. Forrest got tongue tied when he had to speak to five people at once, and this morning he was going to lecture more than 150 legislators from the four corners of the Emerald Isle.

"Daddy, Christopher stopped calling me a cow. Now he's calling me a smelly skunk," four-year-old Elizabeth said tugging on her father's arm. Forrest lifted his little girl in his arms and grabbed his blue pinstriped blazer off the post of his bed.

"Just between you and me," he whispered to the child. "Christopher smells like a Baboon's behind."

Elizabeth laughed as her father kissed her cheek. She wiped off the kiss and pointed to the staircase. "Daddy, we must hurry. You can't be late for your speech."

Forrest carried the curly haired tike down the stairs and into the den. Ten-year-old Christopher was sitting on his father's easy chair watching television.

"Turn that thing off Chris and grab your coat," Forrest ordered.

The boy shut the TV off with the remote control and sulked while putting his arms through the sleeves of his tan jacket. Katherine had finished applying her make up and looked absolutely stunning as she waited for her family at the front door.

"Come now, we mustn't be late for daddy's big day," she said displaying a perfect smile.

Todd Forrest paused a moment to reflect on how truly lucky he was. The former Katherine O'Meara was still the most beautiful woman he had ever seen, and she was smart too. In her previous life, Katherine strutted the catwalks as a sought after fashion model. Now she was a well paid senior buyer for Brown Thomas, Dublin's most expensive department store. They met on a blind date and he was immediately taken by her beauty. She in turn, was captivated by the American's puppy dog eyes and his charming Savannah drawl. Forrest opened the front door and led his family out into the damp Dublin morning.

Seamus Barry watched the family from the passenger seat of a silver Peugeot. He had been parked outside the reporter's flat since 4 a.m. Barry held a small black box in his hands. He looked over at the driver who was also watching the front steps of the apartment building.

"For fuck sake, he's got the family with him," Conor Francis said as Forrest ushered his children into the back seat of his black BMW.

"That's no matter. We have our orders," Barry told his driver.

Forrest's wife lifted their little girl and placed her in a booster seat in the back of the sedan. The woman spent several more seconds buckling the child in. The seconds felt like hours to Seamus Barry.

"This isn't right," the driver protested. "The family isn't part of the plan."

"I swear to God, that if you don't shut the fuck up, I'm gonna put you on sticks!" Barry warned his companion.

Conor Francis knew that his passenger meant every word. Seamus Barry had shot out the kneecaps of five other men who had dared to cross his path.

The two men waited for Forrest and his family to get settled in their car.

Todd Forrest sat in the driver seat of his BMW and patted the breasts of his topcoat.

"Sorry darling, I seem to have left my speech in the study," he sheepishly told his wife.

Katherine rolled her eyes and laughed. She knew how absent-minded her husband could be. Forrest reached for the handle and slowly opened the driver's side door.

"What's taking them so long?" Barry asked angrily with his finger on the detonator. "Fuck it."

Seamus Barry pressed the button with his gloved index finger and smiled as the BMW exploded before his eyes. The ear shattering blast was followed by a huge plume of fire. Todd Forrest was thrown ten feet from the car. He lay semi-conscious on the street. He could feel nothing below his waist, but he smelled something awful. Just then he realized his legs were ablaze. Forrest could also hear the screams of his children coming from inside the burning vehicle. He turned over on his stomach and clawed at the pavement. Forrest yelled as he desperately tried to reach his burning family.

Conor Francis pulled out of the parking space and hit the gas pedal.

"There he is on the street," Seamus Barry pointed out with wild eyes. "Hit that fucker!"

The Peugeot drove over the reporter's burning legs and sped away from the crime scene. Seamus Barry looked into his rear-view mirror.

"He's fucking dead. His whole family is fucking dead!" He declared gleefully.

CHAPTER 18

"Should we wake him?" Timothy Clancy asked nervously.

His companion nodded his reply. The man's jaw was wired shut and he could not speak. He had been in charge of Vincent Logan's abduction and release. When the Dorcha found out how his men had treated his brother, someone had to pay. Ian Greeley paid with a broken jaw. Greeley knocked on the bedroom door. Michael Logan walked out moments later rubbing his weary eyes.

"What is it?" Logan asked his men.

Clancy told him of the attack on Todd Forrest and his family. Logan showed no emotion as he took the news, but inside he was a fiery cauldron of rage. He had met secretly with the reporter on several occasions while Forrest gathered information for his book. Michael Logan was disgusted with the new direction of the IRA and it was he who had become the reporter's most trusted source. Putting a hit on his secret friend was bad enough, but to kill his wife and children also? There was no justification for that. The Dorcha had been one to openly criticize the IRA's bombing campaigns in the past. "Bombers are not soldiers, they are cowards," he had told leaders of the IRA military council. When children were killed in an IRA attack, the council called it collateral damage. Logan called it sloppy work. There was no room for innocent victims in Michael Logan's war. He went back into the bedroom, got on his cell phone and called Martin Barry.

Logan's words were slow and deliberate. "Your brother has ruined us."

"Michael, it is unfortunate the family was killed. But the leadership stands by its decision. Todd Forrest could not give that speech under any circumstances," replied the chief of the IRA military council.

Logan was not interested in excuses. "Seamus has set our cause back twenty years. The pictures of those burned children speak louder that any speech that reporter could have made. The police won't stop now until we're all rounded up. Seamus is a homicidal maniac and I'm sure he enjoyed every minute of it. He's a mad dog and mad dogs need to be put down."

Martin Barry squeezed the telephone receiver and pounded his desk with his fist.

"Do not go near my brother, Dorcha," he shouted. "That is an order! I will deal with Seamus. This does not concern you!"

The phone line went dead. Logan stared at his cell phone and knew what he had to do next.

The Dorcha parked his red Suzuki motorbike in an alley off Aran Quay. Logan was wearing a black leather jacket and matching leather pants. He kept his helmet on with the tinted visor shielding his face. He could hear the thumping techno-music bleeding from the walls of *The Whispering Gypsy*. It was just after 11 p.m. and the line of Euro-trash waiting to get into the club was already twenty deep. The Dorcha walked up to the front of the line and lifted his visor for the doorman.

The bouncer recognized Logan immediately and lifted the velvet rope without saying a word.

"Hey what the hell? We've been waiting here for almost an hour?" complained a tall skinny twenty-something with a nose ring.

The muscular doorman shrugged his wide shoulders and folded his beefy arms.

Logan entered the cavernous club and walked past several drugged out party-goers who were clinging to the walls. The music grew louder as he neared the dance floor. Logan snatched a shot glass filled with vodka off a barmaid's tray and downed it without breaking stride. The angry peroxide haired waitress tugged on his shoulder but the Dorcha paid no attention. He cut a path through the dance floor and began climbing a staircase next to the dee-jay booth. One hand was on the railing; the other was tucked into the right pocket of his jacket. The gun felt warm in his palm.

Logan bypassed the billiard room on the second floor and continued climbing the metal stairs to the top floor of the club. The door was shut but laughter could be heard from within. Logan took a thin piece of metal from his jacket and picked the lock with ease. He closed the visor of his motorcycle helmet to hide his eyes, grabbed the door handle and pushed it open. The Dorcha entered the club's private bungalow.

The walls were draped with red velvet and a disco ball spun from the ceiling. Conor Francis was seated on several large pillows piled up on the floor. In front of him, a young brunette stood on a round table stripping her clothes off to the beat of the music. Despite the erotic display, Francis' eyes were closed as the music penetrated his ears and the heroin coursed through his blood stream. The brunette caught a glimpse of the intruder in the mirror that covered the entire back wall. She spotted the gun in his right hand and shrieked. Francis opened his eyes, but was too slow to react. Logan jumped across the table and rammed his knee into the man's chest. He brought down his pistol and drove it into Francis' forehead.

"Where is Seamus Barry?" Logan shouted from under his helmet.

Francis did not flinch. "Do you know who you're fucking with?" he yelled back.

"Now's not the time for bravery Francis," the Dorcha replied lifting the visor of his helmet.

Conor Francis' eyes went wide. He knew he was now face to face with death.

The Dorcha grabbed Francis by the front of his sweatshirt and lifted the heavy man off the pillows.

"Now I'll ask again fat man. Where is Seamus Barry?"

Francis pointed his pudgy index finger to a door in the back of the room.

Logan held a firm grip on the larger man's shoulder and guided him slowly toward the door. The brunette had covered her naked body with pillows and was now quivering in the corner of the room.

"Get your clothes on girl, and get out of here," Logan ordered. "You don't want to be a part of what's going to happen here."

The dancer grabbed her jeans and silk top and ran out the door.

At that moment, Conor Francis spun around and wrapped Logan in a powerful bear hug. The Dorcha was caught off guard by the large man's quickness. His arms were now pinned under Francis' heavy meat hooks. Logan cocked his head back and brought it forward with lightning speed. The top of his motorcycle helmet shattered Francis' nose. The heavy man let go his grip as the intense pain shot through his face. Logan stomped the man's foot with his motorcycle boot and Francis fell to one knee. "Seamus!" the wounded man screamed.

"See you in hell Conor Francis," The Dorcha said as he brought the silenced pistol down and squeezed the trigger.

He lowered the dead man's body to the floor and continued toward the door that was partially hidden in the wall of glass. Logan found the handle and knocked loudly on the mirror.

"Leave us the fuck alone, Conor!" A voice shouted from within. Logan knew the voice belonged to Seamus Barry.

Barry was lying bare-chested on a water mattress in his private bedroom. He held a short straw up to his left nostril and began snorting lines of cocaine off the naked stomach of his blond mistress.

There was another knock on the door.

"I swear to God I'm gonna kill that fat fuck!" he told his drugged out girl-friend who smiled back at him.

Seamus Barry got out of bed and stretched his tall thin frame.

"I bet he's looking for pointers on how to fuck," he laughed as he strutted naked toward the door.

Logan saw the glass handle begin to turn and stepped back. He brought his right leg up and kicked through the door. The power of the kick knocked Seamus Barry to the floor.

"What the fuck!" he screamed while scrambling to his feet.

The Dorcha stepped into the room with his pistol trained on Barry's chest.

Logan lifted his visor and stared at Seamus Barry. He was searching for any traces of humanity in the man's pockmarked face. The Dorcha was right; Seamus Barry was not human. He was a mad dog that needed to be put down.

Barry recognized Logan and his worried expression turned to a smile.

"What the fuck do you want?" he asked defiantly.

"I've come to put you down," The Dorcha replied softly.

"Are you fucking crazy? You touch me and my brother will have your balls for breakfast!"

Logan lunged at Barry and grabbed him by his frail neck. He turned the skinny man around and threw him against the wall. The Dorcha had his left hand wrapped tightly around the man's windpipe. Barry's eyes were bulging and spittle leaked from the sides of his mouth.

"Leave him the fuck alone," cried his girlfriend who was now sitting up on the waterbed. She had Barry's revolver pointed at Logan's back. Seamus Barry tried to laugh as he was being choked.

"You're fucked," Barry managed to say.

The Dorcha kept his eyes locked on Barry's. With his right hand, Logan brought his gun under his left arm and fired backwards. His shot caught the blond in the center of her chest. The bullet tore through her emaciated body and penetrated the waterbed. Cold water and warm blood oozed out onto the floor. Barry clawed at Logan's vice grip but the Dorcha continued to squeeze with force. Logan heard a crack in the man's windpipe and watched his eyes roll to the back of his head.

He finally released his grip and Seamus Barry's body collapsed to the floor.

The Dorcha looked over to the dead mistress sprawled out on the water bed. "Pity that," he muttered to himself as he closed the visor on his motorcycle helmet and walked back downstairs to the club. No one paid any attention to him as he made his way to the exit. The partygoers were oblivious to the triple murder that had just been carried out above them. Logan strolled out the front door of *The Whispering Gypsy*, and nodded to the doorman. He climbed on his motorcycle and started the engine.

CHAPTER 19

Martin Barry sat at a table in his basement office surrounded by two of his fellow leaders in the IRA military council. Barry dabbed at his tear stained cheek with a white kerchief. He had been sobbing uncontrollably since being brought in to identify his brother's body at the Dublin City Morgue. Jimmy Cahill handed him a hot cup of coffee but he pushed it away.

"Get a hold of yourself Martin," Cahill urged. "There are some decisions to be made here."

Barry kept his head resting on the table and started pounding the wood with his fist.

"He was my baby brother. What do I tell our Ma?"

Barry had another good cry before he sat up in his chair and regained his composure. "There's only one decision to be made here," he said clearing his throat. "I want Michael Logan's balls hanging on my wall!"

There was a knock at the door of the wood paneled office. Jimmy Cahill got up and peeked his head outside. He nodded and opened the door wide to let the young man in. The teenager stood in front of Martin Barry clutching a baseball cap. He was clearly nervous.

"What have you got to say for yourself?" Barry barked.

"Logan has vanished," the teen answered. "We've checked every safe house in Dublin, but we've found nothing."

Martin Barry did not appreciate bad news.

"What about Logan's men?"

The teen smiled. "We worked them over pretty good. If they knew anything, they would have told us by now."

Jimmy Cahill dismissed the young man with a wave of his hand. He closed the office door and sat back down.

"Well, what do you want to do now?" he asked Barry.

"If we can't find Logan, then I want a member of his family!" Barry shouted. "I want the Dorcha to feel my pain."

Cahill glanced over at the third man in the room, Padraig Tully. Both men wrestled with the problem. Michael Logan was revered by the rank and file of the IRA. Privately, Cahill and Tully celebrated the murder of Seamus Barry. He had been an embarrassment to the cause since the day he was sworn in. But Michael Logan had broken a cardinal rule of the organization. He had taken out a hit against one of his own. There was only one punishment to fit that crime, death. If he would not come forward to pay the penalty, someone close to him would.

"Let it be done," Cahill told Barry.

BELFAST

Michael Logan sat at his mother's bedside holding her hand. The woman's golden locks were now streaked with gray. Ann Logan's head rested on a pillow while her vacant eyes stared blankly at the wall.

"I've got to go away for awhile," Logan whispered into her ear.

There was no response.

"Vincent has promised me that he'll visit you more often. You need to know that your boys will always be here for you."

Michael brought a paper cup filled with water to her lips. Ann Logan opened her mouth and drank. Her son then took a cloth and wiped the water that had spilled onto her chin. Orla Madden stood outside and watched Logan from a small window in the door. She couldn't take her eyes off of him. What drew her to this beast of a man? It was a question she often asked herself. He visited St. Mary's Home every weekend under the name, Gabriel Collins. During the visits, Madden would take his signature on the facility's registration form and buzz him into Ann Logan's room. She knew that his name was not Gabriel Collins, and probably should have alerted the police. But there was something about Michael Logan that set him apart from all other men she had known. It was the way he treated his mother. Most people who visited their relatives here spent most of the time looking down at their watches. But not this man, he was never in a rush to leave. Sometimes, he'd spend hours reading to her. Other times, he'd hum a lovely ballad while gently brushing her hair. Ireland's most wanted man never appeared to be looking over his shoulder. All his time spent here was focused solely on her. Michael Logan was a true gentleman. He was not the same man that she read about in the newspapers. Orla Madden would not admit it to herself, but the twenty-four year old receptionist was falling in love.

DUBLIN

The teenager's heart pounded with excitement. He had gone from errand boy to enforcer in just a matter of hours. Martin Barry had scribbled the address on a pad of paper and handed it to him.

"Don't let me down," Barry had told the teen.

The young man was now hiding in the shadows outside Vincent Logan's apartment building. He ached for a cigarette but did not want to chance being seen. Instead, he bit down on the inside of his cheek to calm himself down. The teen waited patiently until the light finally went out in the bedroom window. He looked at his watch again. The time was now 11:24 PM.

Martin Barry retreated once again to the solitude of his basement office. His wife Adele had proved to be no help in this family crisis. She once again reminded him how dangerous his life was and what a burden it had become on her and the kids.

Barry ran his fingers through the gray whiskers of his beard and chuckled. He had either planned or taken part in eleven attacks on British forces during his years with the Provisional IRA. He had stared down the barrel of someone else's gun more than once. But the one person he feared most in his life was the wife he had left screaming upstairs. Barry poured a shot of whiskey in his coffee and waited for some good news.

The teenager looked down the street and saw no one. It appeared that all the neighborhood residents were in for the evening. He held a long bottle in his right hand. The bottle, filled with gasoline had an oil soaked rag poking out from the top.

The young man concealed the bottle in his coat as he walked quickly across the street. He crouched while making his way toward Logan's darkened bedroom window. The teen took out a Zippo lighter from his coat pocket, hit the spark and ignited the rag. He stepped back, the crude explosive device illuminating the soft features of his boyish face. The teen then launched the Molotov cocktail through the bedroom window and heard the sound of shattering glass followed by a loud explosion. He cracked a gap toothed smile and ran down the street away from the flames.

Vincent Logan sat at his computer terminal trying to type with his one good hand. His other arm was in a sling. Logan was transcribing crime scene notes and attempting to find any correlation in a string of recent robberies in the Dublin area. He had arrived unannounced at police headquarters earlier that evening. Vincent told the night commander that he was going stir crazy sitting at home with his injured elbow and yearned for some police work. The night commander agreed to let the rookie stick around. The commander was even able to pass off a little project that he had no interest in doing himself. Logan had taken to this *busy work* like a man possessed. He already discovered that one particular paving company had worked in the neighborhoods where two of the robberies took place. *That could be a possible lead,* he thought.

The police radios had been quiet all evening. It was a slow night down at dispatch. There were seven Guarda officers present in the squad room and each was trying his best to look busy. Some were using the down time to work on old cases while others spent their time trying to find out the latest line on the featherweight championship fight which was about to get underway in London.

"We've got a code twelve; explosion at a residence," the squawk box announced.

"Address is 16 Chardon Terrace."

Vincent Logan's head spun around.

"What address did dispatch just give?" he asked frantically.

"I think it was 16 Chardon Terrace," replied Guarda detective Dick Hanafin.

"That's my place!" Logan screamed.

Hanafin grabbed his coat and pulled Logan up by his good arm.

"Let's go kid," he said as he pushed Vincent out the squad room door.

Hanafin slapped the police light on his unmarked cruiser and drove with abandon.

"This is a multiple assistance call. All available units respond to 16 Chardon Terrace," the dispatcher announced over the radio.

Vincent sat in the passenger seat biting his knuckle and feeling completely helpless.

Fiona … Audrey … Please God let them be safe.

Logan and the detective reached Chardon Terrace eleven minutes later. Vincent went numb when he saw fire crews hosing down what was left of his bedroom. He opened the car door and jumped out while the vehicle was still moving. Logan stumbled until he got his footing and then ran toward the yellow police tape as if it were the finish line of a marathon.

"Fiona, Audrey!" he screamed as he got closer to the fire scene.

Hanafin was right on Logan's heels.

"He's a cop," the veteran detective shouted to the officers on the scene. "This is his place."

Logan tried to push his way past the policemen and into the building.

"Where's my wife? Where's my baby?" he yelled.

Detective Noel Roche ran down the steps of the building and grabbed Logan by the shoulders.

"Relax … just relax," he ordered. "Your wife and baby are just fine!"

Logan tried frantically to push the large detective out of his way.

Roche grabbed him by the chin and stared into his wild eyes. "I said your wife and baby are okay!"

"Where? Where are they?" Logan demanded.

Roche guided him to the back of an ambulance parked on the street. Fiona was lying on a stretcher inside holding their infant daughter. Both had oxygen masks on.

"Honey," Logan shouted with relief. "Thank God you're okay."

He climbed into the ambulance and hugged his wife.

Fiona's cheeks were darkened by smoke and she was wearing the pink nightgown Vincent had bought for her birthday. It was wet and covered with black soot.

"What happened baby? What happened?" he asked while squeezing her gently.

Fiona took off the oxygen mask and started to speak. "Mister Brennan saved our lives. I fell asleep in the nursery and was woken up by a big explosion. Smoke and fire were filling the apartment. The landlord kicked down the door and pulled us out of the building."

Vincent nodded his head but he was still confused. Detective Roche butted in.

"Officer Logan, preliminary reports point to some kind of crude bomb. We think it may have been a Molotov cocktail."

Martin Barry slammed the phone receiver down on the table. The force of the action splintered the plastic and sent shards flying across the room. He had just spoken with his highly paid source at Guarda Headquarters. Vincent Logan had not only survived, but he was not even home during the attack. Martin was seething with anger and his blood lust would not go unquenched on this night. He downed another shot of whiskey and called for his driver.

Nineteen-year-old Brendan Dempsey waited under a tall oak tree at the southern tip of Phoenix Park. He sat on a stone bench clutching his baseball cap.

Dempsey's nerves were getting the better of him again. He tapped his sneakers against the pavement and checked his watch. Dempsey replayed the phone call from Martin Barry in his mind. The IRA leader told the teenager what a great job he had done on behalf of the organization. Barry said the cop was dead and the hit was cause for a little celebration. Sitting on the bench, Brendan Dempsey could only imagine what was in store for him on this night. A whole new world was about to open up for the recovering heroin addict. His excitement grew as he watched Martin Barry's black Saab pull up slowly to the curb. Dempsey smiled and started walking toward the car. He was about a foot way from the vehicle when the black tinted window on the front passenger side came down slowly. Martin Barry smiled back at the young man and waved him over. Brendan Dempsey stuck his head in the window.

"Hey kid, You really fucked up tonight!"

Barry brought his gun up quickly and shot the teenager between the eyes. As the car drove away, Martin Barry laughed out loud.

CHAPTER 20

She had asked him if he would like to grab a cup of coffee and to her amazement, he had said yes. They were now at her cottage and her hands were moving up his bare stomach toward his chest. His body was a textured map of muscle and scar tissue. He flinched as her fingernails traced an old knife wound near his shoulder blade. He took her hand gently and pulled it away.

"Does it hurt?" she asked.

He shook his head. "No, but the memories do. It's the scars that you can't see that cause me the greatest pain."

"What happened to you?" she whispered as she leaned up to kiss him. He took her tongue into his mouth. He had never experienced anything like this. He closed his eyes and felt the warmness wash over him. He was finally home.

"I'm not what you think I am," he admitted to her.

"You're exactly the man I think you are Michael."

He looked at her with curious brown eyes. "I guess I've done a pretty lousy job concealing my true identity."

Her lips moved down to his neck and then his chest. "I know you're not Gabriel Collins, Mrs. Logan's estate lawyer. The way you treat her; that love comes only from a son. The doctors offered me extra money to keep my mouth shut, but I refused to take it."

"I'm sure the police would hand you a nice reward for this kind of information," he replied.

"I don't want a reward," she said softly. "I just want you. I've always wanted you."

With that, she pushed him down on the bed and climbed on top of him. Their bodies were made for each other. She welcomed him between her thighs and he fit perfectly inside her. They made love with a passion neither had felt before. They climaxed together and then drifted off to sleep.

Orla Madden awoke and felt the bed shaking under her body. She looked over at Michael who was twitching violently in his sleep. His tightly fisted hands were swinging in the darkness. *Should I wake him?* She leaned over to the bedside lamp but thought better of it. Instead, she moved closer toward him so that he could feel her warm skin on his. Orla rubbed his arms gently until he calmed down. His breathing was much slower now, his screams had grown silent. She kissed his shoulder and went back to sleep.

Michael woke up hours later to the buzzing sound of his mobile phone. It was on *vibrate mode* and he watched as the instrument danced across his crumpled up jeans that lay on the floor. He gently moved Orla's arm from his bare chest. Logan got out of bed; grabbed the phone and walked into the living room.

"What is it?" he whispered.

"Dorcha, It's Padraig Tully."

Logan paused and walked to the window. He looked outside Orla's cottage but saw nothing.

"Listen, I don't know where you are and I don't want to know," Tully continued. "Martin Barry just tried to murder your brother and his family." He heard Logan take a deep breath on the other end of the phone. "Relax," Tully told him. "They all survived unharmed. You can catch Barry at his mistress's flat over on Mespil Road tomorrow night. Don't forget, he travels with a bodyguard."

The phone line went dead.

Tully hung up the phone and prayed that he had done the right thing. Seamus Barry had been a major liability to the IRA, and now his older brother was becoming one also. It was time for Martin Barry to go.

Logan crept back into the darkened bedroom and grabbed his clothes off the floor. Orla was still sleeping soundly. He hated to leave in the middle of the night like this but he felt that he had no choice. The Dorcha was needed to kill again. Logan got dressed quickly and walked out to his motorbike. He checked the nylon bag he had fastened to the back of the seat. In the satchel were his Walther P99 and five clips of ammunition. Logan put his helmet on; kick started the motorcycle and took off. Orla awoke to the sound of the roaring motor. She reached for her bathrobe and ran outside where she caught a brief glimpse of her lover as he sped away. Orla hugged herself against the cold and walked back inside.

The following evening, the Dorcha parked his motorcycle outside an Indian restaurant on Baggot Street in Dublin. He tipped the valet generously and told him to keep a close eye on the bike. Logan promised that he would be back before midnight. He slung the satchel over his shoulder and began walking. It was the perfect night, the stars were shining luminously in the sky and the temperature was just cool enough for lovers to huddle close together. He passed a couple strolling arm and arm toward Dublin's Grand Canal and immediately thought of Orla. *Will she forgive me for leaving her?* He could not believe that he was asking himself that question. Women had always played a limited role in his life. It wasn't that Logan hated women; in fact it was the contrary. But a woman in his life would mean a soft target for his enemy. *So why can't I get Orla Madden out of my head?* The thought tortured him until he finally reached Mespil Road ten minutes later. He saw the Saab double-parked outside the apartment building. Logan had been to the location before, not with a gun but with a camera. During his previous visit, he had taken more than a dozen photos of Barry with his young Vietnamese lover. That was thanks to a telephoto lens and a rented apartment with windows facing the mistress's flat. The Dorcha did not like playing the role of *Peeping Tom,* but his Russian mentor had tutored him on the advantages of black mail. Logan had built up a deep distrust for the Barry brothers over the years and he wondered whether the compromising photos would come in handy one day.

The Dorcha pulled the satchel off his shoulder, set it down on the ground and opened the zipper. He pulled out his pistol and slid the ammunition clip into the butt of the weapon. Logan waited for two hours tucked into the shadows along the side of the building. His dark brown eyes were focused on the entrance. Martin Barry exited the building just after ten p.m. He walked down the front steps with a wide smile on his face and a delicious memory that would last him until the next time. A few hours with Kim Tran each week had enabled Barry to survive his horrible marriage to Adele. Of course, Adele had no clue about the affair, if she did; Martin Barry's own balls would be hanging on the wall in his office.

Logan crouched down and weaved his way past the cars parked along Mespil Road. He was now just a few feet away from the black Saab. Barry reached the vehicle and opened the passenger door. Logan was now concealing himself by the trunk. Barry stepped into the car and received a knowing smile from his driver.

"How was it?" the man asked.

"She's the best there is," Barry replied.

At that moment, Logan threw the car door open and jumped into the back seat. Without saying a word, he pointed his gun at the back of the driver's head and pulled the trigger. The man's skull partially exploded on impact. The driver's face fell on the steering wheel and his brain matter sprayed the inside of the windshield. Logan then turned the gun to a horrified Martin Barry.

"No sudden movements Martin, my trigger finger is a little itchy this evening," The Dorcha said with a grin.

Martin Barry sat still trying to catch his breath.

"My brother and his family are non-combatants in our little war, yet you went after them anyway. Give me one reason that I shouldn't blow your head off right now."

Barry began reaching into his coat pocket. Logan moved the gun closer to his head.

"That would be a stupid move on your part, Martin."

"No … I'm reaching for a picture, a picture of my kids."

Logan nodded and allowed the man to reach into his pocket. One false move and the Dorcha would send Barry to his maker. The man pulled the photo slowly from his breast pocket. He turned it around and showed it to Logan. The photograph showed Barry and his wife holding their young boys. The image reminded Logan of his own family. Was Logan willing to make orphans out of these children?

"I have money, I'll give you anything you want," Barry pleaded.

"I just want the killing to stop Martin. I'll leave Ireland on the condition that you leave my brother and his family alone."

Martin Barry could not believe that his life was about to be spared, not after what he had done.

"You have my word Dorcha."

"My name is Michael Logan," he replied. "If you should turn your back on this promise, I will find you. And if you make any problems for my brother, I will make sure your wife gets these."

Logan showed Barry a photograph of his own. This picture showed the happy family man on top of his Asian muse. Martin Barry shook his head 'yes' and accepted defeat. But there was still one big problem.

"The military council has already put out the order for your murder," Barry told Logan. "It cannot be rescinded, even by me."

"Then so be it," Logan responded. "We all have our date with the devil sooner or later."

The Dorcha opened the car door but kept his gun pointed at Barry.

"This is farewell for now Martin but just remember this boyo; there is nowhere that you can hide from me." He exited the vehicle and walked off into the night.

Logan returned to St. Mary's Hospital for one last goodbye to his mother and to Orla Madden. He stepped off his motorcycle and heard a familiar voice echo through the parking garage.

"You bastard! Why did you bring my family into your mess?"

Michael turned to find his brother rushing toward him. Vincent had a sling covering one hand and a revolver in the other.

"I thought you weren't supposed to carry a gun," Michael said calmly. "What are you planning to do with that?"

"The policeman in me thinks I should shoot you on the spot," Vincent responded as he continued marching toward his brother.

Michael did not acknowledge the threat.

"How are Fiona and Audrey?" He could feel Vincent's anger grow. "Shoot me, if that's what you're here for Vincent."

Michael held his arms out to his sides. The revolver was now shaking in his brother's hand. Michael reached out for the gun.

"Give it to me brother."

Vincent handed the weapon over and put his head down.

The twins embraced tightly. Michael could hear Vincent crying on his shoulder.

"Your wife and child are safe now," Michael whispered. "I've made it so you'll never be bothered again."

Vincent pulled away from his brother.

"Who did you kill this time?"

"Not the man I had planned to," Michael explained. "But I've promised to leave Ireland on the condition that you are left alone."

The brothers sat down on a bench inside the parking garage.

"Fiona and Audrey are doing okay," Vincent told his brother. "They're staying in the officers' quarters at McCann Barracks back in Tipperary."

Michael was relieved by the news. "I think about your wife and daughter a lot and wonder whether I could have had the same."

"You could have had my life Michael," Vincent told him "But you decided to save my life instead. I wish things turned out differently for both our sake."

Michael placed his arm around Vincent's shoulder. "You're a good brother. You've always been a good brother to me even during the years we've spent apart. I've got to go away again, this time forever." The twins shared one final hug and each went their separate ways.

CHAPTER 21

BOSTON, MASSACHUSETTS 1996

Heath Rosary juggled a bag of popcorn and two large cups of Coca-Cola while searching for a seat in the crowded theater. It was his first night off in a month and his girlfriend had purchased two tickets to the Wang Center Classic Films Series showing of Alfred Hitchcock's *Vertigo*. The lights inside the opulent theater had not yet dimmed and Grace Chen spotted her man fumbling with the food. She stood up and waved him over.

Of course she had to sit right in the middle of the row. Why couldn't she get an aisle seat? Rosary managed to hide his frustration with a smile. He walked over to their row and waited patiently for the other theatergoers to stand at their seats. *This is gonna be a challenge.* Rosary squeezed his large frame between the patrons and the seats in front of him. The former college football star shuffled to his seat without spilling a single kernel of popcorn.

"Nice moves swivel hips," Grace said with a kiss.

"Looks like I didn't miss anything."

"I told the manager not to dim the lights until my tall, dark boyfriend arrived with my popcorn."

"Yessah Miss Chen. Izza comin' wit' da food!"

"Cut the Stepin' Fetchit routine. That's not what I meant," she laughed.

Grace took a handful of popcorn and stuffed it in her delicate mouth.

"Tell me, would you like me better if I looked like Kim Novak?"

Rosary tried to picture his Chinese-American girlfriend with blond hair and a gray suit. "Now if we could just get you to look like Grace Kelly, I'd marry you in a heartbeat."

His girlfriend giggled and punched him playfully in the arm. The couple saw eye to eye on most things, but they vehemently disagreed when it came to their favorite Hitchcock film. Grace loved the exploration of sexual obsession in *Vertigo*, while Rosary opted for the voyeuristic *Rear Window*. Both agreed that although Alfred Hitchcock was a genius, the chubby director had some real issues when it came to women. They settled into their seats as the lights dimmed and the curtain opened. Bernard Hermann's haunting score echoed through the theater. *Now this is how a Hitchcock film should be seen,* Rosary thought. Kim Novak's eye filled the screen as an animated kaleidoscope spun round and round in the background.

Rosary had just put his arm around Grace when the beeper vibrated on his hip.

Grace rolled her eyes while her boyfriend got up and shuffled his way back past five theatergoers who were now clearly annoyed by the interruption. Rosary walked up the aisle just as Jimmy Stewart started his foot chase across the roof tops of San Francisco. He reached the lobby, whipped out his cell phone and dialed his command post.

"This better be good," Rosary warned.

"*Willow* has gone AWOL," the secret service agent replied.

"I'll be right there."

Rosary scribbled a note on a napkin and flagged down the theater manager.

"My name is Heath Rosary. I'm with the United States Secret Service. Can you make sure my girlfriend gets this note during intermission?"

"What does she look like?" asked the theater manager.

"She's Asian with short black hair and a smile to die for."

Rosary ran out of the theater and jumped into his blue Chrysler sedan. The car was parked right outside the theater in a *no parking* spot. It was one of the perks of having a car with U.S. government plates; Rosary could park wherever he wanted to. The agent fired up the engine and switched on the flashing blue lights. He drove the wrong way down Tremont Street and arrived back at the Harvard field office twelve minutes later.

"Brief me on the situation as it stands right now," he ordered immediately after walking in the door.

"*Willow* shook off Agent Patterson at Venus De Milo's. She's been MIA for twenty two minutes."

Venus De Milo's was a trendy nightspot behind Fenway Park. A true Red Sox fan would not be caught dead in the place. Venus catered to the Euro students from nearby Boston University and Harvard.

"Has POTUS been notified yet?" Rosary asked.

"Air Force One is still wheels up over the Pacific Ocean. The President left Hong Kong three hours ago," replied Special Agent Nikki Tavano. "We've still got eight minutes before he needs to be notified."

"Seal off that club. No one goes in or out until I say so."

Agents' Rosary and Tavano arrived at the nightclub on Lansdowne Street a short time later. The line to get in was enormous. Partygoers outside and inside Venus De Milo's were angry and calling for blood. Agent Steve Patterson stood at the door of the club and waved Rosary over.

"What the fuck happened?" Rosary asked his subordinate.

"Boss I'm sorry. She told me she had to go to the bathroom. I did a sweep of the bathroom and made sure it was secure. I waited outside for ten minutes. Finally I asked another girl to check on her and she said the bathroom was empty. It's real dark in that place boss, but I still don't know how she got past me."

Rosary nodded as he looked back at the club. "Let's shed some light on the place then," he ordered. "Get the manager. I want all the lights on and every leather wearin' freak lined up on the dance floor."

Agent Patterson did not need to be told twice. He disappeared into the club.

"We've got a lead on the roommate," Agent Tavano said walking toward her boss.

Both agents had eight years on the job and both had grown up in the Boston area. Nikki Tavano was a tough talking Italian girl from the streets of Revere; just a few miles north of Boston. Heath Rosary grew up a few miles south in the predominantly black neighborhood of Roxbury. Boston was their city, and Tavano was confident they would find the President's daughter. Rosary was not so sure.

"I've got a bad feeling about this one Ginzo,"

"Relax Smokey, she's tried to pull this shit before. We'll find her."

Rosary and Tavano always poked fun at each other's ethnic heritage. It made others feel uncomfortable, but it kept the pair laughing on a very stressful job.

Rosary's Nextel began ringing. The call was coming from the operations center for the Presidential Protective Division of the Secret Service in Washington.

Rosary could picture his boss pacing the floor of Room 10 inside the Executive Office Building. He took the phone off the clip on his hip and placed it to his ear. It was the call he had dreaded.

"Agent Rosary, Give me a status report on *Willow*," barked Marc Lidsky; agent in charge of the Presidential Protection Division (PPD).

"The principal has not been seen for approximately thirty three minutes," Rosary explained calmly. "Principal appears to have purposely evaded her assigned agent inside a Boston nightclub."

"No one goes into or out of the bar until every head is accounted for," Lidsky ordered.

"Already done, sir. We're canvassing the nightclub right now. I'll call you the minute the status changes." Rosary did not wait for a response. He clicked off his Nextel and placed it back on the clip.

Tavano read the frustrated look on his face. "Lemme guess, Washington?"

"Yup, The President will be notified about *Willow* in two minutes. No doubt he'll hit the roof."

"Probably order an air strike right on our command center," Tavano added with a nervous laugh.

Jennifer Bosworth was the only child of President Evan Hamilton Bosworth. The twenty-two-year old Harvard University senior was also one of the most sought after people in the world. With her blond hair and blue eyes, she had helped her father put a compassionate face on the White House. The Secret Service code-named her *Willow* because of her delicate nature but Heath Rosary knew there was darkness behind her winning smile. Her mother Caroline had been killed by a drunk driver when Jennifer was just ten-years old. Her father first made national headlines by serving as lead prosecutor in the case against his wife's killer. When he first ran for U.S. Senate in Virginia, voters were drawn to the story of the widower and single father's quest for justice against the man who had killed his wife. He won the open senate seat in a landslide. Six years later, Evan Hamilton Bosworth ran for President. His daughter Jennifer, young and beautiful, was forced to serve as a de-facto candidate's wife on the campaign trail. Again, her father won the election with stunning ease. The incumbent President's dalliance with a White House intern helped Bosworth secure his victory.

At public events, President Bosworth played the doting father for photographers, but behind the scenes, he was cold and distant toward his only daughter. Jennifer Bosworth arrived on the campus of Harvard University with a big chip on her shoulder, and Heath Rosary was assigned to protect her. The First Daughter wanted to go to Berkeley, but was strong-armed by her father to attend his alma mater. Rosary relished the job at first, thinking it would one day lead to a prized spot on the President's own security detail. Eventually, he came to realize that he was nothing more than a babysitter with a gun. Sweet Jennifer Bosworth was the most unruly subject that he had ever been assigned to protect.

"We found the roommate. A car is bringing her over right now," Tavano informed her boss.

"Let the games begin," Rosary sighed.

The car carrying Jennifer Bosworth's roommate pulled up to the curb on Lansdowne Street minutes later.

Rosary walked over to the vehicle and could see Dolly Martinez smiling inside.

He opened the door and hopped in the backseat with the college student.

"What's so funny Dolly?" Rosary was already annoyed.

"Jennifer really did it this time," she said looking at the line of police cars and people line up outside the nightclub. "It looks like a Chinese fire drill out there."

"I'm glad this amuses you. Now did Jennifer say she was meeting someone at the club tonight?"

"She didn't say a word to me," Dolly answered nonchalantly.

Rosary rolled his eyes and smiled. He wanted to put her at ease, yet a little off balance at the same time. "Come on now girl, you two talk about everything. Now it's my ass if we don't find Jennifer in the next half-hour. I've always been really cool to you ladies. I've always given you your space. If I get busted off this detail, that's all gonna change."

Rosary could see Dolly mulling over her options in her head.

"Okay, Agent Rosary. She was supposed to meet a guy named Ahmet. He's really cute. I think he's Syrian. I know he's a student over at the Mass College of Art."

Rosary cracked another smile but this one was real. "That's great Dolly. Any idea where this guy lives?"

"What's it worth to you?"

Oh how college kids liked to play games.

"I tell you what; I'll spring for dinner and a Scorpion bowl for you and a friend at *Hong Kong's.*"

Dolly flashed her perfect white teeth and brushed a strand of black hair from her pretty Latino face. "Deal," she said with a nod of her head. "He lives a couple of blocks from here over on Park Drive. Don't tell Jennifer that I snitched, she'll never forgive me."

Rosary shook hands with the roommate and stepped out of the vehicle. He waved at Tavano signaling her to come over.

"I think we've got her. Take this down."

Tavano flipped open a notepad and waited for instructions.

"The kid's name is Ahmet," he told her. "He's a student at the Mass College of Art. Dolly says he lives over on Park Drive. Find an address ASAP."

Tavano scribbled down the information and took off.

"Who's in charge here! I wanna speak with him," Nigel Tanner demanded as he pushed his way past Agent Patterson and out onto Lansdowne Street.

Rosary saw the commotion and walked over to the irate man wearing a pony tail, silk shirt and tight leather pants.

Tanner turned to Rosary and jabbed a bony finger in his chest. "Look at the line out here. It's Saturday night and you're killing my business!"

"I take it you are the manager of this fine establishment," Rosary said calmly.

"Fuckin' right I am. Who the hell are you?"

Rosary had just about enough from this little turd. He felt like slapping the brash idiot the way his idol, Humphrey Bogart would have done. *That stuff happens only in the movies*, he reminded himself. "I am Special Agent Heath Rosary of the United States Secret Service," he said flipping open his badge. "We are dealing with a matter of National Security here. If you fail to cooperate with any of my agents, I will have you placed under arrest immediately."

Tanner immediately thought about all the speeding tickets he still owed and quickly backed down. "I'm only trying to run a business here Agent Rosary," he said with an apologetic smile.

Rosary scowled at the manager. "I suggest that you go back inside and await further instructions from Agent Patterson," he said sternly.

Nigel Tanner turned on his heel and walked away. Rosary returned to Agent Tavano.

"What have you got for me?"

"The guy's name is Ahmet Sistani," she said reading from her notes. "518 Park Drive, apartment 5-B."

"Let's go."

518 Park Drive was an old apartment building occupied mostly by students from nearby Simmons College and Northeastern University. Rosary and Tavano

double-parked outside the building along with three other unmarked cars. Rosary huddled with his agents at the front of the building.

"Now I want everyone to relax," he ordered them. "She's probably up there getting a little action with this Ahmet dude. She is a college student, you know? Agent Tavano and I will approach the door." Rosary pointed at Agents Nick Franco and Keith Schofield. Both had scored high marks at the Secret Service training center in Beltsville, Maryland, but this would be their first true test in the field. "You two hang back and provide cover," Rosary ordered. "Agent Tavano and I will take the lead. Let's move." The agents entered the building and climbed the stairs slowly. There was no elevator and the apartment they sought was on the top floor.

Rosary and his team reached apartment 5-B a few moments later and heard music playing from inside.

Ahmet Sistani had Jennifer Bosworth in his bedroom. He was teaching her how to inject a heroin filled needle between her toes. "See sweet thing? This way gives you a buzz but leaves no noticeable tracks," he told her.

The President's daughter injected herself and collapsed on the bed.

The Syrian student heard a loud knock on the door. "Ah, dinner has arrived."

Sistani grabbed a wad of cash off the dresser and walked to the front door. His mouth watered at the mere thought of the pepperoni pizza he had ordered. Sistani looked through the peephole and turned white. Instead of seeing a delivery man, he saw what looked to be two FBI agents with guns drawn. The Syrian looked around the living room of his small apartment and freaked out. The place resembled a chemistry lab. There were a dozen small bags of heroin and cocaine spread out on his coffee table and two large marijuana plants in the corner of the room. Sistani had enough drugs in his apartment to send him to prison for fifty years. *There's no way I can handle prison,* he thought immediately. Visions of gang rape quickly entered his drug addled mind. Totally panicked now, he ran into his kitchen and pulled his gun out of the cupboard. He had never actually shot the weapon before, but it was cool to have around. Rosary knocked on the door once more and received no answer.

"Looks like we'll have to do it the hard way," he whispered to Tavano.

Rosary kicked the door open and entered the apartment with his service revolver drawn. Tavano followed him inside. Both agents saw the drugs scattered about the room and realized that this was more than just a *booty call.*

"Jennifer Bosworth," he shouted over the music. "We need to take you home. Your father is worried about you."

Agent Tavano heard a moan coming from the bedroom.

"She's in there," Tavano pointed with her gun.

The agents moved toward the bedroom. Sistani was still hiding in the kitchen with his small firearm. *There's no fucking way I'm going to jail,* he thought.

The Syrian turned the corner from the kitchen and fired his weapon. Rosary felt a searing burn in his right leg as he instinctively turned and fire back down the hallway. The bullet caught the student squarely on the chin and lifted him right off the floor.

Gary Dupuis had his police scanner on as he drove through the Fenway. The Boston *Herald* photographer had just finished a shoot at the Museum of Fine Arts. Dupuis e-mailed his shots to the photo desk and was then driving to meet a friend for a drink at the *RamRod,* a popular gay bar just one block away from Park Drive.

"Report of shots fired at 518 Park Drive," the dispatcher announced over the scanner.

"Looks like the drink will have to wait," Dupuis sighed as he turned his car around.

Agent Tavano ran toward Rosary who was leaning against the wall with a hand over his blood soaked leg.

"Agent down! Repeat, agent down!" Tavano shouted into her mouthpiece.

"I'm okay, Nikki," Rosary said through clenched teeth. "Go check on *Willow.*"

Tavano followed the order and ran into the bedroom. The First Daughter was passed out on the bed. There was an empty syringe lying on the comforter by her left foot.

"Principal located, but incapacitated. Calling for medical attention."

Tavano grabbed the President's daughter off the bed and shook her.

"Wake up Jennifer, wake up!" she screamed.

Dupuis double-parked his Jeep Cherokee in back of a line of cars along Park Drive. He stuck his *Press* flag on the dashboard and jumped out of the jeep with his camera. Moments later, a stretcher carrying a young woman was taken out of the building. The street light shined on her face.

The Boston *Herald* photographer recognized the girl immediately. "Holy shit!" Dupuis said aloud while he snapped picture after picture. He also got a good shot of a black man being carried out on a stretcher.

What did you do to the President's daughter, asshole?

CHAPTER 22

Heath Rosary felt groggy following surgery to repair his injured leg. The surgeon said he had been very lucky; the bullet came within an inch of the femoral artery.

Had the wound been any lower, Rosary would have bled to death on the spot.

Agent Tavano entered the private hospital room with a cup of Dunkin' Donuts coffee and a copy of the Boston *Herald*.

"How's he doing?" she asked Grace who was sitting at his bedside.

"Doctors say it was a close call, but that he'll be alright."

"Ginzo, I'm right here," Rosary announced with a raspy voice. "Can't you see me?"

"Oh, I thought you were the janitor taking a catnap on my best friend's bed." Rosary laughed so hard it hurt.

"Alright you two," Grace reprimanded them. "Save the jokes until we leave the hospital."

"Congratulations, Agent Rosary. You're a national hero," Tavano said waving a copy of the newspaper. "But you're not gonna like how this one went down."

She handed him the newspaper. Rosary was puzzled by the headline.

Terror Plot Foiled: President's Daughter Safe.

He looked closely at the paper and read out loud. "Jennifer Bosworth, only daughter of President Evan H. Bosworth was abducted Saturday night by a Syrian national with ties to global terrorism. The first daughter was rescued from an apartment at 518 Park Drive by a Secret Service team led by Special Agent Heath Rosary. Rosary was wounded during a deadly gun battle with the suspect. A search of Ahmet Sistani's apartment reportedly found pictures of Jennifer Bosworth and diagrams of her Harvard University dormitory. Sources say the

25-year-old Sistani was clutching a copy of the Koran when he was shot and killed."

Rosary threw the paper across the room. "I know the Koran stuff is bullshit. Is any of the rest of it true?" he asked Tavano.

"Nope. He may have been a pretty heavy drug pusher, but I know my guys didn't find evidence that he was a terrorist."

Rosary started to connect the dots. "Protecting the image of the President's druggie daughter is a matter of national security, I take it?"

Tavano nodded her head. "Elementary my dear, Watson."

"Where is *Willow* right now?"

"She's being treated for post traumatic stress disorder at an undisclosed facility," Tavano with a roll of the eyes.

"You mean she's in drug rehab?"

"Exactly!"

CHAPTER 23

LONDON, 2006

The jogger yearned for a cigarette. He fought the urge to pull out a pack of Dunhill's that he had tucked away in the jacket of his blue tracksuit. Instead, he put his head down and ran deeper into Hyde Park. Today's run was more like an obstacle course; overnight rain had left behind several large puddles along Rotten Row. The lane, a popular spot for runners now, was once the most dangerous place in the city, a place where highwaymen laid in wait for unsuspecting victims. The robberies were so frequent that King William III strung 300 lights up along the avenue making it the first street in England to be lit by night. The park was still a popular place for modern day highwaymen. The jogger pressed on to the bronze statue of J.M. Barrie's Peter Pan, his rendezvous point now in sight.

He ran for another hundred yards before stopping to stretch his legs. His lungs were on fire. The jogger had only picked up the sport a month prior, not for health reasons but as a way to retrieve vital information for his candidate. Mitch Handley served as security advisor to the man he believed would become the next Prime Minster of Great Britain. Handley threw his right leg up on a wooden bench and rubbed his sore calf muscles. He looked straight ahead and paid no apparent attention to the man sitting at the other end of the bench.

"Is it on?" Handley asked under his breath.

The man on the bench nodded his head, yes.

"Time and place?"

"Trafalgar Square, tomorrow at noontime," Muhammad Hamsho replied with a thick Palestinian accent.

Handley retied his running shoes and jogged off. Moments later, Hamsho bent down and picked up 500 euros the jogger had left behind.

The security advisor took the elevator to the top floor of the 800-foot tall Canada Tower. Gone was the tracksuit, Mitch Handley now wore a gray pin-striped suit cut for him by one of London's finest tailors. The suit did nothing to enhance his appearance however; Handley was short and stocky with a face that resembled a bulldog. In fact, that was his nickname. Of course, Handley would argue that people called him *the bulldog* not because of his looks, but because he could be both fiercely loyal and frighteningly aggressive when it came to protecting his candidate. He got off the elevator and entered his master's domain. Handley inserted his security pass into the slot and stepped into the headquarters of Stirling Global Enterprises. The billion-dollar Oil Company was also headquarters for the Robert Stirling campaign. Signs showing the golden haired entrepreneur with his thumb raised high covered every available inch of wall space. Handley walked past the receptionist without saying hello. The woman was not offended, but relieved. Mitch Handley was the scariest person she had ever met. Campaign workers were also advised not to engage the man with pleasantries or chitchat. Like the receptionist, they were too terrified to look up when *the bulldog* marched by. With a strawberry Danish in one hand, and a cigarette in the other, Handley marched down a corridor of kiosks and entered his boss's office without knocking. Robert Stirling stood behind his desk with his back facing the door. He was staring out his large office window at the incredible view of Canary Wharf and the Thames River. Renting the top floor of London's tallest building certainly had its privileges.

"We've got to talk, Robert," Handley told him.

"You sound thinner," Stirling observed still facing the window.

"I think I'm the only man who took up jogging and actually gained weight," Handley growled as took a seat on the white leather couch.

Stirling chuckled at the remark. He turned and sat down at his long mahogany desk. Robert Stirling's office was his seat of power and it certainly looked that way.

There were pictures hung up on the walls showing the CEO with presidents, princes and kings. They all at one time or another had tried to gain influence with him. Robert Stirling was one of the world's richest oil men and he had amassed his great wealth the old fashioned way; he killed for it.

After serving fifteen years in the military, Stirling had returned to the sweeping sands of Oman where his fearsome legend had been born, but this time he had struck an unlikely alliance with members of the Bedouin tribe he had threatened to kill so many years before. At Stirling's urging, the Bedouins' re-instituted their reign of terror against the oil company he had once fought to protect. Workers began disappearing from the oil fields at an alarming rate. Each would turn up again days later at the front gates of the company with their throats slit and their tongues pulled out. The murders sparked a mass exodus among oil company employees. The board of directors at Westbridge Oil was in a panic. The British Prime Minister at the time proved to be no help. She refused to send in the military and told the company that it was on its own. Robert Stirling's plan had been carried out beautifully. The former SAS Commando came forward and told the board that he could quell the uprising, as he had done years before. It would cost Westbridge Oil five percent of its holdings. The board scoffed at the idea and the murders increased to the point where all the oil employees refused to come to work. The oil fields were forced to shut down and the company lost billions. After calculating future financial losses, the board decided that it had no other choice and finally gave in. The company turned over five percent of its control to Robert Stirling and he made good on his promise. He and his Bedouin ally pointed the guilty finger at a group of innocent sheepherders living in the area and slaughtered them without mercy. The uprising was over and Robert Stirling was the new conquering hero of Westbridge Oil. Over the next decade, he built up his holdings through keen business moves, threats and intimidation to the point where Robert Stirling owned fifty-four percent of the company. With controlling interest in Westbridge Oil, he then decided to mold the company in his image. This began with a name change. The name Westbridge Oil was changed to Stirling Global Enterprises. Stockholders did not fight the decision because their quarterly statements had shown a sharp increase under Stirling's leadership.

Robert Stirling had amassed great power and he had more money than he could ever spend. What he wanted now was immortality. He wanted his name to be talked about through the ages of British history. Robert Stirling had vowed to become the Winston Churchill of the 21st Century.

"I hope that you've brought me more than a half-eaten strawberry Danish," Stirling told Handley.

"I have indeed sir. The Fist of Allah will carry out an attack on Trafalgar square at noontime tomorrow." Mitch Handley briefed his boss on the details of the operation. Stirling listened, but did not say a word.

"Here are our options," Handley explained. "We can alert MI-5 about the attack ahead of time and take credit for foiling this murderous plot. You would look like a hero."

The scenario was met with a firm shake of the head.

Handley took a deep breath and continued. "If the attack does happen, we could run into a serious political risk. With the election just four days away, the people may come out and show a united front and place their vote for Meeks. It certainly worked for the cowboy after 9/11."

Stirling placed his strong hands under his chiseled chin. He paused for a few seconds before addressing his trusted advisor. "Conrad Meeks is no George W. Bush. Say what you want about the Yank, but the man has resolve. I think that's why his people supported him for a second term. Prime Minister Meeks has been a great friend to the Arab. He pushed hard to soften immigration guidelines during his days in Parliament. And look at this city now." Stirling got up from his chair and stared out the window again. "London has become Cairo of the north. I've decided against alerting the authorities. We must let history take its course."

Gregory Monroe was not your typical suicide bomber. He had never set foot in a refugee camp nor was he ever tortured by Israel or some other pro-western government; in fact he was raised as a child of privilege. The twenty-two year old had attended the best schools and went on holiday at Europe's most lavish retreats. Monroe's father was professor of neurology at the University of London; his mother was an heiress to a department store empire. The young man lived a typical upper class life until he was exposed to Islam during his second year at Oxford. He had signed up for a class in Middle Eastern studies to get close to a co-ed whom he was trying to charm. His teacher was a radical professor on loan from Cairo University whose words about the purity of the Muslim faith had touched the young man's soul. After a couple of lectures, Monroe found that he was paying less attention to the doe-eyed co-ed sitting next to him and more attention to the one-eyed Egyptian standing at the front of the class.

Soon, the student began accompanying his teacher into London where both would pray at the Mosque in Regent's Park. The city's largest mosque became a second home to Greg Monroe. He grew out his beard and carried a prayer mat wherever he traveled. At first, Greg's liberal parents welcomed the religious experimentation. They even supported his decision to drop his Christian name. Gregory Monroe was now called Mustapha Rahim-Al Qir. But Donald and Marline Monroe's boy horrified his parents when he began interrupting their dinner parties with readings from the Koran. *Infidels!* He called the guests as they sipped wine and ate pastry. Greg's parents had finally told him that it was time to grow up and focus on a career. He told *them* that they would burn in the fires of hell if they did not give their lives over to the great Allah. He had not spoken with them in over a year. But something in his mind told him that Don and Marline would be thinking of their boy on this day.

They no doubt would have approved of his appearance. Monroe was dressed in a crewneck sweater and jeans and he had shaved off his beard after waking up that morning. The young man ate a full breakfast and walked to the bus stop at Cleveland Square. London had experienced a week of rain but now the sun was shining brilliantly in the sky. *Praise be Allah,* he thought. Trafalgar Square would be bustling with people on this day. Monroe formed a line with six others as the red double-decker bus pulled up to the curb. A gray-haired woman at the front of the line carried two shopping bags. The driver stepped off the bus and examined the bags closely before taking her ticket. Like every other mode of public transportation, bus line security had been beefed up following the deadly terror attacks of July 2005. Greg Monroe stood patiently at the end of the line. He was not worried about getting caught. He carried no bag and wore no backpack. The bomb he *had* was being carried inside of him. The plastic explosives were concealed in Monroe's buttocks. The student was given a serum to make him constipated and his ass cheeks were then duct-taped shut. He had practiced all morning, but it was still hard for him to walk. Mustapha Rahim Al-Qir could withstand a few hours of discomfort if it meant eternity in Paradise. *Seventy-two virgins,* he thought trying to encourage himself.

He handed the driver the ticket and boarded the bus. He had taken the route many times over the past month. The professor told him to sit in the middle of the bus to ensure maximum impact. The one-eyed Egyptian would explode the device by remote control as soon as the bus reached Trafalgar Square. *Martyrdom was now just seven stops away.* Monroe found an empty aisle seat five rows back. *Allah is good.* He sat down and opened his newspaper. He looked at the words printed on the page but could see nothing. The student was in deep prayer. He ran through the gospel, as he knew it, in his head. He opened his eyes as the bus came to another stop where a family of Americans boarded the double-decker. *Perfect.* With their *GAP* sweatshirts and boorish manner, Monroe knew they were Americans just by looking at them. The bus started to move again. The double-decker was nearing Trafalgar Square and destiny. Monroe slipped his hand into the pocket of his jacket and took out his prayer beads. *God is merciful. God is great.* He prayed for the strength to carry out his mission. He prayed that the professor was now in place to see their mission through.

Professor Tariq Qawi had also shaved his beard for this occasion. He sat with legs folded under an umbrella at an outside café. Qawi sipped a cup of Turkish coffee and typed on his laptop computer. He was not unlike anyone else in the square taking advantage of this beautiful day and doing a little office work out in the sun.

Bus Number 29 was running right on schedule. The double-decker was filled to capacity and the line to get on the bus was twelve people deep. Qawi typed in his secure five-digit code and waited. He took another sip of his coffee as the bus slowed to a stop. *Praise Allah. Praise Mustapha Rahim Al-Qir.* The professor hit *enter* on the computer and watched as the red double-decker erupted into a massive fireball.

CHAPTER 24

Robert Stirling sat in his office with his feet on the desk. He worked a small remote control with his right hand. He pointed the remote to a row of plasma screen televisions lined up along the wall of the office. The first TV was set to CNN where a young female reporter was in the middle of her live stand-up in front of the burned out shell of the double-decker. A breaking news ticker crawled across the bottom of the screen reading; *Deadly Bus Bombing in London's Trafalgar Square.* The reporter then ad-libbed over video of the bombing's aftermath. An image of a wailing ambulance filled the screen followed by b-roll footage of rescuers pulling charred bodies out of the smoking wreckage. Stirling turned his attention to the second plasma screen, which was set to the BBC. An older male reporter was conducting a live interview with an eyewitness to the attack. The BBC reporter cupped his ear and received instructions from his producer back at the studio.

"Sorry, I must cut you off," he told the eyewitness. "Let's take you live now to 10 Downing Street where Prime Minister Meeks is addressing reporters on today's attack."

The director back in the studio dropped the live shot from the bombing scene and switched to the Prime Minister's residence as Conrad Meeks stepped up to the podium. "I first want to express my sorrow and regret to the families of those killed in today's heinous attack." The Prime Minister paused and bit his lower lip. "This is a dark day in the history of Great Britain. I ask all of you to pray for the driver and passengers on board Bus Number 29. The people responsible for this will be brought to justice. It is still too early in the investigation to point the finger of blame at any one person or group. Please do not take the law into your own hands. You will be prosecuted as stiffly as those who carried out this attack. I ask you again to pray for the victims and their loved ones. Thank you." The Prime Minister returned swiftly to his residence without taking questions.

The director then cut back to his reporter live at the bomb scene for analysis.

"Solemn words from Prime Minister Meeks," the reporter said. "The Prime Minister offered condolences to the families of the victims here, and he also warned citizens against any vigilante justice. A group calling itself The Fist of Allah has claimed initial responsibility for the attack. But as the Prime Minister warned, it's still early in the investigation to identify the culprits. Still, there have been threats against just about every mosque in the city. As it stands right now, there are thirty-six people killed, twenty-nine wounded. Reporting live from Trafalgar Square, Brian Leeds BBC News."

Robert Stirling clicked the televisions off and turned to Mitch Handley.

"It's the opportunity we've been waiting for," he said flashing a devilish grin. "I need a car, not the limo but something more rugged. And find me a bull horn ASAP."

Minutes later, Stirling was sitting in the passenger seat of a Land Rover speeding through the city. *Just like old times,* he thought. He pulled off his 600 euro blue silk tie and unbuttoned his collar. The Land Rover was the second car in the motorcade. Because he was a candidate for Prime Minister, Stirling was granted the same security provisions as his rival, Conrad Meeks. Police officers cleared a path as the convoy of vehicles arrived at the bombing scene. Cameras panned from the wreckage over to Robert Stirling as he stepped out of the vehicle. The superintendent of the London Fire Department walked over to the candidate and briefed him on the situation. Stirling patted the man on the back and began making his way toward the wreckage. He was ten yards away from the site when he stopped and looked down. The tall man leaned over and picked up what looked like a child's doll. The plastic head was burned off and the doll's tiny body was covered in black oil. Cameras flashed and video tape rolled. Stirling shook his head and carried the doll up to the burned out bus. The red double-decker was now a skeleton of smoldering metal. Stirling made the sign of the cross and then turned to face reporters. "We can not stand for this," he said.

His words were muffled by the wail of an ambulance siren. Someone in the crowd stepped forward and handed Stirling a bullhorn.

"I said, we cannot stand for this," the candidate re-stated while pointing to the wreckage. "The animals that did this shouldn't be brought to justice; they should be summarily executed!"

Mitch Handley was taken aback by the harsh words of his boss. But the line drew a loud cheer from the crowd of more than a hundred people gathered at the site.

Stirling paused and looked out over the crowd. Each person was hanging on the candidate's every word. He continued. "I have spent my life fighting terrorists from the sands of Arabia to the sewers of Northern Ireland." The candidate pushed back a lock of golden hair that had fallen down over his forehead. "This country cannot give in to terrorists, not now, not ever!" He raised the scorched doll high over his head. "This doll belonged to a little girl on that bus. What kind of political message do the terrorists hope to send by the murder of a child?"

Handley folded his arms and watched his boss work the crowd. Some were crying; others were clapping but they all seemed to believe what the candidate was saying.

"I've got only one message to send to the terrorists," Stirling said looking directly into the television cameras. "Your days are numbered!"

The speech finished to thunderous applause. People in the crowd pushed forward frantically in hopes of touching the candidate. Robert Stirling seemed overwhelmed by the reaction. He waved his arms and smiled as security agents whisked him back into the Land Rover.

The motorcade sped back to Stirling's headquarters at the Canada Tower. The candidate exited the elevator and was greeted by a standing ovation from dozens of volunteers working on his behalf. He shook hands with his campaign workers, many of whom had tears rolling down their cheeks.

"I'm sorry for letting my emotions get the better of me," he said sheepishly.

He finally reached his office and opened the door. With another wave, Robert Stirling disappeared inside. Mitch Handley followed. The candidate stretched out on the leather couch while his advisor poured two glasses of scotch.

"I guess you were right," Handley said with a grin.

Stirling ran his fingers through his blond hair. "We both shall see come Election Day."

CHAPTER 25

GUADALAJARA, MEXICO-2006

"Come on Michael, we're going to miss her," Orla Madden warned Logan while tugging on his arm as they strolled down Avenida Hidalgo toward Plaza de Armas de Guadalajara. It was now 7:50 a.m. Orla had rousted him out of bed to witness one of the city's most unusual and endearing traditions. Logan could not remember the last time he had gotten such an early start to his day. He hated to admit it, but he was glad that she had accompanied him to Mexico. It was not as if he had much of a choice. The woman had that stubborn *tinker* blood in her veins. Orla Madden was the daughter of Irish gypsies, or *tinkers* as the locals call them. She was accustomed to raising stakes and moving on a whim. He had told her of his plans to flee Ireland and she pleaded to go with him. At first he flatly refused, but after a heated debate, Logan finally gave in.

The pair reached the plaza just before eight o'clock. The square was laid out in the shadows of Guadalajara's most famous landmark, The Cathedral. The twin-towered structure was nearly as old as the ancient city itself. The church was built in 1558. The sweeping towers were added in 1848 after an earthquake destroyed the shorter originals. A large crowd was already gathered in the square to watch *La Pichona*. The small Mexican woman entered the plaza carrying two large plastic buckets filled with breadcrumbs. Pigeons living at the Cathedral and nearby Degollado Theater took her cue and flocked to the square. Soon, *La Pichona (the pigeon)* found herself surrounded by hundreds of small birds pecking around her feet. Tourists snapped pictures and shot videotape while the woman fed the pigeons oblivious to their attention. *La Pichona* fed the birds at the same time every morning. What made this ritual so special was that the woman was carrying on a tradition three generations in the making. The old woman's mother and grandmother had fed the pigeons in the plaza before her. Someday soon, her own daughter would become *La Pichona*. Orla beamed at the spectacle.

"Isn't it beautiful the way she carries out the traditions of her ancestors?" she whispered.

Logan did not answer; he was too busy studying the crowd. His Russian mentor had trained him to commit every face to memory and to look for the unordinary in ordinary things. He pulled his baseball cap down shielding his tan face. Orla sensed that he was getting nervous.

"Let's go darling," she said rubbing his arm. "I didn't realize that this would bother you."

He grabbed her hand and the two left the plaza. They took a right onto Calle de Morelos and sheltered themselves from the hot morning sun under a row of laurel trees.

"I know you were a bit nervous, but what did you think of *La Pichona?*" she asked while staring into her lover's eyes.

"You woke me up early so I could watch an old lady feed the birds?" he jokingly replied.

Orla shot her elbow into his rib cage and giggled.

"I'll turn you into a Mexican gentleman yet Michael Logan."

The couple returned to their spacious apartment in the Analco District. Barrio de Analco is the oldest district in Guadalajara and separated from the downtown area by the river, San Juan de Dios. Michael and Orla were the only two white people living in the neighborhood and both liked it that way. Their landlord accepted cash and asked no questions. It was the perfect place for both to hide. The gringo couple stood out when they arrived nine years ago, but Michael and Orla soon ingratiated themselves with the neighborhood. The gringos were now considered *tapatios* (natives of Guadalajara) by those who lived here. Their apartment was next to the San Jose de Analco Church and overlooked the great garden of Analco. From the balcony, Logan had a sweeping view of the neighborhood square.

They entered the apartment carrying bags of groceries in each hand. On the way back from seeing *La Pichona,* they stopped at the Abastos Market where Orla bought fresh eggs, bacon, green pepper, and cheese. She promised Michael an omelet for accompanying her into the city so early in the morning. Logan took the morning edition of *Publico,* Guadalajara's most popular daily newspaper, and stepped out onto the deck. The smell of bacon sizzling in the frying pan made his mouth water and his stomach growl. He sat down in a white wicker chair and unfolded the newspaper. Logan was a mimic for languages and mastered Spanish much quicker than Orla had done. However, reading Spanish was still a challenge. He scanned the front page and caught an article of interest. There had been another kidnapping in Guadalajara. Kidnapping was now a full-blown epidemic in Mexico. Security experts figured the country averaged 4,000 abductions for ransom each year; the government claimed the real number was about half that much. Kidnappers were no longer targeting only the very wealthy; they were now preying on victims from the middle class. Abductions had become more frequent because the ransoms had gotten smaller. Families were paying anything they had to get their loved ones back safely. Logan shook his head as he folded the newspaper and placed it on the table. "The IRA's not the only group looking to capitalize on human suffering," he muttered to himself.

Retirement had suited Logan fine thus far. Money would never be an issue thanks to his old friend, Viktor Tarkov, the KGB Colonel whom had trained Logan in the sands of Libya and in the classrooms of Moscow. Tarkov recognized early on that there was something special about the assassin from West Belfast. Once the Iron Curtain came down, Tarkov hung out his security shingle and offered his services to the highest bidder. The first contract came from his own government. A Chechen rebel was wanted dead or alive for bombing a Moscow theater. Russian commandos attempted to snatch the rebel leader twice, but each mission ended in their own deaths. Tarkov contacted the Dorcha and asked him if he'd like to go on an extended vacation to Grozny, Chechnya. The mission paid $1 million pounds. Logan accepted the offer and told the IRA military council that he was taking a long break to rehab a wounded shoulder. Twenty-four hours later, he was boots down in Chechnya with plans to infiltrate the rebel's private army. It took Logan just two weeks to complete the mission. The Dorcha's unique skills made the rebel leader take notice right away. One evening, the leader called Logan into his tent and offered him a drink of vodka. As he began pouring a shot into a dirty glass, Logan reached around the man's neck and strangled him with a nylon cord. He slipped out of camp before the rebel's body got cold. Logan signaled for help from a satellite phone and Tarkov's chopper whisked him to safety.

The next victim was a Japanese politician who had foolishly launched an investigation of the country's most powerful automaker. The politician was not acting on principle; instead he had been paid by a rival automaker to manufacture evidence of a price fixing scheme. Logan received the contract and flew to Japan posing as a journalist for the Irish *Times.* He landed an interview with the politician and shot him in the face while the man took a steam inside a Tokyo bathhouse.

The Dorch'a most lucrative payday came next when a Saudi prince took out a contract on his own brother. Logan had used a high powered rifle to take the prince out as he stepped out of the lobby of a Paris hotel. In all, he had earned nine million pounds while working for Viktor Tarkov and it was money the IRA did not know he had. The fortune would allow him to keep running for the rest of his life.

Logan wore a smile as Orla walked out onto the terrace. She was carrying an overstuffed omelet on a warm plate and a tall glass of orange juice. She kissed him on the cheek as she set down the meal on the table in front of him.

"After you finish with that, I've planned a little dessert," she purred.

Logan arched an eyebrow and understood perfectly. He attacked the plate of eggs while Orla retreated to their bedroom. He finished the omelet in a matter of seconds. Logan got up from the wicker chair and stretched his legs. *Maybe a little run after sex,* he thought.

He grabbed his plate and was about to head inside when something caught his eye. He looked down from the balcony to the plaza below. A man with dark sunglasses sat at the outdoor cantina sipping a drink. He was wearing one of those Panama hats that are sold in just about every market in the city. He also had on lime green pants and a navy blue blazer. Logan had seen the man earlier that morning at the Plaza de Armas de Guadalajara. He remembered that the man was the only person who didn't have a camera pointed at *La Pichona.* It could have been a coincidence, but he was trained not to believe in such things. Logan walked swiftly back inside the apartment and toward the bedroom. He opened the door and found Orla lying naked in bed.

"Get your clothes on," he ordered.

"Why, what's going on?"

"I think we've been spotted," Logan replied as he grabbed a sundress from the closet. "Here, put this on, hurry!"

Orla dressed quickly and put on her sandals. They had practiced the scenario many times before, but today was no drill.

"Take the back stairs and meet me in two hours inside the leather shop at the Liberty Market," Logan ordered. "And take this." He handed Orla a wad of cash and a hand written note with a phone number on it. "If you don't see me, call this number. Give the man my mother's name. It's a password that will give you access to the rest of the money."

Orla reached up to kiss him, but Logan pushed her away.

"Just go!"

She turned and ran out of the villa. Logan went back to the bedroom closet and turned on the light. He knelt down and felt for a loose panel in the wooden floor. Logan pulled up the floor board and reached for his gun.

The man paid for his drink and got up from the table. He started walking toward Logan's apartment building. The Dorcha stood in an alleyway and waited for the stranger to stroll by. *So the IRA has followed me all the way here,* he thought. Seconds later, the Panama hat came into view. Logan reached out and grabbed the man by the back of his sport coat. He spun the man around and pulled him into the darkness of the alley. The Panama hat fell to the ground and a large paper bag soon followed.

"Who are you working for?" Logan demanded with one hand gripping the man's shirt and the other holding a gun.

"Michael ... it's me son. It's Father O'Bannon!"

"Shut the fuck up!" Logan shouted back in disbelief.

"It's me, Michael," O'Bannon restated while taking off his sunglasses.

Logan recognized the priest's furry eyebrows, but the once powerful looking man now seemed small and frail. Logan did not let go of the priest's shirt.

"What are you doing here, old man?"

"If you would let me go, I'll show you. I've come to give you something."

Logan unclenched his grip and O'Bannon turned to retrieve the bag that had fallen to the pavement.

"You open that bag, and I'll blow your head off," Logan promised.

"Is there somewhere we can talk?" O'Bannon asked emphatically.

He looked down at the pathetic old man. *If the IRA were going to kill me, they wouldn't send a disheveled priest,* Logan thought. After checking O'Bannon for weapons, Logan led him upstairs to the apartment. The old priest perspired heavily with each step. Logan reached into the refrigerator and pulled out two cold Dos Equis. The Irishman had taken a shine to the Mexican beer because it was impossible to find a bottle of Guinness in Guadalajara. He tossed a bottle to O'Bannon who examined it as if it were a moon rock.

"The best beer in all of Mexico," Logan informed him. "It will cool you off."

O'Bannon ran the cold bottle along his sweaty forehead before opening it.

"How did you find me?" Logan asked with all traces of congeniality gone from his voice.

O'Bannon smiled. "I call it *Divine Intervention*. I happen to share a long friendship with a priest who serves in the church next door. He once told me about a gracious Irish couple that had moved into the neighborhood. Curious, I asked my friend what the Irishman looked like. He told me that the man could easily pass himself off as a *tapatios*. I then asked if the man had any distinguishing features. My friend told me there was nothing extraordinary about the man except that he had a small scar on his forehead. Your mark gave you away."

Logan punched the wall and began shouting at the priest. "So have you come all this way to feast your eyes on the Devil, to denounce me for not following in God's path?"

O'Bannon was frightened but tried not to show it. "No Michael, I have not. I bare the responsibility for the man you've become."

Logan struck a curious look at the priest.

"I've come here to say that I'm sorry," O'Bannon pleaded. "If I had known about that pedophile priest, I never would have sent you boys to St. Christian's."

Logan felt his stomach tighten. He took a long pull from his Dos Equis and wiped his mouth with the sleeve of his white cotton shirt. "You know, when I was thirteen I lived in an abandoned building. On cold winter nights, I would light broken pieces of furniture on fire to keep warm."

Logan paused as tears formed in the corners of his brown eyes. *The emotional scars are the ones that never go away.*

"I'd wrap myself up in a filthy old coat and seek out a warm spot on the concrete floor. I cried myself to sleep night after night. I wondered why God had done this to me. What had I done to welcome his wrath? Once, I even thought of paying you a visit and putting my knife in your back."

"I cannot say that I would have blamed you," O'Bannon replied.

"But I fought the urge and found out later that you'd kept your promise. You took care of Vincent and my mother. It's the only reason that you're still alive."

O'Bannon ran his bony fingers up over his wrinkled forehead and into his bristled hair. "Maybe you should have killed me years ago. I have been wracked with guilt everyday since you fled that place. Did you know that Brother Tobias' death was ruled an accident? The sight of a naked priest outside that bell tower was even too much for Greyabbey police to handle. They helped the friary cover up *his* crime and *yours*. I left the church soon after. How could my God welcome beasts like Brother Tobias into my church? I found out the problem was more widespread than I ever realized." The old priest bit his lip and started sobbing.

Logan walked over and touched his shoulder. "So why have you come, father?" he asked softly.

O'Bannon wiped away his tears and pointed to the large paper bag he had been carrying. "After you killed Brother Tobias, I too became a firm believer in the Old Testament. Have you ever read Leviticus Michael?"

Logan shook his head no.

"Revelation 24:20-21: talks about *Lex Talionis,* which is Latin for *The Law of Retribution.* The quote that I think we both now live by is, *"Life for Life, eye for eye, tooth for tooth, hand for hand."*

Logan had no time for a sermon. "So what's in the bag father?"

"I have come to repay my debt to you. I have been carrying this bag over two continents. What is in it could change your life and possibly the history of Britain and Ireland."

O'Bannon reached into the bag and pulled out a large manila folder that was sealed by two rubber bands. He handed it to Logan.

"Open it Michael."

Logan rolled the rubber bands off and opened the folder. His mouth went dry and his heart pounded inside his chest. He was staring at a black and white photograph of three men. They were in military uniform and wore grease paint on their faces.

The two men on each side appeared to be scowling for the photographer, but the soldier in the middle was smiling.

"Do you recognize that man?" O'Bannon asked while looking over Logan's left shoulder.

"Yes, yes I do. That man killed my father."

O'Bannon let the moment sink in. He waited a minute before continuing.

"Michael, is there any thing else that you recognize about that man?"

Logan shook his head no.

"I want you to sit down son."

Michael's head was swimming. He did what he was told without thinking.

O'Bannon sat on the other end of the couch, giving the younger man space.

"Michael, the man who killed your father has just been elected Prime Minister of Great Britain."

Logan downed the last half of his Dos Equis in one swig. He had searched thirty years for the man who killed his father, and now here he was; the blond haired assassin. He set the photograph aside and leafed through a stack of documents that accompanied the picture. All bore a red stamp that read, *Top Secret.*

"Where did you get this," Logan asked while flipping through the papers.

O'Bannon grinned. "It's another case of *Divine Intervention.* A former SAS commander came to me riddled with cancer and with guilt. His mother was Irish Catholic, you see. Well this man once commanded a rogue unit known as, The Knights of the Round Table. Their mission was simple and it was born at the highest levels of the British government. The Knights were to wreak havoc and create terror like nothing ever witnessed before in Northern Ireland. According to the documents you have in your hand, one of their victims was skinned alive. The man who murdered your father is Robert Stirling. He owned England's largest oil company before turning to politics. According to the SAS officer, Stirling was the craziest of the three. And now he is the most powerful man in Europe."

O'Bannon's words hung in the air like a black cloud. Neither man knew what to say next, but both knew what actions were to be taken. Logan studied the photo once more. "Look how far I've had to run," he told the priest. "Yet, I cannot get away from him. This man has been chasing me in my dreams since I was a boy."

O'Bannon nodded his head. "Your father named you Michael, after the archangel. Like the biblical legend, you too are a warrior of God. I truly believe the Lord tortured you in life, so that you would be ready for this final mission."

O'Bannon lifted his frail body off the couch and walked slowly to the front door.

Logan brought over the Panama hat that the priest had left on the couch.

"God be with you Michael Logan," he said while making the sign of the cross.

"God be with both of us, father."

CHAPTER 26

Orla pretended to browse the items at the Liberty Market. She ran her hands through a rack of *guayaberas* (leather coats) and inspected the price tags. Inside, the woman was wrought with worry. It was approaching two hours since Logan had given her a hasty goodbye at their apartment.

What if something awful has happened to him?

The tinkers' daughter felt like crying, but she had to remain strong for the both of them.

"Would you care to try something on, Senorita?" asked the leather vendor in broken English.

"No thank you," Orla replied with a smile. "I'm waiting for my husband."

Where are you Michael?

Logan entered the Liberty Market and wound his way past the displays of palm leaf crafts and blown glass. He spotted flashes of her blue sundress behind the sea of people crowded into the leather shop. Logan walked up behind and hugged her around the waist. "Everything's okay," he said kissing her neck.

Orla swung her body around and planted her lips onto his. "I've been worried sick about you darling. What happened to you?"

Logan slowly pushed her body away from his.

"We need to talk."

Orla looked at his face for the first time. His olive skin had turned white and he was sweating.

"Michael, you've gone pale. You look like you've just seen a ghost."

"I have seen a ghost Orla, one that has haunted me for a very long time."

The couple left the darkness of the market and shielded their eyes from the bright Mexican sun. They walked in silence until discovering an empty bench next to a glorious stone fountain. Logan reached out and caressed his lover's hand.

"I don't know how to say this, so I'll just say it. I got to leave you and go back to my old life."

Orla was floored by the news.

"What, back to the IRA? I thought you said those days were ancient history?"

"I'm not going back to the IRA. This is personal," Logan tried to explain without revealing too much information.

"Let me come with you," she pleaded.

"It will not be safe for you. Trust me; you do not want to be a part of my plans."

Orla saw that there was no talking him out of it. Feeling completely helpless, she started to weep uncontrollably. Logan hated to see her cry.

"I've set aside money for you. I've made it so you can live comfortably for the rest of your life."

Orla's sorrow turned to anger. "Please don't treat me like some kind of prostitute," she shouted. "I don't care about money Michael. I care about you! Do you not love me?"

Logan swallowed hard. "There is no place in my heart for love," he replied coldly.

He got up and left her crying on the bench. Logan's heart broke as he walked away.

Orla returned to their flat later that afternoon. In her heart, she hoped that he changed his mind. She opened the door to find the apartment empty. She walked into their bedroom. A picture of the two of them was missing from her dresser. She opened his closet and saw a row of empty hangers. Michael Logan had left no trace of himself behind. She went into the kitchen and pulled a bottle of red wine off an iron rack. On the kitchen counter was a page of instructions showing her how to withdraw her fortune from an offshore account.

"My reward for nine years with that man," she said aloud.

She took the piece of notepaper and tore it up.

Orla looked back toward the front door and noticed what looked to be a cut-out newspaper article lying on the floor. She bent down to pick it up and saw of a mature blond haired man with his arms held high. The caption read *Prime Min-*

ister-elect Robert Stirling celebrates his sweeping victory. Someone had used a red magic marker to draw an X over the man's picture.

Dear God in Heaven, Orla thought.

CHAPTER 27

Professor Tariq Qawi left his one bedroom flat on High Street and began a ten-minute walk to his small office at the Divinity School at Oxford University. He was forced to cancel classes again that morning after yet another anonymous threat to the university. Qawi had already been questioned by Scotland Yard and university officials about Greg Monroe, also known as Mustapha Rahim Al-Quir. The professor told them truthfully that Monroe was a passionate student who had turned his life completely over to Islam. Qawi also said that he soon became frightened by Monroe's extremist views and banished him from class. University records showed the professor was telling the truth. Qawi had ordered his young martyr to stay away from his Middle Eastern Studies class so that he would have some level of deniability after the mission was completed. The professor told authorities he had no knowledge of the group calling itself, *The Fist of Allah*, which claimed responsibility for the deadly attack aboard Bus Number 29.

The one-eyed Egyptian smiled as he passed Magdalene College, considered by many to be Oxford's most beautiful building. A strong wind whipped up bushels of leaves that floated freely around the 15th century quadrangle. The crisp air penetrated the scar tissue around the professor's left eye and it felt good. Qawi had always refused to wear a patch over the grotesque scar. It was something that he had used to great effect when recruiting martyrs. The professor told them he had lost the eye when he and some fellow students traveled from Egypt to Israel to protest the Jews illegal occupation of the West Bank. Qawi claimed that his eye was shot out by an Israeli soldier who fired rubber bullets into a crowd of demonstrators. The truth was far less dramatic. He had actually lost the eye while trying to climb a cedar tree in the backyard of his home when he was eight-years-old. The young Qawi slipped and fell face first into a tree branch. That secret was now held by only Qawi, his parents, and Allah.

He crossed Magdalen Bridge, which spanned the River Cherwell. The Coxswain of Oxford's rowing club could be heard underneath the bridge shouting directions to his teammates. Three minutes later, Professor Qawi reached the Divinity School, located inside the southern wing of the Bodleian Library. Even a *chosen one* like Qawi had to marvel at the infidels' breathtaking architectural design. The gothic library was erected in 1320 and expanded by the brother of Henry V in 1426. Humphrey, the Duke of Gloucester added onto the already massive structure when he realized the original library was too small to house his collection of manuscripts.

The professor entered the library annex, known as Duke Humphrey's Library and passed under a collection of ornate ceiling panels that carried Oxford's crest and Latin motto: *Dominus Illuminatio Mea* (the Lord, my Light). *Right idea; wrong God,* Qawi thought. He reached the Divinity School and continued toward his small office. Like the annex, the Divinity School's lecture hall also showcased an intricate ceiling design. Built in 1488, artists had carved 455 biblical scenes into the vaulted ceiling of the large hall. The one-eyed Egyptian was surrounded by Christian symbols at every turn. And if that was not insult enough, the Divinity School Chair had put him in an office adjacent to Oxford's resident rabbi.

Qawi retrieved his key and entered the security and serenity of his small corner office. He sat at his desk and unfolded the morning edition of the *Times* of London.

The new Prime Minister was not paying lip service in his promise to crackdown on Islamic radicals. The *Times* reported overnight raids in Arab communities in North-West London, Luton, Bedfordshire, and Blackburn. Inayet Shadjareh, from the Muslim Council of Great Britain called the anti-terror raids, *Islamophobia*. Qawi's heart ached when he thought about innocent Muslims being rounded up and detained at places like the Paddington Green Police Station in London. *Still, each brother has a role to play in the jihad against the Infidels,* he thought.

Qawi's spirits were raised by a sidebar story which detailed the bus bombing's psychological effect on Londoners. The head of the London Transit Authority admitted that ridership was way down despite a major increase in security. City attractions like the British Airways London Eye also reported a loss in revenue.

Qawi smiled and sipped from his cup of Turkish coffee. He set the newspaper down and opened his laptop computer. The professor logged onto the Internet and typed in the address: roadkillfansrule.org. It was a website for fans to discuss their favorite heavy metal band, *Road Kill*. It was also the method Qawi used to communicate with leaders of Al-Qaeda. He had not heard from his superiors since the bombing more than a month ago. Qawi was nervous. *Were they not pleased by my operation?*

He found the website's home page, which showed a picture of an electric guitar plastered to the grill of a speeding Mack Truck. The professor clicked on a link called, *talk back* and began scrolling through the messages.

-Did u C Cyrus's house on MTV'S CRIBS? Crime does pay! (Motercity madman)

-I don't care if he did deal drugs as a kid, I'd still have his baby! (Christina from the marina)

The professor grew to hate the West more each time he was forced to log onto this website. Still, he kept reading.

-Caught the double-bill, pyrotechnics were trippin' Hope to see it again real soon! (Tony in Toledo)

Qawi grinned. Tony's real name was Omar; he was not messaging from Toledo, Ohio, but Manila, Philippines. *So, they would like to see another one ...*

The professor logged off the computer and folded the laptop. He left his office at the same time Rabbi Levi entered his. The colleagues looked at each other, and then looked away. Neither man had acknowledged the other's presence in the two years they taught at Oxford. *You're day will come too Jew.*

Qawi shuffled down the steps of the Boldleian Library and began walking west across the courtyard toward The Radcliffe Camera, a domed rotunda built in 1748 as a memorial to the physician Dr. John Radcliffe. Special agent Phillip Sparks of Scotland Yard peered out a window of the Baroque rotunda with a pair of binoculars. His team was acting on an anonymous tip given to Prime Minister Stirling's office.

"Qawi has just exited the building. Stand by Team One, he's coming your way," Sparks said into his mouthpiece.

Frank Judge and Denise Russell walked arm and arm across the courtyard.

They were about ten paces behind the professor and gaining ground quickly, but not quietly. Qawi heard their affectionate laughter in the background but paid no attention. He could not know the collegiate sweethearts were actually highly trained members of Scotland Yard's Anti-Terror Task Force. Another undercover officer approached from the front. The man wore a tweed coat over a crew neck sweater. His long brown hair bore the disheveled look of a student or teaching assistant.

The man smiled and nodded to the professor who returned the gesture.

"Take him down now," Special Agent Sparks ordered.

Judge and Russell came up from behind and locked their hands under the professor's elbows. Before he could react, the undercover officer with long brown hair grabbed the front of Qawi's coat and pulled him to the ground.

"What, what is happening? What are you doing to me?" the professor screamed.

The officer took out his badge and held it an inch away from the Egyptian's scarred face.

"Tariq Qawi, you are under arrest for the murders of thirty-six people aboard Bus Number 29."

The following morning, Mitch Handley laced up his sneakers and went out for his daily run. He hated to admit it, but he actually enjoyed the exercise. It was too bad that this would be his last jog through Hyde Park. Muhammad Hamsho sat on the bench waiting for the rendezvous. The Palestinian's conscience weighed heavily on him. He had sold out his people for a few thousand euros; Allah would no doubt be setting a special place aside for him in Hell. Muhammad's fear of Allah was strong, but not stronger than his growing gambling addiction. Those seeds were planted with a few horse bets at his local coffeehouse, but his life soon began spiraling out of control. Muhammad kept the bookies at bay with money he received for ratting out his fellow Muslims. Now his brothers were sitting in jail getting tortured by the *infidels*. He had been seduced by the fat jogger with the thick wallet. *Here he comes now.*

Robert Stirling's words echoed in Handley's mind. "We must tie up all loose ends," his boss had said. He could see the informant a few yards ahead. Muhammad looked quite relaxed as he slouched on the wooden bench. *Good,* thought Handley. He placed both hands in the front pockets of his nylon running jacket as he casually scanned the perimeter of the park. *We're alone.* Muhammad grew puzzled as he watched the jogger continue past the bench without breaking stride. Suddenly, he noticed the man pull something out of his pocket. Muhammad's eyes showed fear when he realized what it was. Handley fired his silenced Walther twice hitting the Palestinian in the stomach. He kept jogging and did not look back as the informant rolled off the bench and hit the soft ground. *No loose ends.*

CHAPTER 28

LONDON, TEN
MONTHS LATER

The motorcade carrying Prime Minister Robert Stirling weaved its way through the line of protesters surrounding 10 Downing Street. BBC reporter Brian Leeds stood shoulder to shoulder with the protesters as he described the scene on live television. "Prime Minister Robert Stirling is just returning from the House of Commons, where he was once again asked to explain the beating deaths of fourteen British Muslims being held by the government. There are still more than three hundred Muslims who are detained without formal charges."

The cameraman panned off the reporter and focused on the crowd. Leeds ad-libbed over the live pictures. "I have never seen a protest quite like this one. There has to be at least a thousand people here. Most are carrying signs urging the Prime Minister to resign. You can see another sign that says *Police State* and another one that we won't show you on live television. Let's just say the sign compares Robert Stirling to a great villain of history. Reporting live from 10 Downing Street, Brian Leeds BBC News."

Prime Minister Stirling looked out at the crowd from the tinted and protected windows of his limousine. His Chief of Staff, Mitch Handley sat opposite of the Prime Minister in the back seat.

"Just look at these jackals. One would think the bombing of Bus Number 29 never happened," he said in disgust.

"The attack happened nearly eleven months ago," Handley pointed out. "That's a life time in politics, sir."

The limousine pulled up in front of the Prime Minister's residence. The back door was opened and Robert Stirling stepped out waving defiantly to the protesters.

His security detail surrounded the Prime Minister and whisked him inside. Stirling's smile disappeared as the doors closed. He tugged at his tie while marching passed various advisors who knew not to approach him at a time like this. As always, Mitch Handley was right on the Prime Minister's heels. Both men entered the Prime Minister's office and closed the door.

"I gave up my shares in Stirling Global for this?" The Prime Minister asked aloud.

"Leadership can be very lonely sir," Handley replied while pouring his boss a scotch.

Stirling sat at his desk under two large portraits of Winston Churchill and Margaret Thatcher.

"This never happened to them," Stirling said referring to his legendary predecessors.

"Well sir, Winston Churchill was a man on an island in the years leading up to World War Two. If you remember, most Britons either feared or admired Adolf Hitler."

"That reminds me," Stirling laughed. "Did you see that poster of me wearing a Hitler mustache?"

Handley had hoped the Prime Minister had not seen it.

"Yes sir, I did. They do it to Bush all the time in America."

Stirling rolled his eyes. "That's another thing. His Iraq mess has not helped the situation one bit. I keep asking him for a timetable on bringing soldiers home and he just says, when the mission's over. As if he'd ever known what a real mission looked like."

"We cannot bring our troops home because it would look like we are weak," Handley pointed out.

Stirling ran his hand though his golden hair. "So where does that leave us?"

Handley took a sip of scotch before speaking. "Sir, I think you need to keep your boot on the neck of the Arab. History will show that you did the right thing. But you also need to be, dare I say it "compassionate". What about floating an olive branch over the Irish Sea? The Catholics and Protestants are finally making great strides toward peace. The IRA appears to be no longer a threat. You could really score some points there."

Prime Minister Stirling got out of his chair and stretched his legs. He paced the room for several minutes with his hands on his hips. Handley knew his boss's mind had floated back somewhere in his dark past.

"The Irish and the Arab are not that dissimilar," The Prime Minister lectured his Chief of Staff. "Both races are quite savage you know. I've shed a lot of blood on that island. I don't think that I could ever go back."

Mitch Handley remained calm. "Sir if I am to protect you, please don't ever repeat those words to me or anyone else again."

"So where does that leave us Mitch?"

It was the first time Robert Stirling had ever referred to his subordinate by his first name. Handley knew his boss was troubled. "Let's do it in America, for maximum impact. I'll phone Belfast and the White House immediately."

Stirling contemplated the idea and rejected it.

"I don't want the cowboy anywhere near this summit. In fact, I'd like to rub it in his Texas face a bit. Is there one person the President dislikes most over there?"

Handley thought for a moment and smiled.

"Prime Minister, have you ever been to Cape Cod?"

C H A P T E R   29

ROXBURY,
MASSACHUSETTS

Heath Rosary crept silently through the shadows of the darkened corridor. He saw a light coming from the open door of a small room at the end of the hallway. His strong shoulders hugged the concrete wall as he inched his way closer to the door. His target was now in sight. The man was sitting at a desk with his back facing the door. He appeared to be doing paperwork with the aid of a small desk lamp. Rosary was now only five feet away.

"Heathcliff, didn't I teach you how to knock," the man said still staring down at his paperwork.

"Damn, I was so close," Rosary laughed. "When are you going to learn to lock this place up at night?"

"I've been here for twenty-six years," James Rosary reminded his nephew. "So far, you've been the only one foolish enough to come in here and test his fate."

The older man got out of his chair and walked over with his arms stretched out.

Heath stepped forward and embraced his uncle.

"Got a message you wanted to see me?"

"In a moment son, follow me into the dojo where we can talk."

The men walked down the narrow hallway that opened up to a large empty space with padded floors. James Rosary had owned and operated the Jeet Kune

Do Studio on Blue Hill Avenue for the past two decades. The elder Rosary stepped behind a heavy bag and called his nephew over.

"Show me what you got."

The younger man cracked his knuckles and threw a spinning back fist toward the bag. The sound of the punch echoed through the room.

"Not bad son. Talk to your sister lately?"

"We had dinner a couple of nights ago at a place on Longwood. She got called back to the hospital just after the appetizers had arrived."

"Carla's gonna make a fine doctor one day."

"Sure, if she doesn't die from exhaustion before her residency is over."

Heath continued to pound the bag with a flurry of punches. His uncle stood on the other side holding the bag close to his body.

"I see you haven't lost any of your power," James Rosary observed as he absorbed the punches with his chest.

"I had a great teacher," Heath replied throwing a straight right jab followed by a left hook.

"So did I," Heath's uncle reminded him.

James Rosary was one of the only certified Jeet Kune Do instructors on the east coast. He was also one of the few people to actually train with the founder of the hybrid martial art, a young man named Bruce Lee. Rosary met Lee while both were attending the University of Washington in the early 1960's. Unlike other kung fu instructors in the Seattle area, Bruce Lee was the only teacher to open his doors to non-Chinese. Rosary became an early disciple after seeing Lee perform his one-inch punch technique in the school cafeteria. The five-foot-seven Chinese man stood just one inch away from his towering opponent and with a slight jerk of his wrist, the 150-pound Lee took the man off his feet and sent him flying over a chair. A skeptical James Rosary thought it was a parlor trick and offered his own body up for the exercise. Bruce Lee smiled and repeated the drill sending Rosary two feet further than the previous man. When Rosary finally caught his breath, Lee helped him to his feet and handed him a sign up sheet. It was the beginning of a special relationship between teacher and student.

Like a mechanic building a hot rod from a collection of spare parts, Lee created Jeet Kune Do by picking and choosing from various martial arts. He only took the most useful techniques from each and discarded the rest. Lee not only opened Rosary's mind up to an unorthodox fighting method, he also taught his friend the philosophy behind Jeet Kune Do. "Use no way as way. Seek no limitation as limitation," Lee would urge his students. After three years of training, Bruce Lee went off to Hong Kong in search of movie stardom. James Rosary went off to Vietnam where he survived two tours of duty before leaving the army and heading home to Boston. Upon his return, Rosary became the instant father of two young children when his drug addicted sister Darlene disappeared with a man she had met at a bar.

James Rosary opened a kung-fu studio and raised his niece and nephew as his own. By all accounts, he was successful. Carla Rosary had graduated Boston University Medical School and was now completing her residency at Beth Israel Hospital. Heath had graduated from the prestigious Boston College High School and went on to Boston College on a full football scholarship. He played cornerback for the B.C. Eagles and secured his place in local sports lore by intercepting a pass and running it back for a touchdown in a last minute Fiesta Bowl win against the University of Michigan. Boston College capped off its only undefeated season with a national title. The following spring, Heath was selected by his hometown team, The New England Patriots in the second round of the NFL draft. Dreams of a pro career were dashed however when he suffered a major knee injury during a pre-season game against the New York Jets.

With his signing bonus and money from his insurance company, Heath Rosary returned to Boston College and earned his law degree. He couldn't see himself arguing cases in a courtroom, so Rosary applied for and was selected into the United States Secret Service. It all felt like a lifetime ago to him now. It was before he was assigned to protect Jennifer Bosworth and before he took a bullet for her inside the apartment on Park Drive. Once Rosary recovered from his gunshot wound, he resigned from his post. He did not lose his nerve, but he lost his faith in the Secret Service. Ahmet Sistani had gone down in history as the Arab terrorist who kidnapped the President's daughter. After the attacks of September 11th, the Sistani myth became even more of an insult, especially to the families of those who died at the hands of the real terrorists.

Now he made his living as a private investigator. *Not a very good living,* he reminded himself, but at least it was an honest one. Honesty was a character trait instilled in him by his Uncle James. Heath called him, Uncle, but in reality James Rosary was the only father he had ever known.

"How's Grace doing?" James asked Heath bringing him back to the here and now.

"She's doing just fine. Grace likes producing TV news, it's like she feeds on the stress level."

"That girl has definitely got it together. Any change in attitude with her family?"

This was a real sore spot for the couple.

"Her father still hopes our relationship is just a phase. He can't see his Chinese princess marrying a black man."

"Tommy Chen has a doctorate from MIT and heads a billion dollar pharmaceutical company, but if you ask me the man's still a damn fool!" scoffed Uncle James.

Heath stopped hitting the heavy bag and inspected his raw knuckles.

"C'mon Uncle, you didn't ask me to meet you here late at night to talk about my love life."

"No I didn't son."

The two men walked over to a row of mirrors along the wall where they instinctively began throwing kicks in the air. It was how they communicated with one another. They always had their best conversations while training.

"May Galvin came to see me," James said while practicing his sidekick. "She's got a thirteen year-old grandson who has found himself in a bit of trouble."

"What did the kid do?" Heath grunted as he hooked his right leg and flicked it out toward the wall.

"The kid found an envelope filled with cash in a trash can outside the Curley Housing Project. It seems he and his friends went on quite a spending spree. They bought bikes; some of those damned X-Boxes, and some clothes. The money's all gone and now the man who lost it has come back for it."

"How much money did the kids take?"

"May tells me it was around ten thousand."

Heath's eyes went wide. "That's a lot of money for a thirteen-year-old."

"Hell, that's a lot of money for a fifty-five-year old."

The men started laughing and stopped their exercises.

"Seriously Heath, her grandson is a good kid. He stays out of trouble and scores well on his report cards. I guess he thought it was found money."

"Found money always belongs to someone else. Whose money was it?" Heath inquired.

"A nasty little pusher named, Ossie Bramble. He's Jamaican which means that he won't think twice about blowing this kid's head off."

"Let me ask around and see what I can do."

"How much do you charge for something like this?" Uncle James asked sincerely.

"For you the usual fee," Heath replied. "Nothing."

Rosary left his uncle's dojo and drove back down Blue Hill Avenue toward his condo in South Boston. It was a warm spring evening and young black toughs were hanging out on stoops and outside liquor stores. They eyeballed Rosary's silver Jaguar as it idled at a stoplight. The car was the only extravagant gift he had purchased for himself after signing the contract with the Patriots. The Jaguar was now nearly twenty years-old but Rosary kept it in mint condition. The light turned green and he hit the gas. One punk with a red bandana chucked a forty-ounce bottle of Miller Light in Rosary's direction. He heard the sound of shattering glass as he sped away. *There but for the grace of God,* he thought. If it had not been for his uncle, he would have ended up like the other kids from the neighborhood, either dead or in prison. But while those kids were getting schooled in the ABC's of the streets, Heath and his sister were taking piano lessons or wandering the exhibits of the Museum of Fine Arts on Huntington Avenue. Uncle James was the first person in the family to get his college diploma and he made damn sure he wasn't the last.

CHAPTER 30

LONDON

Brian Leeds was sitting on the toilet when the story crossed the Associated Press wires. He was trying to shake off the dizzying effects of a brutal hangover and he was also hiding from his producer who had demanded a noon live shot on the latest foxhunting debate in Parliament.

"Where the fuck is he?" the producer yelled while searching the BBC newsroom for his chief correspondent.

"Check the bathroom," the anchorman suggested. "Brian smelled like a bottle of whiskey when he walked in here this morning."

The producer threw open the door to the men's restroom and noticed a familiar pair of tan loafers under one of the stalls.

"Read this," the producer said while slipping a piece of wire copy under the stall door. "Don't wipe your ass with it. I'll need you at camera five in four minutes."

The reporter's head started to clear after reading the first paragraph. He pulled his pants up, flushed the toilet and ran out of the bathroom.

"Tell master control that we want to break into this soap opera," the producer shouted into his headset. He then searched the wires for more information as the director cut into the soap and rolled the breaking news animation.

"Good Afternoon, I'm Jack Shields," the anchor announced. "We have breaking news now on the peace process between Great Britain and the Catholics of Northern Ireland. The Associated Press reports both sides are headed back to the negotiating table in hopes of resurrecting the Good Friday Peace Agreement. BBC Senior Correspondent Brian Leeds joins us live in the newsroom with the very latest on this breaking story."

Leeds finished putting in his ear piece just seconds before the director took his picture in a double box effect with the anchor.

"Brian, what can you tell us?" the anchor asked.

"Well Jack, this is truly unprecedented. According to this report, Prime Minister Robert Stirling will bypass the Secretary of State of Northern Ireland and lead the negotiations himself. As you know, the Good Friday Peace Agreement was shattered back in 2002 when the British Government suspended elections. The British government said it could not negotiate with Sinn Fein if the IRA did not disarm but now, four years later there has been a major shift in policy. It all comes following a 60-page assessment from the Independent Monitoring Commission. The four man panel has concluded that the IRA has begun reducing its membership. According to the report, the outlawed group has also shut down key units responsible for weapons-making, arms smuggling and training. The commission believes the Irish Republican Army is no longer in the terrorism business."

Leeds paused and waited for another scripted question to come his way. He could not believe this blow-dryed anchorman made nearly double his salary.

"Brian, we understand this peace summit will not take place in Ireland or the United Kingdom?"

"That's right Jack. The details are still coming in but here's what we know. Both sides are scheduled to meet in the United States at the historic Kennedy Compound. Call it the Cape Cod Accord, if you will. The Prime Minister and Sinn Fein leader Gerry Adams will be hosted by Senator Edward Kennedy who has been named special U.S. Envoy to the negotiations."

The anchorman nodded to his colleague. "Chief Correspondent Brian Leeds, thank you. We'll bring you much more on this breaking story on the news at noon. For now, I'm Jack Shields BBC News."

Leeds took out his earpiece and stepped off the newsroom set. Jack Shields walked out of the main studio toward his old friend. "Nice job Brian," Shields said with a grin. "You can go back to the toilet now."

The line drew a chuckle from a group of news writers sitting nearby.

"Fuck off Jack," Leeds grumbled as Shields strolled by.

DUBLIN, IRELAND

Vincent Logan sat as his desk picking at his lunch. It was supposed to be steak salad, but the detective still could not find a sliver of beef hidden among the greens. He thought about sending his lunch to the forensic lab for further analysis. Fiona said she was worried about her husband's eating habits and the long hours he was putting in at the office. *This is her way of getting back at me,* he thought.

He had just finished writing a performance report on the Italian Prime Minister's recent visit to the Republic of Ireland. As commandant of the Special Detective Unit (SDU) of the Guarda Siochana, he was now responsible for the protection of all VIP's who landed on Irish soil. In Logan's opinion, the security operation had run quite smoothly, from the time the Prime Minister's plane touched down at Shannon Airport, to the moment he kissed the Taoiseach of Ireland goodbye on both cheeks.

His decision to include two decoy vehicles in the Prime Minister's entourage drew praise from Logan's superiors, because even they did not know which limousine the VIP was in. It was an idea he had picked up during a training exchange in the United States.

He pushed his salad away and picked up a framed photo of Fiona and Audrey. He had taken the picture during their trip to the south of France. It was their last vacation and it was more than a year ago. It was time to recharge the batteries and reconnect with the two most important people in his life. Using the Internet, Vincent was able to book a trip for the three of them to Disney World. He could just imagine the look on his little girl's face when he told her the news after he arrived home that night. Audrey owned just about every Disney DVD there was. Still, it was *The Jungle Book,* which she watched over and over again. No doubt Audrey would be humming the tune to *The Bear Necessities* from Dublin all the way to Florida. The pleasant thought was interrupted by a knock on the door.

"Sorry to bother you sir, but there's a woman here to see you," receptionist Helen O'Keefe informed Logan. "I told her that she needs to make an appointment, but she won't go away."

"Did you catch the woman's name, Ms. O'Keefe?"

"Orla Madden, sir."

Vincent's blood ran cold. *Something has happened to Michael.*

"Oh, I remember her now. She did make an appointment. I must have forgotten to put it in my daybook. Please tell her that I'll be right with her."

The receptionist nodded her head and closed the door. *He sure is acting peculiar,* O'Keefe thought. *His eyes nearly popped out of his head at the mere mention of her name. Vincent Logan is not the type to be cheating on his wife, but if he is, then he's got a big surprise waiting for him.* O'Keefe shook her head as she walked back to her desk.

Logan left his office and walked toward the reception area where he saw a woman seated on a long wooden bench. Hung directly overhead was a large portrait of Michael Staines, the first commissioner of the Garda Siochana. There was a quote from Staines written on a gold plaque at the bottom of the portrait that read, "The Garda Siochana will succeed, not by force of arms or numbers, but by their moral authority as servants of the people." Logan wondered whether that statement still rang true today. The problems facing the Garda were not unlike the problems facing any other modern police force. The public appeared to be more concerned with the rights of the criminal than with the rights of the cops.

The woman seated on the bench was not the Orla Madden he had remembered at his mother's hospital. Her brown hair had been bleached by the sun and her creamy white skin was now the color of light caramel. She also appeared much heavier than Logan had remembered. He found out why when she stood to shake his hand. Orla Madden was eight months pregnant.

"Vincent, thank you for seeing me today," Orla greeted him formally.

"It looks like we have a lot to talk about," he replied uncomfortably. "Please let me take you to lunch. Do not say a word here," he said putting his finger to his lips.

Logan walked her out of police headquarters and toward his car. An awkward silence hung over them as they drove to lunch at the Diep Noodle bar on Ranelagh Street. He chose the restaurant for two reasons, first because it was far way from Garda headquarters, and secondly because the spicy Thai food would help him forget about the steak salad minus the steak.

The two entered the small restaurant and found a corner booth. A smiling Vietnamese waiter approached quickly with menus in hand. Logan knew what he wanted but waited patiently for his companion to make her decision. He ordered the red snapper vermicelli; Orla chose a dish of seafood rice noodles.

"So what can I do for you?" Vincent asked while reaching out for her hand. *Clearly my brother has run out on you and the baby,* he thought.

"I've debated coming to see you for months," she admitted. "But I wanted my baby to be born here in Ireland, so I've come home."

"I take it that Michael is the father of your child?"

"Yes, but he doesn't know it. He left me before I found out. I want you to find him; I want you to find him before he does something awful."

"Okay, lower your voice," he advised. "What is my brother fixed up in now?"

Orla told Vincent the story about Guadalajara and Michael's sudden decision to abandon her. "I thought he was happy and then he just walked away. At first, I was so angry but I couldn't stay mad at the only man I've ever loved."

Vincent listened patiently before asking his next question. "Orla, you said Michael was going to do something awful. What were you talking about?"

"He told me that it was *personal.* You know how he feels about the British. I think he wants to derail the peace process."

"Why do you think that?"

"Because I found this," Orla replied as she pulled a folded newspaper article out of her coat pocket and slid it across the table. Vincent unfolded the clipping and saw the marked up photograph of Prime Minister Stirling. He refolded the paper and put his head in his hands.

"I tried to get it out of my mind until I read about that peace summit planned in the states," Orla continued.

Vincent agreed. "It would be the perfect place for him to operate. They don't know him there."

"I want you to stop him Vincent," Orla whispered. "I want you to save him from himself."

C H A P T E R   31

BOSTON

The man whose passport read, *Roberto Tomba* stepped off a British Airways jumbo jet and walked through the tunnel into Logan International Airport. He followed the signs toward the customs checkpoint where he waited patiently behind his fellow British Airways passengers. This was not the time for the histrionics he had performed as Senor Tomba when he first flew into Heathrow. Logan was too close to his final goal to take any unnecessary chances now. He stood in line with his nose in a mystery novel, apparently uninterested in the scene around him. His eyes moved slowly from the open page to two national guardsmen standing by the windows of Terminal E, both carrying M16 Rifles.

Logan reminded himself that this was the same airport used by ten of the nineteen hijackers as a portal to unspeakable horror on September 11th 2001. *Cowards,* he thought. In Logan's mind, he saw no similarity between himself and terrorists working for Al Qaeda. They went after soft targets: women, children and the elderly. These victims were the unwitting spectators to an ancient battle of ideals. Michael Logan had always targeted the men on the battlefield itself.

He finally took his place at the head of the line and handed his passport over to the immigration official, an overweight woman with frosted hair and a large gap between her front teeth. "Are you here on business or pleasure sir?" she asked dropping her R's.

"Pleasure," he answered with a Spanish accent. "I am a great admirer of your city's Colonial history."

His comment seemed to break her sullen mood. The immigration official was also a proud member of the Daughters of the Liberty Tree, a group whose goal was to keep the memory of 1776 alive for future generations. "Everyone comes to see Paul Revere's house and the Old North Church," she informed him. "But your best bet is the Old Granary Burial Ground down on Tremont Street. That's where Samuel Adams and John Hancock are buried. It's quite small, but you can still spend hours in there."

"Gracias," he replied.

The woman stamped the passport and handed it back to him. Logan placed it inside the pocket of his leather jacket and continued toward the main concourse. He approached the counter of Avis Rent-a-Car and ordered a small Toyota Camry. The saleswoman handed Logan his key along with a map covering Boston and the rest of New England. He picked up the car and spent the next twenty minutes trying to leave the airport. Because of the massive *Big Dig* highway project, the roads leading to and away from the airport were a confusing collection of detours where one wrong turn could add another hour to your travel time. Logan finally spotted a sign for Route 1 North and steered the Camry across three lanes toward the exit.

The rest of the drive was long but fairly simple. He followed Route 1 through the suburbs of Revere, Peabody, and Danvers. The nine-mile stretch was a dizzying array of neon signs, which pointed to roadside restaurants and strip joints. Logan had his map unfolded in front of him on the steering wheel. The directions told him to follow Route 1 to Route 16 North. He turned on the car radio and scanned the dial for a news station. He settled on WBZ Radio 1030. Logan sat through the weather and sports reports. Apparently, a team called the Boston Celtics had just won their first playoff game. Logan had no idea what a *Seltic* was. The announcer promised a look at the day's top stories after a commercial break. The station played three minutes of advertisements including a clever jingle for a local glass company. *Who do you call when your windshield's busted? Call Giant Glass! 1-800-54-GIANT, done right, done fast!* Logan was about to change the station when suddenly the announcer came back on.

"Good morning, It's nine o'clock and forty five degrees outside our Brighton studios. I'm Gary Lapierre, WBZ News. Next week's Anglo-Irish Summit is being met with guarded optimism by members of the local Irish community. Teddy Jones is a Belfast native who immigrated to South Boston three years ago."

The announcer's smooth voice was replaced by Jones' thick Irish brogue.

"The Good Friday Peace Accord was a sham," Jones said. "They ordered the IRA to disarm but didn't go after Loyalist groups that have shed more blood than the republicans. They'll only achieve peace if they get the Unionists to disarm as well."

The announcer returned to the air and pitched to another sound cut.

"We also spoke with Nancy Griffin from the Fletcher School at Tufts University."

The announcer's deep voice was replaced by another sound bite. "I think Sinn Fein leader Gerry Adams should proceed with caution here," the expert said. "Prime Minister Robert Stirling is the same man, who is being roundly criticized in his own country for what some call his harsh treatment of members of the Islamic community," Griffin pointed out. "He is not the type of man that I would choose to broker a peace deal."

"The world must wait and see," Lapierre continued. "Both sides will sit down seven days from now at the Kennedy Compound in Hyannisport. In other news …"

Seven days and the nightmare will finally be over, Logan thought.

The blue Toyota Camry arrived in Conway, New Hampshire just before noon. It was still mud season in New Hampshire so there was not a steady stream of tourist traffic rolling through the resort town. Logan turned left off Route 16 onto West Side Road. The scenery was brilliant. Out his car window, he could see the majestic peaks of the Presidential Mountain range disappearing into the clouds. It reminded him of Black Mountain back home. He passed a red covered bridge and two farms before he spotted the address he was looking for. It was painted on an old tin mailbox that was planted into the muddy ground on the side of the road. He put his blinker on and turned left down a long dirt driveway.

Viktor Tarkov was growing frustrated with the New York *Times* crossword puzzle. The former KGB Colonel was nearly finished when he got caught up on one riddle. *Heisman Trophy winner from Stanford.* Damn these American sports. Tarkov knew the Heisman Trophy winner was a football player and that his name was Jim something or other. *Elway? Staubach? No, it is an eight-letter word.* He gnawed on his pencil and waited for the answer to come to him. Tarkov stared over to his computer. *Should I look it up on the Internet? No that would be cheating.* Tarkov smiled to himself. *Since when did you ever play by the rules?* He started walking toward his computer when an alarm sounded. Lying at their master's feet, Tarkov's Doberman Pincers craned their long necks at the high pitch of the alarm.

"Boris," Tarkov ordered. "Alexander, come!"

The dogs followed their master out of the study.

Tarkov walked across the hall and into a spare bedroom. He opened the closet door and pulled out a rifle. He did not need to check if it was loaded. Viktor Tarkov was always prepared. His Japanese wife Koki saw the weapon in his hands.

"What is it?" she asked nervously.

"Nothing dearest," he assured her. "Probably some kids trying to scare the horses again."

The Russian looked out the kitchen window and saw the Toyota Camry come to a stop at the end of the driveway. He opened the back door just wide enough for the Dobermans.

"Go!" he ordered the dogs in Russian.

Boris and Alex both shot out of the back door and pounced on the Camry within seconds. Their sharp claws scraped the blue paint, their hot breath fogged up the driver's side window. Logan jumped in his seat and instinctively reached into his pocket for a gun that he knew was not there.

"My dogs have been known to break through glass," the Russian warned as he approached the Camry with his rifle aimed high.

"Viktor I need you!" shouted a voice from within the car.

Tarkov moved slowly closer. "Logan, is that you?"

"You really know how to make an old friend feel welcome."

A smile came over the old Russian's wrinkled face. "Alexander, Boris heal!" he commanded in his native tongue.

The animals, frothing at the mouth came to immediate attention for their master.

Logan brought his window down slowly.

"Did you think I was an old nemesis coming for revenge?"

"No, I thought you were a Jehovah's Witness. They've been coming around my farm for weeks."

Tarkov opened Logan's door and invited him out of the car. The Irishman kept his eyes on the killer dogs as he slowly stepped out of the vehicle.

"Michael, I would like you to meet Boris and Alexander," Tarkov said waving toward the animals. "I named them after Alexander Pushkin and Boris Pasternak, two of the greatest poets in Russian history. These dogs are the best bodyguards that money can buy."

"I'll take your word for it Viktor."

The men laughed aloud and hugged each other warmly. Logan eventually broke the embrace and looked around the spread. Tarkov owned thirty acres of rich New Hampshire farmland. There were endless rows of corn waving in the breeze and heads of lettuce and cabbage as far as the eye could see. It was clear that Viktor Tarkov had a green thumb connected to his iron fist. There was also a two-story barn adjacent to a horse stable. Logan counted six horses.

"Beautiful are they not?" Tarkov said reading his former student's mind. "Those Morgan stallions are my pride and joy. The Morgan is a true American original. The entire breed can trace its heritage back to a single horse. Just look at their gleaming, muscular bodies. Their chestnut coat is the finest I've ever seen."

Tarkov shook his head and chuckled. "Look at me carrying on like a proud papa. Come, we've got so much to talk about."

The Russian led the way toward the farmhouse. Tarkov's wife stood with arms folded at the door.

"Koki, a dear friend has come to visit," he shouted. "We'll take our coffee outside on the porch."

The woman nodded and disappeared back inside.

"Your maid?" inquired Logan.

"No, my wife actually," the Russian smiled. "I met her during that job we pulled in Tokyo a few years back. Her knowledge of our target was indispensable. But she's even more indispensable to me now."

"Aw, spoken like a true romantic," Logan kidded his friend.

"Not a romantic Michael, a realist. I'm getting old you know."

Tarkov must have been over seventy years old, but Logan would never ask. He was fully bald and wore a little more padding around the waistline, but still looked spry for his advanced age. The men walked along the side of the one hundred-year-old farmhouse toward the screened in porch. Two cups of coffee awaited them on a small iron table surrounded by a pair of white wicker chairs. Logan noticed the difficulty to which Tarkov took his seat. The older man balanced both hands on the arms of the chair and slowly lowered the rest of his body down.

"Doctor says I'll riddled with arthritis," Tarkov told Michael. "I bet that I can still beat him down the mountain on a pair of skis."

Logan had no doubt in his mind. He remembered the treacherous obstacle courses and grueling hikes he was forced to go on as part of his training. Viktor Tarkov had always performed the challenges with his men, most of the time leading the pack himself. Teacher and student both sipped their coffee in silence not wanting to spoil the special moment with words. Tarkov pulled a pack of cigarettes from his pocket; placed one between his lips and lit it.

"I guess you're wondering how a sworn enemy of capitalism ended up here?"

"The question did cross my mind," Logan replied.

"After you disappeared, I could never find anyone to equal your ... special talents. So I took a break from the wet work and hired myself out as a sort of corporate spymaster. Instead of working for countries, I did the dirty work for major companies including some here in America. The heads of those companies, all big political backers, greased the way for my private relocation here in the bosom of the White Mountains."

The men went back to their coffee while admiring the farm's panoramic view. Tarkov's porch looked out over the jagged side of Cathedral Ledge, a mountain that appeared to be sliced in half by nature. It was midday and the sun splashed on the tiny climbers trying to conquer the mountain's unforgiving face.

"Unlike some of your Irish comrades, you never bought any of the Marxist dogma that we tried to force down your throat in the training camps. That is why I liked you most of all Michael."

Logan nodded his head.

"Do you know why Communism failed?" the Russian asked.

The younger man thought for a moment. Logan felt like he was back in the classroom in Moscow. "I believe it was a number of factors," he explained. "Military overspending by the Americans, lack of production by the Russians ..."

Tarkov cut his former student off.

"It's because of this," he said staring at the burning end of his Marlboro. "I spent decades smoking those awful East German cigarettes. But the first time I tasted a Marlboro, I had an epiphany. The country that made these had to be better than mine."

Both men laughed as they finished their coffee. The conversation then turned from the philosophical to the practical.

"So why have you come after all this time?" Tarkov asked.

"I need your help Viktor. I have found the man who murdered my father."

Tarkov watched Logan's placid eyes fill with fire.

"I see," the Russian responded. "And who is this man?"

Logan leaned closer. "He's the Prime Minister of Britain, Robert Stirling."

Tarkov leaned back in his chair and took another drag from his cigarette. "I'd love to say you are crazy but unfortunately, I believe you. Robert Stirling, I've heard some very bad things about that man. My friends in the Arab world say he's as crazy as Saddam ever was."

Logan took another sip of his coffee and stared off toward the mountains. "He has cancelled all public appearances back in Britain while he prepares for next week's summit," Logan told Tarkov. "That's what has brought me here."

The Russian lifted himself off the chair. "Follow me dear boy," he grunted. Tarkov led Logan off the porch and over to the two-story barn. They bypassed the livestock stalls strewn with hay and climbed a wooden ladder up to the loft.

"This is my work shop," Tarkov said with a smile.

It appeared to be just that, but along with the mitre saws, tools and sawdust, there was a wide array of hi-tech weapons lining the walls of the barn.

"I still consult from time to time," Tarkov said with a grin as he walked over to a small flat screen computer in the corner of the loft. "Now, this summit is scheduled to take place in Hyannisport, Massachusetts." He typed the location into the computer and waited for a response. A multi-colored image of Cape Cod appeared on the small screen. "According to this map, you couldn't have chosen a more difficult location." Tarkov waved his young guest closer. "Unless you flee by boat, your only route of escape is here and here." He pointed to the Sagamore and Bourne bridges that connect Cape Cod to the mainland. "The map also shows the Massachusetts Military Reservation right here." Tarkov pointed to the village of Sandwich. "The reservation is home to Camp Edwards, Otis Air National Guard base and the Coast Guard. Are you sure you don't want to wait until he returns to London?" he asked.

"I don't need an escape plan Viktor," Logan replied softly.

The words caught Tarkov by surprise. "Is this a suicide mission Michael?"

"He took my soul the day he murdered my father. How can I kill myself when I can't feel that I'm even alive?"

Tarkov walked up and put his arms around his troubled young friend.

"If this is your decision, then let me help you," he whispered into Logan's ear.

Logan shook his head. "No Viktor, I can't drag you into this. You've built a nice quiet life for yourself here."

"Bargaining chips my boy," Tarkov said as he tapped his bald skull with his index finger. "I have enough information up here and elsewhere to sink the past five presidential administrations. If I get caught, I can assure you that I'll be back here tending to my Morgans' within a week's time."

"Only if you really want to do this."

"Look around my workshop," Tarkov laughed. "Do I look like a man complacent with retirement?"

Logan scanned the walls of the loft. Hung on wooden pegs was a vast collection of handguns, assault rifles, rocket launchers and explosive charges. Viktor Tarkov was a one-man militia group. Logan's eyes moved from the arsenal of weapons to an impressive array of surveillance equipment that was laid out on a long wooden table. He walked over for a closer look. Logan inspected a dozen small bugging devices along with a lipstick camera fitted into a pair of eyeglasses. In the corner of this hi-tech loft stood three small video cameras fixed on top of their tri-pods. A plan began to form in Logan's mind.

CHAPTER 32

"He seems to be making himself at home," Grace Chen whispered.

Grace and Heath Rosary stood in the galley kitchen of his South Boston condominium. Thirteen-year-old Jamal Galvin sat quietly in the living room watching a cartoon on television. The youngster had just finished a plate of chicken and two bowls of macaroni.

"First the kid hijacked my leather couch, and now *Sponge Bob Square Pants* has taken over my plasma screen," Heath grumbled.

Grace wrapped her arms around her man. "Oh, you poor dear. You've been waiting for that special on the History Channel haven't you."

"FDR: A Presidency Revealed," Heath reminded her. "Don't worry, I've got the Tivo going."

"Yah, like you even know how to use it," he laughed. "Have you been this grumpy all day?" she asked elbowing him gently in the ribs.

Rosary rolled his eyes. "If you had the day I've had, you wouldn't be little Miss Sunshine either. I took Jamal to school and walked him from class to class. It was like reliving junior high all over again. I think I even sat on some gum."

Grace was doubled over with laughter. "Anything else exciting?"

"Actually, I got a call from a cop buddy over in Ireland. We trained together at the Rowley Center in Maryland. Of course that was in my past life. Anyway, he's in town and wants to meet me tomorrow about a job. It sounds like he's looking for a long lost relative or something."

Rosary took out a pair of long stemmed wineglasses from an overhead rack. He then opened a bottle of Francis Coppola's Black Label Claret. It was one of twenty bottles they brought back from a tour of Napa Valley, California six months before.

Grace loved the wine but what she could not stand was the *Godfather* impression that always came with it.

"Don't ask me about my business, Kay," Rosary joked as he filled two glasses halfway.

Grace raised an eyebrow and cocked her head to the side. "Do I look like Diane Keaton to you?"

"*Annie Hall* can't hold a candle to my baby," he said handing her a glass.

Rosary raised his glass for a toast. "Here's to adventures in babysitting,"

"Just one Heath, we're on duty," she whispered.

Jamal Galvin had been staying with Rosary since three gunshots had shattered his bedroom window two nights before. Fortunately, the boy was brushing his teeth in the bathroom of his grandmother's cramped tenement apartment and was not hurt. Rosary offered to take Jamal and his grandmother in while he and the police tried to track down the Jamaican drug dealer responsible for the attack. May Galvin was too proud and too stubborn to make such a move but she did accept the offer on behalf of her grandson. "Protect my baby," she ordered Rosary.

May Galvin's "baby" was an overweight, undersized boy with few friends in the dreary housing project in which he lived. The lonely kid thought the fortune he had found would impress the other boys in his building. Rosary quickly learned that the introverted Jamal was not the type of kid who would throw around ten grand without some coaxing from his so-called friends. The other kids used Jamal to get their toys and then left the poor boy holding the bag. Now there was a price on the Jamal's head and there was no telling when the Jamaican pusher, Ossie Bramble would come to collect. He had vanished after the shooting and there was some hope the cornrow-wearing thug would never return, but Rosary did not think this was the case. *The stupid ones always come back.*

He wanted to be on the street himself hunting this slime down. However, someone had to stick like glue to the boy he was trying to kill. Rosary had to rely on his detective buddies in the Boston Police department in hopes of finding the Jamaican. Instead of acting as an investigator, the former secret service agent found himself playing protector again. This time, the principal was not a rich white girl with abandonment issues, but a kid from the old neighborhood who was just hoping to stay alive through junior high school. Rosary had some help too; a detail cop was parked across the street from his condo just in case his hunch was correct.

"Jamal, time to hit the books buddy," Heath said pointing to his watch.

The teenager flicked off the television and grabbed his book bag.

"What are you working on? Maybe I can help."

"I have to write an essay about a hero of mine," Jamal answered.

Math I can help you with, but writing? "Uh oh, my writing skills have eroded a little over time," he told the boy. "I'll bet Grace here can help. You know that you're in the presence of a real life journalist?"

"For real?" Jamal asked turning his attention to the lady of the house.

"C'mon Jamal, Heath is great at a lot of things but writing isn't one of them," she laughed. Grace tossed her arm around Jamal's shoulder and walked him down the stairs toward the spare bedroom, which Rosary used for an office. The room had a large desk and a couch that folded out to a bed. It was also filled with mementos from Rosary's past. His jerseys from the Boston College Eagles and New England Patriots were framed on the wall. His game-winning ball from the Fiesta Bowl however, was back at BC in the lobby of the Conte Forum. It shared the rarified spotlight next to Doug Flutie's 1984 Heisman Trophy. Rosary also kept a few memories from his life in the Secret Service. A picture of him shaking hands with the President sat in a frame on his desk. There was another photo of Rosary with his Secret Service team at the Harvard command center. Two items that were not shown off were the cover stories about Rosary in *People Magazine* and *Newsweek* following the Sistani shooting. The cover of *People* showed his picture with the headline: *Meet America's Last Line of Defense.* Rosary had refused to grant interviews for the articles and tossed out the magazines, but unbeknownst to him Grace kept a few copies stashed away in her condo.

"Did Mister Rosary really do all this stuff?" Jamal asked touring the office as if it were a small museum.

"He did it and then some," Grace answered proudly.

Rosary pounced on the remote control and collapsed on the leather couch. *Maybe I can catch the FDR documentary after all.* He left his glass of wine untouched on the kitchen counter. He never took a drink while he was on the job. He only poured a glass for himself for Grace's sake. She had been a little nervous about babysitting. Grace Chen was the most beautiful, caring woman he had ever laid eyes on, but she constantly felt the need to be liked. It made her a little uncomfortable around people she did not know. Heath felt that he had a cure for that, he just didn't give a shit what people thought of him.

"So when you think of the word *hero*, what person comes to mind?" Grace asked Jamal as she leaned over him at Rosary's office computer.

"Martin Luther King, I guess."

"That's a good choice. He was an incredible man who accomplished a lot for African-Americans and other people of color like me. Did you know that we both went to the same college? Dr. King got his doctorate from Boston University. Pretty cool, huh?"

"Yah, that's pretty cool."

"You know who my hero was when I was your age?"

The boy shook his head.

"It was Mary Lou Retton," she laughed. "I saw her in the 84' Olympics and was blown away. But when I got a little older I realized who my real hero was. It was my mother who came here from China and kept our house in order while my dad went to school. She didn't know a word of English but she taught herself and raised three kids virtually on her own. Is there a person like that in your life?"

Jamal shrugged his shoulders. "My grandma I guess."

"I think that she would be a great choice for your paper," she told him. "Why don't you just write down all the things you like about her and we'll find a way to make a story out of it."

"Okay Miss Grace."

She rubbed the boy's head. "Are you hungry?"

He nodded yes.

"I'll go up to the kitchen and get us both some brain food."

Rosary's condo on Telegraph Hill was laid out awkwardly, but that is why he liked it so much. The front door opened to a hallway between two bedrooms. A staircase led up to the second floor, which housed a galley kitchen and a living room built with a cathedral ceiling. The biggest selling point for Rosary was the condo's spectacular view. The living room led out to a large deck that overlooked the skyline of Boston. He bought the place for a song before the gentrification of Southie in the early 1990's. Rosary had been told by a pesky real estate agent that he could sell it for a cool million now. He wouldn't even entertain the idea.

Grace climbed the stairs and noticed Heath sprawled out on the couch.

"Don't you look comfy," she observed.

"How's it going down there?"

"Jamal's a real sweet kid. He says I'm Phat!"

"The boy better get his eyes checked. You look damn sexy to me."

She giggled. "Phat means cool you old fart."

"I know what it means. I grew up in the hood you know."

Grace walked by the couch and Rosary reached out his long arms, pulling her toward him. The two shared a deep kiss before she let go.

"I promised Jamal some popcorn. Now watch your show," she demanded.

"How's about we get to know one another after the boy goes beddy-bye?" That was Rosary's code word for sex.

"Are you crazy? You know how loud it can be," she said in mock horror.

"Who could blame you for screaming?"

"Me? I was talking about you!"

Ossie Bramble sucked on a blunt as the red Grand Marquis cruised along West Broadway. A sub-machine gun sat on the passenger seat; it would be his only companion on this night. Bramble did not like to roll with a posse when it was time to take someone out. Accomplices could make for good prosecution witnesses if they got caught. Bramble looked at the address once again. *10 Thomas Park* was scribbled on the back of a brown paper bag. The Jamaican was beginning to make a name for himself on the tough streets of Roxbury and he could not afford for some snot nosed kid to make him look stupid. Bramble could hear the whispers. *Dumb niggah drops 10 G's in a trash can, then gets taken by a little fat kid and his friends.*

He would have to send a message. *Fuck with Ossie Bramble-Get Dropped!* He turned up his *Ludicris* CD and kept rolling.

Boston police officer Ross Peterson had his radio tuned to WEEI. The Red Sox were in the middle of a three game home stand against the New York Yankees at Fenway Park. The dreaded Yanks were leading the Sox by a score of 5 to 2. Slugger Manny Ramirez was stepping up to the plate. The game was in the 6th inning and the Sox outfielder was 0 for 3 on the night. Peterson kept his ears on the game and his eyes on the building across the street. Heath Rosary's place was on the first floor and both bedroom windows faced the street. There was a light on in just one of the rooms, a pair of shadows moved behind the curtains inside. Peterson returned his attention to the game. Manny Ramirez swung on the first pitch taking Yankees starter Mike Mussina deep. The ball disappeared in the seats atop the Green Monster and the Sox star began his home run lap. The cheers of the crowd were drowned out by an announcement on the police radio.

"All available units. Officer down at the Andrew Square T-stop. Possible hit and run."

Peterson grabbed his two-way and reported in to dispatch.

"I'm about three blocks from there. I'm on my way."

The officer slammed the cruiser in *drive* and tore out of Telegraph Hill.

Ossie Bramble nearly shit himself when he saw the police car approach with its lights on and sirens blazing. Fortunately for Bramble, the cop drove right past him.

He breathed deeply and snuffed out his marijuana cigarette in the ashtray. The Grand Marquis rolled slowly up Telegraph Street and turned right onto Thomas Park. Bramble passed the Telegraph Hill Monument, which was majestically illuminated at night.

The five-story monument was erected in honor of General George Washington's troops who fortified the hill in 1776. From the high vantage point, Washington's soldiers could attack Boston from the west and the harbor from the south. Fearing such an attack would destroy their only outside line of communication, the British evacuated Boston and sailed for home. Another battle was waged on the other side of Telegraph Hill two centuries later during the 1970's when white residents lined the streets tossing bottles and shouting racial slurs at yellow buses filled with black students on their way to South Boston High School. A judge ruled that black students were at an educational disadvantage in their own neighborhoods so he forced the desegregation of Boston's predominantly white schools. The ruling was met with violent protest. The Busing Crisis was a sorry chapter in the otherwise proud history of Southie.

The Jamaican did not know the history and couldn't give a shit. He counted apartment house numbers while making his way around Thomas Park. The street was shaped like an oval around the top of Telegraph Hill. He came around the front of Southie High and knew he was close.

Rosary hit *stop* on the Tivo button, rolled off the couch and walked to the kitchen. *The detail cop must be a little hungry,* he thought. Heath placed a bag of popcorn in the microwave and hit *start.* The kernels began to pop one after another. Rosary opened the refrigerator door and pulled out two cans of Diet Pepsi. He was startled by the sound of five pops much louder than those coming from the microwave. *Oh shit!* He heard screams and leaped down the flight of stairs to the first floor. Another round of shots shattered windows and tore through walls. Rosary made a full sprint down the corridor and dove into the spare bedroom. Grace lay on the floor shielding Jamal with her quivering body. Both cried uncontrollably as Heath crawled toward them.

"Are you okay? Are you hit?" he screamed.

Grace yelled back. "No we're alright! Jesus Heath, what's going on?"

Rosary did not answer as he crept toward the window.

"Baby, what are you doing?" Grace cried.

He looked out the window searching frantically for the police cruiser.

"The detail," he shouted. "It's gone!"

Rosary turned to Grace who was picking shards of glass out of Jamal's afro as he continued to cry in her arms. All three were startled once more by the sound of a violent crash outside. Rosary jumped to his feet and ran for the door.

"Where are you going?" his girlfriend cried.

"Just stay right there!"

He pulled his snub-nosed revolver out of his sock and bolted through the front door of the building. Rosary looked up the street and saw the Grand Marquis wrapped around a telephone pole. The front of the car was nearly split in two and smoke was coming from the engine. He also noticed a dark figure scaling the iron fence surrounding the monument. Rosary gave chase and called upon the speed that had once made him such a defensive threat at Boston College. He jumped the iron fence and quickly gained ground on the shooter who was dazed after driving straight on into the utility pole. Bramble had fired the shots into the building while pointing his automatic weapon out the passenger side window. Before he knew it, the Grand Marquis jumped the curb and slammed into the pole. Bramble ran with the weapon in his hand as he heard footsteps coming up close behind him. The Jamaican turned wildly and squeezed the trigger. Rosary saw the motion, hit the ground and rolled. Bramble turned back and started running again. Heath got up on one knee and aimed the revolver at the man's legs. He fired one shot and Ossie Bramble went down. The Jamaican let out a scream that echoed through the park. Rosary saw that he was still clutching the machine gun.

"Drop the weapon or I'll blow your fucking brains out!"

Bramble hesitated briefly then tossed the machine gun to the ground a few feet away. Boston Police detective Alan Otis got to the scene seconds after the gunfight. "Rosary, you okay up there?" Otis shouted as he made his way up the hill followed by two uniformed officers.

"What happened to the fucking detail?" Rosary asked with his gun still trained on Bramble.

"MBTA police officer got run over at Andrew Station. Your detail was the first on the scene."

Detective Otis grabbed Rosary's arm gently. "Heath, let these boys take over now."

The two uniformed officers made their way over to the Jamaican. One hand-cuffed him while the other inspected his wound.

"After I saw what he did to your place, I thought I'd be calling for a coroner not an ambulance," Otis whispered.

"Little fuck caught me on a good day," Rosary growled.

CHAPTER 33

Rosary sat on a stool at *Sligo's Tavern* sipping a 16-ounce glass of Sam Adams.

He replayed the excitement of the previous night in his mind while waiting for his friend to show up. *Should've checked on the detail before letting the two of them go downstairs. Actually, I shouldn't have let them go downstairs in the first place. Windows facing the street! What were you thinking Rosary? You weren't thinking, that's the problem.* The windows were now being replaced by reinforced glass three inches thick. Grace was back at her condo and Jamal had returned to his grandmother's house. That morning Grace played the loyal girlfriend and told Heath that she was fine and that she'd call him later. It was now pushing 6 p.m. and he still had not heard from her. *Is she second-guessing our relationship? After what she went through last night, who could blame her?*

Rosary had just returned from the Boston Medical Center where Ossie Bramble was arraigned in his hospital bed. The Jamaican was being treated for a deep gunshot wound to the back of his right thigh. His right wrist was handcuffed to the side of the bed. Bramble kept his eyes closed while the judge read off the attempted murder charges. His court appointed lawyer issued a *not guilty* plea on his behalf. Rosary stood alongside Detective Otis and two other cops in the corner of the room. *Ossie Bramble could put the fear of God in a kid but he didn't look like much of a bad ass now.* The Jamaican's thumb worked the morphine button as if it was the joystick of a video game. *Boy's in pain, good.* Bramble's court appointed weasel was already threatening to sue Rosary for shooting his client. Heath was tempted to put his fist through the lawyer's forehead. *What's another lawsuit?* Instead, he flipped the attorney off and walked out of the hospital.

Now he was sitting at the bar polishing off his third tall glass of beer. *Sligo's Tavern* was a short walk down the hill from Rosary's condo, and as Irish a bar as you could find in the newly yuppified neighborhood of South Boston. It had become Heath's favorite watering hole and he was certainly a cherished customer. The owner was a BC grad and once offered Rosary drinks on the house for life. Heath said no thanks, but asked the owner if he wouldn't mind taking down a poster of him holding the national title after the Fiesta Bowl. The owner obliged and Rosary started frequenting the pub in relative anonymity.

The door of the tavern opened and Vince Logan walked through. Rosary's spirits were immediately lifted. "Sully I want you to meet the best cop in Ireland," he told the bartender.

Sully smiled. "If he's a friend of yours, he's a friend of mine."

Rosary stepped off his stool and greeted Logan with a tremendous bear hug.

"What's the matter, drink all the Guinness in Ireland, and now you're coming to clean us out?"

Logan smiled slightly but did not laugh. "I wish that were the case my friend. I've come here with my hat in my hand to ask for your help."

Rosary guided him over to a table and motioned to the bartender.

"Sully, two more over here okay?"

The bartender nodded and reached for two clean glasses.

"Sorry Heath, I didn't know where else to turn. I want you to help me find my brother."

Rosary nodded. "If he draws a paycheck anywhere in the U.S. I should be able to find him using Auto Tracker," he informed his friend. He suddenly lowered his voice to a whisper. "Now if he's here illegally, that's gonna be a little harder. I guess we could start with some roofing companies here in Southie and see if anybody's heard of him."

Logan shook his head. "Listen, this isn't your ordinary missing persons case. Yes, I'm sure my brother is here illegally, but he didn't come here to work."

Rosary looked puzzled. "What did he come here to do?"

"I think he's going to kill the Prime Minister of Britain."

Rosary waited for the punch line but there was none. "You're shitting me."

"No, I think he wants to destroy the peace process. I need to stop him before he does something crazy and gets himself hurt."

Rosary put his glass of beer back on the table. "Vincent you're a cop, why don't you just call Scotland Yard or MI-5 and report this."

"Because I know they won't arrest him, they'll kill him." Logan looked his friend in the eye. "Heath, have you ever been sodomized?"

Rosary spit out a mouthful of *Sam Adams*. "What? Fuck no!"

"Neither have I and I only have my brother to thank for that."

Over the next twenty minutes, Logan told him about the attack on his parents, the murder of the pedophile priest and his brother's bloody career in the Irish Republican Army. Rosary did not say a word but soaked in every detail.

"So you see Heath, my brother saved my life and now I must return the favor. I'll pay you double whatever your normal fee is."

Rosary felt torn, he had already refused payment in the Jamal Galvin case and the bills were beginning to stack up on his front door.

"Vincent, I'd do it for free if I could but I've just begun some emergency remodeling at my place. I'll do it for fifty percent of my normal rate. I just hope that we can find him before they do."

The friends sealed the deal with a knock of their beer glasses.

"Hey Sully, how about another round over here?"

Rosary's order was drowned out by three large white men with loud voices. The trio had just knocked off work at the docks on Atlantic Avenue. They looked and smelled like they had been packing fish all day. The dockworkers took a table directly in back of Rosary and Logan. Sully brought over a pitcher of beer and three mugs before heading back into the kitchen.

"So that nigger's been tryin' to steal my shifts again," One worker said to his friends. "Do you believe that? I swear to God I'm gonna kill that spear-chucker."

"You can't walk three feet down there without stepping on a nigger or a spic," a friend chimed in.

Rosary shook his head and sipped his beer. "Fucking rednecks," he said under his breath. Incredibly, it was the first time he had heard the word *nigger* said in his presence since he had moved to Southie. Uncle James had warned him that just because he was something of a hero in Boston, it did not mean that he had the key to the entire city. He could still hear his uncle's words ringing in his ears. *With a bistro popping up on nearly every corner, Southie may look a little different these days, but it's still Southie!*

Logan saw his friend growing anxious. The Irishman got up from his chair and approached the table where the dockworkers were sitting.

"Listen lads, my friend and I are trying to enjoy a late day pint," he said in a singsong Irish brogue. "We'd appreciate it if you kept your blinding ignorance and intellectual deficiency to yourselves."

The dockworkers sat speechless for a moment while the insult sunk in. All three then stood up off their stools and crowded around the Irishman. Each man weighed over two hundred and thirty pounds. "Listen up Paddy," one worker said jabbing his finger into Logan's chest. "Why don't you come back when you get a green card. And tell your nigger friend that the world was a better place when he was just a commodity."

The line drew a hearty laugh from the other dockworkers.

Rosary had heard enough. He drained his glass, hopped off his stool and joined his friend. "I suggest you boys finish your beers and head on back to your mama's basement," Heath told them. "Otherwise things could get ugly, and I have to admit I'm in a real ugly mood tonight."

One dockworker took a swing at Rosary who deflected it and returned a thundering back fist to the bridge of the man's nose. His companion grabbed Logan's jacket and was met with an open hand strike to his larynx. Both men fell back in their chairs. The third dockworker stood with his fists held high.

Logan smiled at Rosary. "What was that move you showed me in the gym?"

Rosary walked up to the man and waited for him to throw a punch. This time, instead of merely deflecting it, he caught the dockworker's arm and twisted it up behind his back. Rosary then slammed the man's face down on the table.

"I could easily break your arm right now," he said calmly. "You'd probably stumble home; ice it down and show up to work tomorrow. Now I figure that's when you'd do a slip and fall job and file for workman's comp. But I ain't your lottery ticket boy. So I suggest you pay up and leave a nice big tip for my friend Sully over there."

The dockworker nodded his head and Rosary let go. He and Logan returned to their table and watched as the rednecks paid their bill and left quietly.

"Now can I put your poster back up?" Sully asked.

Rosary laughed. "Fuck you Sully."

CHAPTER 34

He ran shirtless through the streets of West Belfast; the blond haired assassin had found him again. This time, the man in black wore a suit and tie; his blond hair now showed signs of gray. Logan was no longer a boy; he was a man who had killed several times himself. Why couldn't he simply turn around and confront his pursuer? This man had been chasing him in his dreams since he was thirteen, but tonight it was going to stop. The assassin had a name now, Prime Minister Robert Stirling. The chase continued down a narrow alley that led to a dead end. Both men were trapped now. The bells of Old Gomery chimed in the distance. Michael Logan turned to face his life long antagonist; all traces of fear were gone.

"Hello, Michael I am Hell. Remember me?"

Stirling pulled out his long steel blade and approached slowly. Michael Logan reached for his gun and fired. He shot six rounds through the blond assassin's heart, yet the man kept coming. Stirling now stood just inches away; Logan could smell the mixture of tobacco and peppermint on his breath. Michael tried to speak, but once again could not find his voice. He was frozen with fear once more. No, I'm stronger now. I am not afraid of you. Logan's body did not respond to his thoughts. He stood motionless while the blond haired assassin brought the cold blade up to his neck.

Logan shot up out of bed and rubbed his wet neck. *Oh God, am I bleeding?*

He ran into the bathroom and flicked on the light. He looked at himself in the mirror and realized he was just covered in sweat. *Jesus Christ, I am going mad!*

What would Orla say if she saw me right now? Oh Orla, How I miss you. Logan had forced himself not to think about her, but the task was impossible. He remembered how she looked the last time he saw her, sitting on that bench in

Guadalajara weeping as he walked away. Where was she now? God only knew. Hopefully she had decided to take his fortune for herself. *Maybe she's found someone.* He tried to get the thought out of his head. He could hardly blame her though. Logan stared in the mirror and wondered whether she'd be repulsed by the life he had returned to. He had killed three times *after* telling himself that the killing had to stop. Geoffrey Ferguson and Malcolm Rogers had to pay for their sins, but what about Corly Cunningham? Logan couldn't shake the vision of her blood soaked body. *It was either you or her.* The logic still did not lessen the guilt. Was the bloodshed worth it? Just to relieve himself of a nightmare? The dreams were coming every evening now and he was afraid to fall asleep. He had bags under his brown eyes and he looked like hell; still he refused to take a tranquilizer. His mind or what was left of it had to remain sharp for the mission ahead. *Just a few more days,* he told himself.

Logan reached over and turned on the clock radio, which sat on the nightstand. His dark thoughts were interrupted by the newscaster. "Good morning, it's 5 a.m. and forty-three degrees. Accu-Weather says expect plenty of sunshine today with highs in the mid-sixties, I'm Gary Lapierre WBZ News. Today's top story; History in the making on Cape Cod, the Prime Minister of Great Britain and the President of Ireland's Sinn Fein party arrived under the cover of darkness this morning at Camp Edwards in Sandwich. Their respective motorcades then drove down Route 28 to Hyannisport and the famed, Kennedy Compound. The Irish-Anglo Summit is expected to begin there later today. Both sides say they will not address the media until a peace deal is struck. In other news, police are investigating an apparent carjacking in Everett …"

Logan turned off the radio and walked toward the shower.

Heath Rosary was dragged out of bed before dawn. "An early morning run will do us both good, clear out the cobwebs," Vincent told him. Rosary was not exactly sure how many beers he had put away the night before, but he knew that he stopped counting after ten. The evening ended with a drunken phone call to Grace. She told him to get some sleep and that they'd talk about it in the morning. *What was there to talk about?* Rosary didn't feel like talking, he felt like throwing up, which he did just moments after stepping out his front door.

"I know what it feels like to put your loved ones in danger," Logan said as they jogged up East Broadway toward Castle Island on the northern point of South Boston. "My flat was fire bombed while Fiona and Audrey slept. It was payback against my brother for murdering two comrades in the IRA. My wife and daughter weren't hurt, thank God, but I'll never forget the look in Fiona's eyes when I arrived at the scene that night. It was as if I had lost her trust. I still feel guilty about it."

Rosary slowed his stride to keep pace with his friend. "I told Grace that I'd never put her in danger. Maybe that was a stupid promise to make."

They stopped talking and picked up the pace when they saw Castle Island illuminated in the distance. Logan considered himself to be in good physical shape, but he was no match for a former professional athlete like Rosary. He knew his friend was taking it easy on him.

"You're right," Rosary told him when they finally reached Castle Island, which was actually a small peninsula. "A morning run was just what I needed to get over this hangover." *The aspirin did not hurt either.*

They walked toward a massive granite garrison that dominated the landscape of Castle Island. "So professor, what is this place?" Logan asked.

"We also had a little war going with the British," Rosary replied. "It's called Fort Independence and it dates back to the 1600's. The British destroyed it in 1776. It was then rebuilt under the command of Paul Revere. It was expanded again in the early 1800's and later served as a POW camp during the Civil War."

"How the hell do you know all that off the top of your head?"

"The History Channel, and the fact that I'm reading from a plaque embedded into the ground in front of me. It also says the fort covers more than 172-thousand linear feet. How about a race around the perimeter? The loser can buy breakfast."

"How about I just hand over my money now and be done with it?" Logan laughed.

"Deal," Rosary replied. "Only I'm buying and I know just the place."

"That's what you said last night, and we ended up in a fight!"

"I promised you that I'd show you a good time didn't I?"

Rosary brought Logan over to Mul's Diner on West Broadway. The décor inside had not changed since the 1960's. They sat opposite each other in a booth with vinyl seats and selected their breakfast from a large sign that hung behind the lunch counter. The sun was just rising over Boston Harbor yet the small eatery was bustling with business. Mul's was packed with workers from the MBTA and the nearby Gillette Headquarters. The two friends got back to business over the sounds of clanging silverware.

Rosary took a bite of his western omelet. "So your bosses back in Dublin know you're here?" he asked.

"Not exactly," Logan replied. "They think we're down in Florida visiting Mickey Mouse. I told Fiona to stay with her parents for the week. She's been my rock through all of this; she's even caring for my brother's girlfriend who's expected to give birth soon. I think that's how I may be able to talk him out of his plan, Michael does not know that he's about to have a son."

Rosary had been waiting for Vincent to bring up his brother again. He opened two pink packets of *Sweet and Low* and stirred the confection into his coffee.

"Now, about keeping Michael's plan a secret, I don't work for the Secret Service anymore, but I cannot disregard a possible threat against a visiting head of state."

Logan's brown eyes narrowed as he looked across the table. "What are you telling me Heath?"

"I'm saying that I need to let my government know what's happening. Your brother's life isn't the only one at stake here."

Logan wiped his mouth and tossed his napkin onto his plate. "I guess that I shouldn't have come here. I'll go it alone."

He tried to stand up but Rosary tugged at his arm.

"You won't be able to find him, much less stop him, Vincent. You don't know the terrain, or the people involved. I can get us inside the security perimeter down at the Kennedy Compound. It will be our best hope of finding Michael before the British do. My old colleague is coordinating the security operation. She can help us, trust me."

CHAPTER 35

Special Agent-in-Charge Nikki Tavano huddled with her Secret Service team at the top of Marchant Avenue in Hyannisport. The wind was blowing loudly off Nantucket Sound and Tavano was forced to shout out instructions to her crew of twenty agents.

"As all of you know, the principals have arrived with their own security details. Our colleagues from across the pond are now being shown their quarters over on Squaw Island. Senator Kennedy's former wife was nice enough to let us use the place. As you can imagine, the Brits are pissed at the quarter mile travel time between here and there."

Tavano's team nodded in agreement, no security professional would allow his or herself to be so far away from the person they were guarding.

"I know," said Tavano. "I'd be pissed too. But thanks to Presidential Decision Directive 62, this is our show. Anything coming into this area, or leaving it must go through the United States Secret Service."

The presidential directive had been issued in 1998. A portion of PDD-62 outlines the coordination of federal anti-terrorism assets for events of national interest. The Anglo-Irish Summit was declared a National Special Security Event, which meant the Secret Service had a mandated role to lead and enforce the operational security plan. Because of the limited accommodations, only Tavano's team would be housed directly inside the Compound.

"Each of you has been assigned a specific security area," she continued while reading her clipboard. "The code names should be easy to remember. Summit negotiations will take place in the main house. We'll call that location, *Joe* after papa Joe Kennedy. Prime Minister Sterling is staying at President Kennedy's former house directly behind me. We'll call that location, *Jack*. Mister Adams and his people are staying across the road here at Ethel Kennedy's home. That location now has the codename, *Bobby*. Our command headquarters has been set up inside the Shrivers' home next door. We'll call that location, *Sargent.*"

Tavano's longtime colleague, Special Agent Nick Franco raised his hand trying to lighten the mood. "Governor Arnold spends his summer's there, and now you'll be sleeping in that house. Instead of *Sargent,* shouldn't we call it *Terminator?*"

Tavano smiled briefly. "Thank you Special Agent *Wise Ass!* Seriously people, the eyes of the world are going to be on this summit; that makes it a perfect target for our friends in Al Qaeda. Please take a look at your maps."

The agents pulled out a set of diagrams from their operational packets.

"Coast Guard crews will be patrolling this area from Hyannis Point to the breakwater. F-15's from Otis Air Force Base will provide us with some eyes in the skies to look out for any possible aerial assault. The road leading down to the Compound will be closed at the corner of Wachusett and Irving Avenues. We will be employing the *three perimeter philosophy*. The outer perimeter will be guarded by troopers from the state police manning barricades. The middle perimeter will be manned by members of this team positioned on roof tops of houses within the compound area. The inner perimeter will be the detail immediately surrounding the principals. The latest itinerary states that Senator Kennedy will give the principals a private tour of the grounds after lunch. Let's show our foreign guests why we're the best damned security force in the world. Dismissed."

The team broke away as agents reported to their assigned stations. Tavano marched back to her command post at *Sargent* and tried her best not to look overwhelmed. This was the biggest assignment of her career and high marks would possibly lead to a coveted spot on the President's personal security team. Tavano passed the white clapboard structure that was once JFK's summer home and realized that she was walking in the footsteps of history. There were more secret service agents at the compound now than anytime since *Lancer* was president. Those in Tavano's line of work had the habit of referring to presidents only by their Secret Service codename. The compound's commanding view of Nantucket Sound and its plush lawns were impressive by anyone's standards. *Were Lancer's agents taken in so much by the beauty that they could not contemplate the horror that would eventually befall them in Dallas? Or were they too preoccupied by the seemingly nightly challenges of sneaking in Marilyn Monroe, Judith Campbell or any number of his mistresses?*

Like many of her fellow agents, Tavano considered herself to be an expert on the Kennedy Assassination. She had been forced to study it over and over again as part of her training. *I've probably seen the Zapruder film more times than Oliver Stone.* She thought. Tavano did not believe the conspiracy theories put forth in the Hollywood director's movie *JFK.* To her, the assassination of John F. Kennedy was simply a classic breakdown of operational procedure. The first mistake was that the secret service allowed Kennedy to ride through the streets of Dallas without a protective bubble top covering his Lincoln convertible. The parade route had also been publicized in advance letting his assassin know exactly where the President would be at a given time. Much has been written and discussed about Lee Harvey Oswald's vantage point inside the Texas School Book Depository. It was a great location for a sniper. Oswald could shoot in a straight line as the motorcade moved past the building. It would have been much more difficult for Oswald to fire three shots from right to left. Tavano lived by the old adage, *those who do not learn from history are condemned to repeat it.*

Rosary returned to his condo with a full stomach and a clear head. He had two phone calls to make; the question was which one would be easier? Telling your best friend that an IRA assassin was planning to crash her party? Or hearing your girlfriend tell you what a drunken fool you were the night before? He opted for the first choice. Rosary took out his Nokia and punched in the number. Tavano answered the call after one ring.

"Special-Agent Tavano speaking."

"Ginzo it's me. Is it a good time to talk?"

Tavano looked around the Shriver's living room, which was now filled with computers, fax machines and an infrared map that told her exactly where the principals were at any given time.

"I'm kinda busy here Smoky. Can I get back to you in a few days?"

"I have information about a possible threat to the summit."

Tavano sat up in her chair. She placed her small phone into a special recording machine at her desk and hit *record.* "I'm listening."

"Subject's name is Logan, Michael Logan. He is a former assassin for the IRA, but apparently has had a falling out with the old gang. I have credible information that Logan could be planning an attack against Prime Minister Stirling at the compound."

"We're did this information originate?"

"I got it from Logan's brother who is a Special Detective with the Irish Police. We met a few years ago as part of an exchange at the Rowley Training Center in Maryland. Look, it's a long story. I'd like to bring him down to meet you since he's the only one who can identify the guy."

"What does this Michael Logan look like?"

"Well, that's the odd part," Rosary explained. "He and his brother are identical twins. I'll send a photo image of the brother over by cell phone. At least that way, you'll have an idea of what to look out for."

He pointed his cell phone at his friend. "Smile for the camera, Vincent."

Tavano kept the Nextel to her ear and pulled her own cell phone out of her coat pocket.

"I see the image now," she told him. "Jesus, he looks just like Clive Owen."

"Who?"

"Dammit Smoky! You know; the actor from *Sin City, Closer?*"

"I don't know who you're talking about," Rosary replied truthfully.

He could hear laughter coming from the other end of the phone.

"I don't know how Grace puts up with you. Can you please rent a movie that's been made within the past twenty years? How soon can you get down here?" Tavano was all business again.

"Drive time's about an hour twenty from here," Rosary replied looking down at his watch. "Give me sixty minutes."

Rosary packed a bag and drove his Jaguar over to the Seaport Hotel on Atlantic Avenue. Vincent Logan ran into the hotel and quickly retrieved his luggage. The Irishman hopped in the passenger seat and Rosary drove off cutting through the *Big Dig* maze to the Southeast Expressway. It was time to call Grace.

"Good luck," Vincent offered as they rolled down the highway from South Boston into Quincy.

"See that beach over there," Rosary pointed out forever playing tour guide. He was also trying to buy a little time before the nerve-wracking call to his girlfriend.

"We had a gangster around here named Whitey Bulger. Ever hear of him?"

Logan nodded. "Oh yes, your FBI came over a couple of years ago to let us know that he might be hiding somewhere in Ireland."

"That's right. Whitey is wanted for more than twenty murders. He even strangled his partner's daughter to death and pulled out her teeth. He took off though before federal racketeering indictments came down in 1995. A real scumbag of a federal agent named John Connolly helped Bulger escape. Well Whitey used to drive by the beach everyday after seeing his girlfriend in Quincy. The feds, the honest feds I should say, bugged his car. Every time he'd drive past Tenean Beach, he'd tell whoever was riding with him; Tip your hat to Tommy boys, tip your hat to Tommy. The FBI guys on the other end of that wiretap were scratching their heads; they didn't know what the hell Whitey was talking about until a few years ago. The state police used a backhoe to do a little digging there and sure enough they found the body of this gangster Tommy King. King was one tough mother; he beat the shit out of Whitey one night at a bar. Bulger had him whacked and buried there a short time later."

"Tip your hat to Tommy, boys," Logan repeated. "If he's in Ireland, we sure don't want him. We've got enough psychopaths roaming about."

The two continued to drive through Quincy and along the South Shore. Rosary's cell phone rang and he checked the caller ID. He paused for a moment before answering.

"Hello Grace."

"Hi baby, I've been worried sick about you."

Heath was relieved to hear those words.

"You're not mad at me?"

"No honey, not at all. You sounded a little drunk last night, but you were also very cute. You sang a Barry White song to me over the phone," she laughed.

Rosary winced as the memory came back to him.

"What about the little thing about being shot at?"

"I was scared for sure, but that doesn't mean I'd ever stop being with you. I'm afraid you're stuck with me."

He hoped that she meant for life.

"I love you Grace."

"Ditto darling."

Rosary hung up the phone and looked over at Vincent who was clearly eavesdropping.

"She's a very special girl," Logan told him.

"The best," he replied meaning every word.

Ted Kennedy walked out of the main house and up Marchant Avenue to meet his guests. The senior senator from Massachusetts wore a blue blazer and tan slacks; he was also wearing a broad smile and felt quite vigorous, even though he battled chronic pain from a broken back he suffered in a plane crash back in 1964. The Kennedy compound had been dubbed the Summer White House when his brother Jack was president. It was once the most important place on earth, and now it was again if only for a few days. He waved to his guests who were standing outside their cottages.

Kennedy quickly wondered what the protocol should be. Whom should he greet first? Fortunately he did not have to answer that question. Prime Minister Stirling and Sinn Fein President Gerry Adams both walked forward and met their host in the middle of the road. Kennedy placed his hands on the shoulders of both men.

"On behalf of the United States and the Kennedy family, I welcome you to Hyannisport," he said with a toothy grin.

The Prime Minister bowed slightly. "On behalf of the people of Great Britain, I thank you for opening up your lovely homes to us."

Gerry Adams was not going to be outdone. "The people of Ireland, your people thank you as well Senator Kennedy."

"Shall we gentlemen?"

Kennedy guided his guests back down the road toward the biggest of the gabled Dutch Colonial homes on the compound. The mansion sat back from the bluff, its wrap around porch offering a magnificent view of the ocean.

"My father bought this house in 1929," Kennedy told them. "My fondest memories are the times that I spent here with my family."

The senator guided the prime minister and Gerry Adams up the front porch steps and into the home. The main house was laid out with a living room, dining room, sunroom and a bedroom used by Jack Kennedy before he purchased his own home a few yards away. There where six more bedrooms on the second floor and four servant's quarters. The basement was equipped with both a motion picture theater and sauna. Each room appeared as if it was frozen in time. Although family members still stayed there from time to time, it was more of a museum than a vacation home. The rooms were decorated in the same fashion as they were during the days of Camelot. Photos of the Kennedy brothers and their wives were hung up in nearly every room of the house.

"Your formal negotiations will take place here in the dining room," Kennedy told them. "Your staff will also be allowed to work in any of the downstairs rooms."

The senator continued his tour outside where clouds were giving way to bright sunshine. "The President taught me how to sail out there," he said pointing to the ocean. "We still have Jack's boat, a *Wianno Senior* on display at his presidential library," he said proudly.

"And this is where you played those famous games of touch football?" Stirling asked pointing to the grassy area in front of the main house.

"That's right, of course it's not the same football you play over there."

Stirling and Adams both smiled.

"I must tell you Senator that there is a picture of your brother Jack hanging up above the mantel in nearly every home in Ireland," Adams told him.

"President Kennedy was a man of peace," Kennedy replied. "That is why we're here today gentlemen."

Stirling saw an opening and could not resist. "Yes, but your brother was also a shrewd cold warrior. He won the peace by bargaining from a position of strength."

"Let's save that talk for the negotiating table shall we?" Kennedy replied with a nervous laugh.

Special-Agent Tavano watched as the principals shared a chuckle on the front lawn of *Joe*. She had already run off thirty copies of the Logan picture and had handed them out to each member of her team. Handing out more copies over to the Brits and Irish would take a little diplomacy. Tavano approached Mitch Handley first.

"Sir I want you to be aware of a security situation that has come to my attention," she said offering him a folder with the picture and brief CIA summary of Michael Logan's operational background.

Handley took a pair of wire rimmed eyeglasses out of his breast pocket and leafed through the folder.

"Are you sure that he's coming here?" he asked while looking down at the photograph.

"It's a strong possibility sir," she replied. "The photo you are looking at is actually a picture of Logan's twin brother. No picture of Michael Logan exists."

Handley looked up from the folder. "How did you get the brother's picture?"

"He's the one who tipped us about the possibility of an attack. He's actually on his way down here to help us."

"That's quite unusual isn't it? I'll choose the moment to tell the Prime Minister," he told Tavano. "He's under tremendous stress as it is right now. I'll have members of our security team meet with you for a complete briefing on the matter."

"That is already being coordinated sir."

"Good," said Handley with a smile. "Then we have nothing to worry about."

He walked away with his hands clasped tightly behind his back. Tavano turned and walked toward *Bobby* with one remaining folder tucked under her arm. She dreaded the prospect of letting the Irish delegation know that one of its own was hoping to spoil the summit.

The silver Jaguar roared over the Sagamore Bridge and the Cape Cod Canal. Rosary was making better time than expected. He was doing about eighty miles per hour the entire ride and was fortunate not to get pulled over by the state police. Once over the bridge, he pulled off Route 3 and took back roads from the village of Cotuit down to Hyannisport.

"You sure know your way around here," Logan observed.

"Grace and I have been coming here for years. She owns a little cottage about a mile and a half from the Kennedy compound. That's where we'll be staying tonight. It'll cut down on expenses."

They entered Hyannisport and drove down Scudder Avenue which was lined with million dollar summer homes and came to a stop at the police checkpoint near the corner of Irving Avenue. A large state trooper waved the Jaguar away. Rosary rolled down the window but did not move the car.

"You blind buddy?" the trooper shouted as he marched toward the car. "This road is off limits, you'll have to turn left right here."

"My name is Heath Rosary, I'm a former Special-Agent for the United States Secret Service. We have an appointment with the Special-Agent in charge of this operation, Nicole Tavano."

Rosary handed the trooper his driver's license and badge that signified he was a retired federal agent.

"Wait here a sec," ordered the trooper who then began talking into a small microphone attached to his collar.

"You both can come in, but your car can't. Park it on the side of the road and then follow me."

Rosary pulled the Jaguar off Irving Avenue and under a row of tall pine trees. He stepped out to stretch his legs while Vincent Logan did the same. The trooper ushered the pair past the security checkpoint and down Scudder Avenue, the white picket fences surrounding the Kennedy compound were coming into view.

"It looks just as it does in the magazines," Logan commented.

Rosary smiled. "I could give you the history of the place, but we don't have time."

"Is there a plaque under your feet that I don't know about?" Logan snickered.

Special-Agent Tavano met them both at the front gate. "I'll take 'em from here trooper, you can head back to your post."

The state police officer turned on his heel and marched away.

"Smoky, you really know how to screw up a party," Tavano said under her breath.

"What did I always teach you? It's better to be safe and real fucking sorry," he replied. "I truly hope that we came down here for nothing."

He turned to his friend. "Special-Agent Nikki Tavano, I want you to meet Special Detective Vincent Logan from the Garda Siochana."

The two professionals shook hands. Logan was surprised by the woman's firm grip. She stood five foot seven inches tall, and Logan guessed that she weighed roughly 120 pounds. Tavano's black hair was short but stylish; her brown eyes were pools that immediately drew you in. The fact that she never wore makeup only enhanced her natural beauty. Her good looks came with a tough as nails attitude.

"I briefed the Irish delegation on the situation and they threatened to walk out of the summit," she told them. "Sinn Fein claims that it's some kind of hoax perpetuated by the Brits to take them look bad. Fortunately, Gerry Adams told his people that he wasn't leaving until there was a peace agreement signed, sealed and delivered. The principals have just sat down for their first negotiation session," she said pointing to the large white house in the background. "Let's go some place we can talk in private."

Tavano led them down Marchant Avenue to her command headquarters inside the Shriver house. They entered through the kitchen and walked past the spacious living room where three staffers were busy working on their laptop computers. She led them both upstairs to the master bedroom, where her quarters doubled as her office.

"This is the first time you've invited me to your bedroom," Rosary joked.

"My father would kill me if he found a black man in my bed," she shot back.

Vincent Logan stayed quiet; Tavano saw a look of confusion in his eyes.

"Don't mind us Detective Logan, a few minutes with him and it's like getting the old act back together."

They entered the master bedroom and closed the door. Rosary's focus turned to pictures of the Kennedy family on the walls.

"So I bet *Rancher's* pissed that he's being kept out of this little party."

"I'm sure the President is angry as hell," Tavano replied. "Senator Kennedy blasts his Iraq policy and demands a complete troop withdrawal. Now *Rancher's* forced to name Kennedy special envoy to the summit? I'd be pissed off too."

Tavano walked over to a small, elegant writing table and punched up her laptop computer. "So what do you say we start from the beginning?" She asked.

Logan told her the same story he had told Rosary. Tavano nodded as she banged away at her keyboard. She waited for him to finish before she spoke.

"So Detective Logan, you've got a crossed out picture of Robert Stirling and an ex-girlfriend's wild story. Is there anything else to suggest that he's coming here?"

"I know he's here," Vincent said with passion in his voice.

"How do you know for sure?" she pressed.

"He's my twin brother, I can feel it."

Tavano rolled her eyes. "So we've now got a crossed out picture, an ex-girlfriend's wild story and a brother's sixth sense."

Rosary felt a little disappointed in his former second in command. He had trained her to take every threat seriously, even the most outlandish ones.

"Hey Ginzo, you shouldn't just dismiss my friend here. He's also a cop, you know. I believe him and I think you should too. You could have a very dangerous man on your hands."

Tavano shrugged her shoulders. "Yes, you're right. I'm sorry for acting like a bitch, but as you know I've got a lot on my plate right now. I'll send some agents into town to sniff around and check if anyone's seen him." She turned to Logan. "Now, your brother's not working for the IRA, but you think he wants to destroy the peace process. Could he be working for a foreign government?"

Logan nodded reluctantly. "Irish Intelligence believes that my brother once sold his skills to foreign powers like Russia and Saudi Arabia."

"If he's getting bank rolled by a terrorist group or our other enemies in the world, well, that's a whole new ball game," Tavano told them. "If he's here and we find him, we're gonna take him down." She then looked over at her best friend. "I'm sorry Heath, but that's the way it is."

Rosary walked over and gently rubbed her shoulders. "I'd do the same thing if were in your shoes. We'll just have to find him first."

C H A P T E R   36

Prime Minister Stirling grabbed a cigarette from his silver case and collapsed on the bed. He lit the Dunhill and inhaled deeply. The prime minister kept the smoke swirling around in his lungs until he felt a little light headed, and then exhaled with eyes closed. He had just taken part in his first international negotiation as leader of Great Britain and he was exhausted. Robert Stirling felt that his instincts were correct; *the Irish were savages.*

The current sticking point was the same issue that had destroyed the Good Friday Peace Accord. Stirling insisted that Gerry Adams force the IRA to cooperate with Northern Ireland's police force. This meant a promise from the IRA that it would not exchange its military objectives for criminal ones. Adams called the request an insult. The Sinn Fein leader pointed to the fact that the IRA had turned over its weapons stockpiles to the disarmament chiefs. "The IRA has become defenseless," Adams stated during negotiations. "You talk about the IRA engaging in crime? I'm talking about unarmed Catholics getting wiped out by gun toting Loyalists!" he shouted as he pounded the table with his fist to heighten the drama. Adams wanted assurances that international inspectors would also force Protestant paramilitary groups to drop their weapons as well. Stirling knew that loyalist groups like the *Orange Order* would not accept such an agreement without bloodshed.

"What shall I do?" he asked Mitch Handley who was sitting in an antique wooden rocking chair in the corner of the room.

Handley contemplated the question for a moment. "I think that we play hard ball for a few more sessions and then give them what they want. You came here for peace, remember?"

"The Protestants won't accept such a measure," Stirling warned his chief of staff.

"Fuck the bloody Protestants," Handley replied angrily. "We'd have been off that miserable island decades ago if we hadn't felt an obligation to protect those ungrateful bastards. It's high time that we start thinking of ourselves and your legacy."

"I wish that I could use your language at the negotiating table," the prime minister laughed.

Handley had some good news and some bad news to report to his boss, first the good news. "The latest poll numbers are out sir. According to the BBC, your popularity numbers have jumped fifteen points, to fifty-two percent."

A smile came over the Prime Minister's face. It was the first time that Handley had seen his boss grin in weeks. "The summit is working sir."

It was now time to tell his boss the bad news. "We have received information about a possible threat against your life, right here on Cape Cod."

Stirling chuckled. "I am the Prime Minister of Great Britain; there have been countless threats against my life since taking office at 10 Downing Street."

"This one appears different sir."

"How so?" Stirling asked.

"The man in this case was once the most feared assassin in the IRA."

Handley handed his boss the file.

"His resume, if that's what you call it is quite frightening. His name is Michael Logan and MI-5 believes he could be responsible for as many as twenty murders. Our guys say that he likes to kill and he that he seems to be holding a grudge. Logan was an eyewitness to the murder of his father back in 1981. Apparently his parents ran a grocery in West Belfast."

Handley saw a glint of recognition in the Prime Minister's eyes.

"Does the name ring a bell to you sir?" Handley asked.

"No Mitch, I've never heard of this Michael Logan," Stirling lied. "It's been a terribly long afternoon and I'm quite tired. I must rest for a couple of hours before dinner and the evening session. Please make sure that I am not disturbed."

Mitch Handley took the order and left the bedroom. *There is something that he is not telling me,* Handley thought.

The prime minister waited for the bedroom door to close before picking up the file again. *It's very Shakespearian, the son coming back to avenge his father's death,* he thought. Stirling closed his eyes and replayed the event from two decades ago in his mind. *Why didn't I kill that boy?* It had been his only mistake in a lifetime of cold-blooded decisions in the field. *I am Hell, and Hell will come back for you one day.* He remembered the look in the boy's eyes when he said those words; it was not a look of fear but one of vengeance. *I should have killed you when I had the chance,* he thought staring at the folder. *It appears that the game is a foot.*

Rosary and Vincent Logan arrived at the cottage on Nautical Way after dark. They had spent the last six hours canvassing every motel and tavern in Hyannis. So far, no one had seen Michael Logan.

"It's amazing that you knew every bartender by their first name," Vincent laughed.

Rosary chuckled and shook his head. "It goes back to my football days, and of course the Sistani case. Sometimes being a small time celebrity helps open a few doors."

He walked into the cozy dining room and laid out their dinner. The last stop of the day was Baxter's Fish and Chips on Hyannis Harbor. Rosary knew that he could not leave there without a double order of Baxter's famous fried clams. He opened the refrigerator and took out two cans of Diet Coke. Logan was still in the living room examining the large bookcase that was built into the wall of the fifty-year-old cottage.

"*Patton: A Genius for War,* biographies of John Adams and Eisenhower. You do a lot of light reading I take it?"

Rosary walked into the living room. "What can I say? I'm a real history nut."

Vincent eyed a collection of paperbacks on the bottom shelf. Pictures of bare-chested, longhaired men were painted on the covers. "You like romance novels too?"

"Grace gobbles that stuff up with a spoon," Rosary laughed. "She's the smartest woman I know, yet she loves reading that trash."

"Try walking around the house with your shirt off. Maybe she'll pay more attention. How did you two meet anyway?"

Rosary took a swig of his Diet Coke. "I met her while guarding Jennifer Bosworth. The president's daughter was attending Harvard for the first time, and the White House wanted to lay down a few ground rules with the media. I went to the local television stations and asked them to leave the poor kid alone. When I spoke at Grace's station, I couldn't believe what a pain in the ass that woman was. She complained about the freedom of the press and all that shit. Finally, we came to an agreement that reporters would stay away from Jennifer when she was on campus, but when she went out on the town, she was fair game."

"So it wasn't exactly love at first sight then?"

"Hell no, I couldn't wait for that meeting to be over so I could get away from that woman. I remember walking toward the front door when she grabbed my shoulder. I'm not used to getting grabbed from behind like that. I spun around quickly and it frightened her a little. But she stood there and had the nerve to ask me where I was taking her to dinner that night. This Asian woman had some balls, plus she was beautiful. That's when I fell in love with her. Alright, now you know my story, what's yours?"

Vincent thought for a moment. "I met Fiona where every young lad meets a girl in Ireland. We met at a pub. I had a few pints in me and asked her to dance. She told me that she'd meet me out on the dance floor. So there I was dancing by myself for what seemed to be an eternity. Luckily, Fiona took pity and finally joined me. We've been together ever since."

Rosary raised his can of soda. "To the women in our lives."

"Indeed," Vincent smiled returning the salute.

They finished their overflowing plates of fried clams and both men retired for the evening. Logan entered the guestroom and collapsed on the bed. Although he felt exhausted, sleep would not come easy. He lay there in bed staring at the ceiling. *Where are you Michael? I know you're close, I can feel it. Please God let me find him before he goes too far.*

Michael Logan sat on a bench at the Ocean Street dock in Hyannis. The early morning fog was finally burning off and that meant visibility would not pose a problem. He thumbed through a stack of brochures for everything from deep-sea fishing to a moonlight jazz cruise on Hyannis Harbor. Logan checked his watch. It was now 8 a.m. Viktor Tarkov walked past Logan's bench and over to the ticket booth for Hy-Line cruises. He purchased one ticket for the 8:15 harbor cruise, checked his watch and strolled over to the waiting area where five tourists stood in line. A man in a long blue rain coat walked up to the line. He appeared about the same age as Tarkov. The man's face bore a wrinkly map of decades spent in the sometimes harsh, unpredictable weather on Cape Cod.

"Is this the line for the 8:30 cruise?" The old man asked Tarkov. *Were you followed?*

"No, but you can still make the 8:15." *All clear.*

Logan walked over to the Hy-Line booth and purchased a ticket with cash.

"Sir, you are eligible for our senior citizen discount," the cheerful attendant explained. "Your ticket is only eight dollars instead of fifteen."

The disguise is working, Logan realized.

He got his ticket and waited patiently while the 150-seat *Prudence* pulled up slowly to the dock. Logan watched as Tarkov walked up the metal plank and moved toward the back of the vessel. Logan was the last passenger to step aboard the Maine coastal steamer. He walked to the bow of the vessel and sat down on a wooden bench and watched the pristine landscape pass slowly by as the *Prudence* steamed her way through Hyannis harbor. A fleet of small sunfishes with multi-colored sails lay in a row on the white sandy beach. Fellow passengers snapped pictures as the vessel came upon a small freshly painted lighthouse at the tip of Channel Point. *Orla would love this.*

Logan tried blocking memories of his lover out of his mind, but the images of her soft skin and bright smile kept coming back to him. Fortunately, the thought was interrupted by a voice over the loud speaker. "Ladies and gentleman, welcome aboard the *Prudence*. I am your captain Eric Cox. In just a few moments, we will be passing by the John F. Kennedy Memorial on your right hand side. Please feel free to take pictures or videos. Normally, the *Prudence* is allowed to pass the Kennedy compound just ahead in Hyannisport. But as you may know, that area is currently off-limits because of the ongoing Anglo-Irish Summit. However, our friends at the Coast Guard say that we can travel as far down as Sea Street Beach. You should be able to take some pictures of Hyannisport from there."

Logan got up out of his seat and walked along the rod iron railing toward the middle of the boat, Viktor Tarkov did the same. The Russian pulled out a pair of binoculars and surveyed the coastline.

"That could be a good launch site. It's covered by sea grass and appears to be a private beach," Tarkov whispered.

Logan opened a small map that he had purchased at a souvenir shop. "It says here that the beach is at the end of Estey Avenue. You'll need to drive to the end of Ocean Street and turn right onto Hawes Avenue. Estey Avenue is about a quarter of a mile down on the left. Good luck my friend."

He handed Tarkov the map and walked slowly back to his seat. The Russian stayed by the railing with arms folded staring out at the sandy beach. "I pray for soft soil so that you may rest in peace Michael Logan," Tarkov muttered to him self.

CHAPTER 37

He stared at his tired face in the mirror of his motel room. His brown eyes were blood shot and heavy bags appeared under the lids. He had only slept a few hours over the past three days. The nightmares made it almost impossible to sleep, and now it was making it nearly impossible for him to concentrate. A local radio station had just reported that a peace agreement had been struck in Hyannisport. A formal announcement was to be made the next morning. Logan stood patiently while re-applying the latex rubber to his face. The old man disguise would not work for him any longer; the Dorcha knew that he had to appear younger for the next phase of the operation. It took him two full hours to transform his face, and another hour to dye his black hair blond. He looked into the bathroom mirror again, this time staring at the image of a total stranger. Satisfied with the makeup job, Logan grabbed his keys and left the motel room.

Prime Minister Stirling and his entourage entered the sprawling white tent set up on the front lawn of *Joe*. Senator Kennedy was already there, as was Gerry Adams and twenty members of the Irish delegation. In the back of the tent, a six-piece brass band played an instrumental version of Bing Cosby's *You got me where you want me.*

The senator does have a sense of humor, Stirling thought.

Senator Kennedy approached the Prime Minister with his right arm extended.

"Congratulations Prime Minister," Kennedy offered while shaking Stirling's hand.

"You've made history here today sir."

"A new dawn has come for both Great Britain and Ireland," Stirling replied. "If two sworn enemies can achieve peace, it gives hope to every other nation in the world, including your own."

These were noble words; but inside, Stirling was still seething. He hated the thought of kow-towing to an IRA coat holder like Gerry Adams. He glanced over at Adams who was holding court near the small bar in the corner of the tent. *Twenty years ago, I would have cut out your heart and fed it to you.*

A waiter walked up to Stirling and Kennedy and offered them champagne. Kennedy accepted a glass, but the Prime Minister waved the waiter off. Stirling looked at the young man suspiciously. Anxiety washed over him. *Is Michael Logan lurking about somewhere in this tent?*

"Call over that American Secret Service agent," He ordered his chief of staff.

Mitch Handley parted the crowd; strolled up to Nikki Tavano and whispered something into her ear. She nodded and made her way over to the prime minister. Until that moment, Stirling had not realized how beautiful the American was. He wondered what kind of scandal would be created if the Prime Minister of Great Britain bedded an American Secret Service agent here at the Compound. He smiled at the mere thought, *delicious.*

"You asked to see me Mister Prime Minister?"

"Yes," he replied while trying to read the identification badge on her breast pocket. "Special Agent Tavano, I've been told by my security staff that I may be receiving some company here on the compound. How seriously are you taking this Logan fellow?"

"Sir, I have a team of agents investigating and assessing the threat as we speak."

Tavano watched Stirling's eyes move across the tent.

"Mister Prime Minister, you have nothing to worry about. The dinner has been catered by *The Paddock,* one of this area's finest restaurants. Each member of the wait staff has been screened by my agents and again by members of your own security detail. Each member of the brass band had to endure the exact same scrutiny. They're instruments were also inspected sir. It may be the reason the band sounds a little off key," she laughed.

Stirling gazed into the agent's eyes then moved down to her chest. "I see that you have the situation well under control Agent Tavano. Will you be available if I have any further questions later in the evening?"

Tavano felt a pang in the pit of her stomach. His intense stare told her what he really wanted. "If I am tied up for some reason, I will make sure that one of my agents is available to answer any of your questions. Enjoy your evening sir."

Tavano winced while walking away from the prime minister. *Should never have used the words, tied up. Lord knows what that creep is thinking now.*

Michael Logan sat in the lobby of the Tara Hyannis Hotel; his nose was buried in a copy of the Cape Cod *Times.* It was just after seven p.m. and the lobby was bustling with activity. The Tara was the largest hotel in Hyannis and the closest in proximity to the Kennedy Compound. The hotel had been transformed into a media compound for visiting journalists from all over the world. All the networks were there. The Anglo-Irish Summit was the biggest story at the moment, although most of the jaded journalists felt peace would never be realized in Northern Ireland. A long table was set up in the middle of the lobby where members of the press stood in line to receive their media credentials.

"A bunch of us booked reservations at the Silver Shell for dinner. You want in?" Kent Earle asked his fellow videographer Jamie Kimball.

The free-lance cameraman waved Earle off.

"That's fine and dandy for you married guys, but it's Friday night and I'm on a trim hunt," Kimball replied with a grin. "I'm gonna head over to Baxter's and see if I can scare up some tail."

Kent Earle was thankful Kimball declined the invitation. The freelancer was good for a few laughs every once in a while, but the act got old real quick. With an orange Hawaiian shirt barely covering his large belly, Jamie Kimball reminded Earle of those middle-aged Margaritaville refugees searching for their lost shakers of salt at Jimmy Buffet concerts.

The Dorcha overheard the conversation between the two men. He folded his newspaper and casually exited the lobby for the parking lot. He sat in his rental car for several minutes waiting for his *mark* to appear. The car radio was tuned into WBZ 1030. The Boston station had just reported that the summit news conference on Cape Cod was scheduled to begin at noontime tomorrow. WBZ promised its listeners complete live coverage of the event. Logan watched as the horny cameraman entered the parking lot. Although night was falling, the photog slid on a pair of wraparound sunglasses and opened the car door of his Ford station wagon, which was painted Robin's egg blue. Jamie Kimball bent down and fussed with his long hair in the driver's side mirror. *This guy is too much,* Logan thought. Finally, the man climbed into the driver's seat and turned the ignition. Logan left the parking lot a few minutes after the photographer. Thanks to his fold out map, he knew where he was headed.

Heath Rosary and Vincent Logan returned to the Nautical Way cottage after another day of fruitless pavement pounding. They had just come from a run-down two-story house near the Barnstable Municipal Airport. Rosary had received a tip from a bartender at the Quarterdeck lounge that an Irishman fitting Logan's description had turned up asking questions about the Kennedy compound. They drove the Jaguar over and found the house overrun by Irish college students who had traveled to the Cape in search of summer jobs. They found the Irishman in question who bore a slight resemblance to the Logan brothers. The kid merely wanted to take a few pictures of the famed compound to send home to his family. In all, the students were quite jovial and even offered the investigators a couple of cans of *Guinness* for their troubles. They declined the offer although now both wished they had not. The search for Michael Logan had become extremely frustrating and it was now getting close to crunch time.

"We've covered just about every inch of Cape Cod over the past few days. What haven't we thought about?" Vincent asked.

Rosary laid out a security map of the compound on the dining room table. He had managed to sweet talk Tavano into giving him a copy. "We've seen the security around the compound. The Coast Guard has five boats patrolling the water surrounding the back of the estate. They sweep for mines every four hours. Even if your brother were an expert diver, it would be impossible to launch a successful attack from the ocean."

Vincent agreed. "He'd have to penetrate the area on foot. But with security patrols and surveillance cameras, I don't see how he can make it three feet inside the perimeter without getting spotted."

Rosary shook his head no. "From what you told me about your brother, he knows this all too well. Hell, he's probably got a copy of this map with him right now. To get on the grounds he'll need a Trojan Horse of some kind. The question is; what will he use?"

CHAPTER 38

It's just not my night, thought Jamie Kimball. He sat on a stool and looked around the bar. Half the women he saw were just months shy of collecting social security, the other half appeared to be right out of college and way out of his league.

Kimball drained his third bottle of Budweiser; paid his tab and sauntered toward the door. He would not be deterred. *Next stop; Fresh Ketch, the place should be packed with drunken karaoke singers about now.* Kimball walked across the dimly lit parking lot toward his station wagon. The cameraman noticed a car with its hood up parked next to his. The driver stood in the darkness shaking his head.

"Car die on ya?"

"Yup," the driver replied. "Engine's shot. I've got some cables if you wouldn't mind giving me a jump?"

Looks like the karaoke girls will have to wait, Kimball thought. "Sure, I'll give you a hand."

The driver motioned Kimball to the back of the vehicle. "My cables are in the trunk. But now the bloody trunk is jammed."

"Shit, I thought I was having a bad night."

The photographer stepped forward to offer some assistance. As he did, Logan moved behind Kimball's back and brought his left arm up under the man's neck. The Dorcha's right hand shot up and covered the man's mouth with a rag soaked in chloro-hydrate. Kimball was shocked by the smaller man's strength. It was the last thought that went through his mind. Seconds later, Jamie Kimball collapsed into Logan's arms.

Michael opened the side door of Kimball's station wagon and lay the man down gently on the back seat. He pulled the car keys from Kimball's coat pocket and quickly covered him up with a blanket. The kidnapping took less than three minutes. Logan looked back toward the bar and was relieved to find no one else outside. He fired up the dent-riddled station wagon and started back to the Craigville Motel.

Robert Stirling sat alone in the master bedroom of *Jack;* Michael Logan weighing heavily on his mind. The prime minister pressed the intercom button on the side of his bed and summonsed Handley.

"Mitch, can you come here for a moment?"

He's calling me Mitch again; something must really be troubling him.

"Right away sir," the chief of staff replied.

Handley was staying just two doors down in what appeared to be the children's room. Photographs of a young Caroline Kennedy and JFK Jr. lined the walls. A very elaborate dollhouse sat on a table by the window. Covered by a layer of dust, it looked like it had not been played with in years. The chief of staff straightened his red tie and walked down the corridor. He nodded at the security officers guarding the entrance; one was British, the other American.

"You wanted to see me sir?" Handley said as he entered the room.

"Yes, please close the door."

Handley did as he was told.

"I would like Scotland Yard to bring me briefing materials on the recent deaths of two men," said the prime minister.

"Shouldn't you be going over tomorrow's speech sir? It could be the biggest speech of your career."

Stirling waved his subordinate off. "There's plenty of time for that," he said angrily. "Right now I need to know how two old friends of mine were killed."

Mitch Handley was puzzled. "Which friends are you referring to sir?"

Stirling wrote the names on a piece of stationary. "Get me the information and then burn this note."

The Dorcha turned the station wagon's headlights off as he pulled the vehicle around to the back of the motel. The next several minutes could make or break the mission. *How can I get this guy into the room without waking the other guests?* He found a parking space directly in front of his motel room. He stepped out of the station wagon and walked up to room eight. At that moment, a middle-aged woman popped her head out of room nine.

"Excuse me sir. Can you point me to the ice machine," she asked waving an empty ice bucket.

"I believe it's up by the manager's office. Let me show you."

Logan walked the woman across the courtyard to the ice machine. She swayed slightly and her speech was slurred. Logan kept a steady hand on the small of her back.

"Are you enjoying your stay on Cape Cod?" he asked.

"Oh, it's just lovely. We spent the whole day browsing the galleries in Provincetown. And you?"

"Well not at the moment," he told her. "I'm here for a wedding and we had the bachelor party earlier this evening."

"I hope you behaved yourselves," she said playfully.

Logan laughed. "I did mum, but the groom did not. He's passed out in the backseat of my car. I just hope that I can get him into the room, he's a large fellow."

"My Harold can help you," she offered.

"That's a kind gesture," Logan replied. "But I couldn't impose on your dear husband. However, if you could forgive any noise you may hear from room eight, I'd greatly appreciate it."

They stood together at the ice machine, the drunken woman seeing his face clearly for the first time under the bright porch light. She gazed up at him for several seconds without speaking. Logan grinned as he realized they were both in disguise. She also dyed her hair, and hid behind several layers of heavy makeup.

"Hey," she slurred. "You're kind of cute."

He smiled back at her. "Aren't you a wicked woman. We'd better get back to our rooms before Harold sends out a search team."

He walked her to her room and waved goodnight. He opened the door to room eight and walked back to the station wagon. Logan opened the side door and pulled the unconscious man out by his legs. He stood the cameraman up against the station wagon and hoisted him up over his right shoulder. Seconds later, both men were safely in room eight. Logan dragged the body into the bathroom and handcuffed Jamie Kimball's left wrist to the base of the sink. Tarkov had told him the potent dose of chloro-hydrate would last twelve hours. Logan made a mental note to apply another dose the following morning. Just to be on the safe side, he also covered Kimball's mouth with a thick strip of duct tape.

Logan grabbed the cameraman's press pass and went to work. He placed the credential on a towel in the center of the bed. He plugged in a hand iron and waited for it to heat up. Who would he be working for the next day? The media pass identified Jamie Kimball as a freelance videographer hired by the BBC. Logan grabbed the iron and ran it back and forth over the credential, its plastic cover peeling off almost immediately. Using an Exacto-knife, he cut his own picture to fit directly over that of Jamie Kimball's. It was a photo he had just taken of himself in the bathroom. He then ironed the lamination back on and waited for it to cool.

"I've just received the case files you requested," Inspector George Mason told Handley.

"Thank you for meeting me out here."

The men stood together on Squaw Island road looking out at Nantucket Sound. Lights coming from the coast guard vessels rose and fell in the distance. It was a chilly spring night and the evening air was thick with salt.

"Has Scotland Yard found any connection between the deaths of Charles Geoffrey and Malcolm Rogers?" Handley inquired.

"As I'm sure you know, Geoffrey was murdered but Rogers' death appears to be accidental," the inspector replied.

"What about the victims, any connection there?" Handley was growing frustrated by the inspector's question and answer game.

"We did find one, yes. Both men served in the SAS. It's very odd, but Scotland Yard has had no luck pulling their operational backgrounds. It's as if both men never existed."

"Who knows the file request came from the prime minister?"

"Just you and me," Mason replied.

"Good, hand over the files," Handley ordered. "And don't you breathe a word of this to anyone or I'll make sure your next job will be picking up shit left behind by the mounted police."

"You're quite a bugger, Mister Handley," the inspector told him point blank.

Handley shrugged his shoulders. "I had my scruples scraped off years ago, inspector."

Mitch Handley arrived back at the prime minister's bedroom suite five minutes later. Robert Stirling relaxed by the fire wearing a red silk bathrobe. Handley was relieved to see his boss going over notes for tomorrow's speech.

"Here are the files you requested sir. May I ask why you feel the pressing need to look at this material now?"

The prime minister got up from his rocking chair and yanked the files from his subordinate's hands. Handley stood his ground.

"Sir, I cannot protect you if I don't know what's going on."

"I should have inquired about this when it happened, but I became so wrapped up in this summit nonsense."

Stirling turned his back to Handley; opened the top file and read aloud. "Charles Geoffrey shot once through the back of the head. Ballistics indicate the shooter was at least ten feet away, yet he was able to hit a moving target with pin-point accuracy without injuring the woman in Geoffrey's bed. Police have yet to crack the husband's alibi that he was working in his law office that evening. The security guard says the husband left the office twenty minutes after the shooting."

The prime minister opened the next file and continued reading. "Malcolm Rogers killed in a fall on his reserve in the Scottish Highlands. Rogers' grandson says it was an accident, yet the autopsy report suggests signs of a struggle. By God, the medical examiner found an imprint of a man's boot on Rogers' chest. Police interview an innkeeper who tells them that a Spanish looking man inquired about Rogers the day before he was killed. This is ruled an accident?"

Handley was still trying to figure out where the prime minister was going with this.

"That photo of Logan's twin brother, I want it shown to the inn-keeper right away," Stirling ordered. "You see Mitch, I served with these men," he said holding up photos of both Geoffrey and Rogers. "We killed Michael Logan's father in 1981. The bloody scab was hiding an IRA bomber in his grocery store. The boy is now a man and he's trying to take us out one by one."

CHAPTER 39

Michael Logan placed Jamie Kimball's video camera on the bed. The Panasonic DVC-PRO 3 chip digital camera was the most popular model used by videographers in the field. Following a diagram drawn up by Tarkov, Logan used a small screw driver to pry open the camera's plastic shell. He then carefully removed the digital chip board and roller spool from the guts of the deck. Logan grabbed his loaded 38 snub-nosed revolver and placed it inside the camera. It was not the most accurate weapon, this he knew, but the gun fit perfectly inside the machine. He replaced the hard plastic shell in the back of the camera with a synthetic breakaway material that would allow him quick access to the weapon. Logan looked at his watch, which now read 3 a.m. He knew that he needed at least two hours of sleep in order to perform at his highest level later that day. He set the alarm for 5 a.m. and nodded off.

The prime minister's personal valet climbed the staircase of JFK's former summer home carrying a silver breakfast tray. Mitch Handley cut the young attractive girl off at the top of the stairs.

"I'll take it in to him, Vanessa," he said grabbing the tray away from her.

The valet bowed her head slightly and retreated down the stairs. Handley carried the tray to Stirling's door and opened the silver lid for the security detail. No weapons just scrambled eggs, sausage and bacon. The agents nodded their approval and opened the prime minister's door. Handley set the tray down by the bed and waited for his boss to exit the bathroom.

"Ah, breakfast," Stirling said clapping his hands. "I am absolutely famished."

The prime minister's jovial mood caught Handley by surprise.

"Before you begin your breakfast sir, I must give you an update on the Logan situation."

Stirling was already crunching away on a strip of bacon. "I can listen and eat at the same time dear boy. Say what you have to say."

"We found the inn-keeper and showed him the photograph. He made a positive ID. As you surmised sir, it is now believed that Michael Logan murdered Malcolm Rogers. That's not all. There's a page missing from the Geoffrey file. A source at MI-5 told me the killer left a calling card."

"What was it?" Stirling asked while bringing a spoonful of eggs to his mouth.

"The killer left behind an old photograph taken of Charles Geoffrey and two other soldiers. Their faces are covered in grease paint but my source told me that one man could be Malcolm Rogers. He thinks the other is you."

Stirling remembered posing for the picture. *They were young men then, fearless. Long live the Knights of the Round Table.* Despite his immense wealth and lofty seat of power, Stirling's tour of Northern Ireland was the one period in his life that he had truly felt alive.

"I strongly suggest that you cancel today's news conference." Handley had been spinning the situation around in his head for the past two hours. "We can send out a press release saying that you've got something like a stomach virus, but that you will address both houses of Parliament upon your return to London."

Stirling took a sip of tea and looked up at his chief of staff. "Mitch, I've been thinking about this long and hard as well. If I cancel my speech, then this entire summit was all for nothing. This is what we came here for remember? If I don't address the world, you can bet that Adams still will. We cannot have that now, can we?"

Handley mulled over the question and reluctantly agreed with his boss. The prime minister's positive new attitude belied a growing fear in his heart. *The hunter had become the hunted.*

Michael Logan rubbed his tired eyes and looked down at his watch. "Jesus Christ," he yelled. Frantically, he reached over and grabbed the bedside alarm clock nearly pulling it out of the wall. The clock's digital face flashed 12:00 a.m. repeatedly. *We must have had a power outage.* He had planned on getting up at 5 a.m., but it was now quarter past ten. He ran into the bathroom and reshaped the latex on his face. Jamie Kimball still lay unconscious on the floor. Logan pulled gently on the rubber cheeks to give him bigger jowls. He then molded another layer of putty onto his bulbous nose. Logan added Kimball's sunglasses and the disguise was complete. He placed the media credential around his neck and grabbed the video camera. The moment he had worked his entire life for was now less than two hours away.

Grace Chen huddled with her fellow producers in the newsroom of CBS4. Her boss, news director Gus Cooper ran over the game plan once more.

"The network is planning to cut into local programming at 11:50 a.m. I want to cover that time with our own people." He pointed at Grace. "Please let Master Control know that we will not be handing our time over to CBS News. This is a major story and it's happening right in our own backyard. We need to be the ones covering it. Grace, I need you to have the anchors in place at quarter of, that way we can get on before the network does."

She nodded. "I also have Dave Robichaud and Kent Earle set up and ready to go if we want to do a little Q&A before the newser starts."

Cooper then handed out Xeroxed copies of the graphics list.

"Our graphics package will be called, *History in Hyannisport*. Please make sure those words are in our copy. Let's kick some ass people."

The meeting broke and Grace began typing a script in the special event queue of her computer. *History in Hyannisport … Great Britain and Ireland agree on a deal that could bring centuries of armed conflict to an end …*

"So what do we do now?" Vincent asked as they climbed into the Jaguar.

"We try to get as close to the compound as we can without getting arrested," Rosary replied. "Hopefully, we'll find him before they do."

His cell phone started to ring.

"Rosary," he answered.

"This is Brendan Monaghan over at the Craigville Motel," the caller announced. "You asked me to call if I had information."

"That's right," Rosary replied calmly.

"We've got something here you need to see," Monaghan explained. "I think the man you're looking for rented a room here last night."

Rosary looked at his watch. The news conference was set to begin in one hour. *Shit, there's not enough time.*

"We'll be over in five minutes," he told the motel manager.

"You'd better put that seat belt on Vincent."

Rosary dialed Tavano's Nextel and was immediately put through to voice mail.

Damn woman, pick up the phone!

"Nikki, it's me. We may be getting close to finding him. Call me when you get this message."

Tavano stood with her hands balled into fists at her slender waist. She had just returned to the command center after monitoring microphone checks at the lecterns where the two principals would be speaking. She watched her agents run from room to room, up and down the stairs of *Sargent*.

"I appreciate the sense of urgency people, but would someone tell me what the hell is going on?"

Agent Nick Franco tore a piece of paper off a small printer and handed it to his boss.

"We've got a lead on Michael Logan. On your order, we sent the brother's photo to every airport in the country. Turns out, an immigration official in Boston remembered our boy; told her he was a history buff."

"When did he arrive?"

"Seven days ago, boss. He rented a car under the name Roberto Tomba. We ran the tags and they matched a car that was found abandoned this morning."

"Where was the car?"

"In a restaurant parking lot here in Hyannis," Franco answered.

Tavano took a deep breath. *Shit, he really is here.* "I don't want the locals going near that car. Get a forensic team over there to comb the vehicle for fingerprints, fibers, and residue of any explosives. Give that rental car a colonoscopy for God's sake."

CHAPTER 40

The Russian sat in his small Toyota truck at the top of Ocean Avenue waiting for the traffic light to change. Winds were gusting up to forty miles per hour off the ocean. Another truck pulled up alongside the green Toyota. The driver rolled down his window.

"Hey buddy," he called to Tarkov. "You're not planning to go out in that thing today are ya?"

The man was pointing to the rear of the Toyota. The Russian turned and looked out the back window of the cab.

"Naw, I'm just towing the boat to by brother's house. It could sure use a good paint job."

The driver smiled and waved as the traffic signal changed. Tarkov let the man pass before pulling off onto a side road. He waited for five minutes before turning out onto Ocean Street again. *I hope this rickety old girl can get where we need her to go.* The Russian drove to the end of Ocean Street and got his first look at the ten-foot waves whipping off Kalmus Beach. The harbor was overrun by whitecaps and there appeared to be no other boats in the water. Tarkov turned right onto Hawes Avenue and followed along the coastline to the predetermined launch point. The bad weather did bring one good fortune; the small beach was deserted. He parked his truck, and then lifted the tarp-covered rowboat off its rusty iron trailer. A family of piping plovers looked on curiously as the man dragged the 14-foot vessel toward the ocean. Tarkov grinned through his arthritis pain as he noticed the small birds following in line. *March my little comrades' march.*

The Dorcha had never seen such security in all his years as a hired assassin. The security checkpoint entering the Kennedy compound had been moved back from Irving Avenue to Overlea Road three blocks away. Logan parked the station wagon on the side of the road and fetched his gear. A Massachusetts state trooper approached as Logan closed the trunk of the automobile. The officer held a sixty-pound German Shepard tightly by the reign.

"You're gonna have to reopen that trunk sir."

Logan did as he was told and the dog went to work sniffing every possible inch of trunk space. The trooper then ran a small mirror attached to a metal pole under the station wagon.

"Can you open the doors of the vehicle sir," the officer asked politely.

"No problem."

The bomb-sniffing dog walked along the vinyl seats giving the wagon's interior a thorough examination.

"Well, looks like Chappy's happy," announced the trooper as the German Shepard wagged its tail. "Just one more thing; can you operate your camera for me?"

Logan called the officer over and told him to look through the viewfinder. He then hit record and a small red light appeared in the lens. After receiving the okay sign, Logan was ordered to hand over his press pass.

"Who are you with, Mr. ah Kimball?" the trooper asked eyeing the credential closely.

"I'm freelancing for the Brits today. Know where I can find the BBC truck?"

The trooper shook his head. "Good luck, It's like the O.J. trial down there. Trucks are lined up everywhere. Haven't seen this much media since JFK Jr.'s plane went down off the Vineyard."

"Yah, I remember. I covered the tragedy," Logan lied.

He threw the camera over his shoulder and made his way toward the media circus.

The camera was about six pounds lighter now that Logan had pulled out the deck equipment to make space for his revolver. "You can tear out the intestines of the machine, and yet the camera will still work," Tarkov had told him. Logan would not be able to roll tape however. He hoped his reporter wouldn't know the difference.

He walked three blocks south on Scudder Avenue and then followed the trail of network flags waving proudly atop the armada of satellite trucks. Suddenly, his eyes fluttered and the scenery began spinning around him. He took his sunglasses off and leaned against a news van. *Keep it together boyo,* he told himself. He pinched the bridge of his nose with his thumb and index finger and waited for a few seconds. He opened his eyes and was relieved to see that the spinning had stopped. Logan's vision was clear but his mind was clouded. The sound of the bells was ringing loudly in his ears. He fought both his body and his mind as he hoisted the camera over his shoulder and continued on. Logan had to show his credentials twice more, this time to agents from the United States Secret Service. The security professionals nodded their approval and walked away. His confidence was starting to grow.

Rosary pulled into the parking lot of the Craigville Motel and was flagged down by the manager.

"Meet me in room eight," the man shouted.

The jaguar pulled up in front of the motel room and both investigators stepped out of the car. They entered the small, but tidy room and saw a man and woman sitting on chairs in front of the television set. The woman wore a satin orange tracksuit with makeup smears lining the collar. She was no health nut for sure, the tracksuit was merely a decoration and not for practical use. She appeared to be in her mid-fifties and her hair was dyed jet-black. *She's definitely ready for her close up,* Rosary thought. It was impossible to tell what the man looked like; a wet towel covered his head.

"We found this guy about an hour ago handcuffed to the bathroom sink," the manager informed them. "He doesn't know how he got here and is still pretty groggy."

"First of all, I found him," the older woman butted in. "My Harold heard some loud banging on the other side of the wall, so I went over to see if the boys were alright."

"How did you know who was in the room?" Rosary asked.

"Last night, I met the nice man who rented it. He told me that his friend," she pointed over to towel head, "that one there, got stinking drunk at his own bachelor party."

Vincent stepped closer to the older woman. "Did he look like me, madam?"

"No," she smiled. "But he had your accent."

Rosary and Logan looked at one another.

"I never saw him," the manager chimed in. "My sister took the reservation before she left for Nantucket. I've got the ledger right here." He held up a clipboard. "He paid in cash and registered under the name Ambrose Chapel."

Rosary saw the irony. "At least your brother's got good taste in movies," he told Vincent. "Ambrose Chapel was the name of the villains' lair in *The Man Who Knew Too Much.*"

Logan looked at his watch; then walked over and yanked the towel off the mystery man's head. "Alright, we're running out of time, it's time to reveal the man under the mask. What's your story boyo?"

Jamie Kimball tried to look up but had trouble focusing his eyes. "I don't know what happened. I'm supposed to be over at the compound right now."

"What's your job there?"

"I'm a photographer; I'm supposed to be shooting the news conference."

"Looks like we have our Trojan Horse," Vincent said aloud.

Both men raced out of the motel room and into the Jaguar.

Brian Leeds had not been this pissed off since the day someone stole his specially ordered therapeutic chair out from under his desk at the BBC. Oh how they loved to prank the senior correspondent. *They were fucking with me then, and they're fucking with me now. Where the bloody hell is my photographer?* He was about to place his third emergency call to London when he noticed a cameraman making his way toward the truck.

"Are you working for the BBC?" Leeds asked angrily.

The cameraman nodded.

"Well it's about fucking time," the reporter said pointing at his watch. "We've just been given a fifteen minute warning. You still need to set up on sticks, white balance your camera and give me a fucking microphone check!"

Logan remained silent and began setting up his equipment. The reporter then turned his anger toward the person at the other end of his cell phone.

"He just got here!" he informed his producer in London. "I told you to spend the extra money to fly out one of my guys. Now I'm at the mercy of this bloody Yank. I think he's a fucking mute."

CBS4 photographer Kent Earle was set up next to Logan's position. "What an asshole," Earle whispered over to his colleague. He had never seen the cameraman before, but had certainly worked with reporters like the one from the BBC. Kent Earle despised *prima donnas.* "I thought Kimball had the British gig. What happened?"

Logan tucked the stolen credential into his sweatshirt. "He got bagged for drunk driving last night. I got the replacement call about an hour ago."

"No way," the CBS4 photographer responded wide-eyed. "That sucks for Kimball."

Logan shrugged his shoulders. "Ah, what are ya gonna do?"

Viktor Tarkov peeled off the heavy-duty plastic tarp that covered the small boat.

Lying down in the middle of the small vessel was a full sized crash test dummy, which Tarkov had purchased at an on-line auction conducted a year earlier by the National Transportation and Highway Safety Board. The crash test dummies fetched the biggest price at the on-line auction. Tarkov bought one for two thousand dollars. He had no idea what exactly he was going to do with the dummy, and had almost given up hope of finding an actual use for it. His Japanese wife had called it the most expensive scarecrow she had ever seen. He had regretted making the purchase until now. Tarkov dressed the dummy in a long yellow rain coat and matching hat. The long coat concealed thirty pounds of C4 plastic explosives strapped around the dummy's torso. It looked like the *Gorton Fisherman* from ten yards away, and that was all the distance Tarkov would need. The dummy also wore a pair of sunglasses equipped with a small antenna. The Russian sat the fake body down on a plastic bench in the middle of the boat. Using a nail gun, he then fastened the dummy to the bench before checking the pair of sunglasses once more. *Everything appears to be working perfectly. Let's go fishing.*

"It's almost showtime," Tavano alerted her team through the microphone hidden near her wrist. "Senator Kennedy will escort the principals from *Joe* to their respective lecterns at the top of Marchant Avenue. Remember; give each man a wide berth, but not too wide." She looked out at the press corps and watched as several reporters battled the gusty weather. Their meticulous hair-dos and notepads blew wildly in the wind.

"Due to the weather everything is moving, the bushes, trees, sea grass. Use your best judgment," she told her agents. "But if you see something out of the ordinary, come down hard!"

CHAPTER 41

Rosary had the silver Jaguar doing eighty miles per hour down Old Stage Road in Centerville. Hyannisport was four miles away. Drizzle now accompanied the high winds, which made the driving even more treacherous. The sports car slid along the wet surface around every curve. Vincent grabbed his side of the dashboard with both hands, his knuckles turning white under the skin. Rosary had one hand on the steering wheel, the other on his cell phone. He flipped open the lid and punched in Tavano's Nextel number. A message flashed on the screen indicating that the phone was low on battery.

"Not now!" Rosary screamed. *How could I have forgotten to charge it last night?*

"What's the matter?" Vincent asked.

"Phone's dying, that's what's the matter!" Rosary clicked off his small Nokia phone and slammed it down on the center console.

"A television cameraman, how come I didn't think of that?" he continued his rant.

Vincent was angry also but he knew it would not do either of them any good. "Come on, Heath it got past me as well. There's still time to end all of this. We can make it."

"I've got a small throw away pistol strapped to my ankle," Rosary told him. "Remind me to give it to you when we get there."

Vincent shook his head. "No, I don't need a gun. He's my twin brother, remember?"

"If it's all the same to you Vincent, I'll keep my gun just in case."

Grace wore a sleek headset and stood with arms folded inside the control booth at CBS4 News. Twenty plasma screens covered the wall in front of her. The live shot coming in from Hyannisport was up on a monitor labeled Sat-19.

"They're walking out now," reporter David Robichaud whispered over the IFB system and into Grace's ear.

"Okay here we go," she yelled out to the director and the rest of the booth crew. She pressed the intercom button and spoke calmly to her anchors. "Here they come, you can toss to the newser right now," she said seeing the relief in their eyes. The anchor man and woman had been adlibbing to fill time for the past nine minutes.

"It's History in Hyannisport," the anchorman announced over live pictures. "Senator Edward Kennedy is walking across the lawn of the house that once belonged to his millionaire father with British Prime Minister Robert Stirling and Gerry Adams, leader of Ireland's Sinn Fein party. The mere fact that these two men are walking together is a powerful image to see. Now they are expected to announce a new treaty and a new era in Anglo-Irish relations. Let's listen in."

The leaders stepped up to the microphones, their respective delegations forming a human chain behind them. The Prime Minister looked over to the Sinn Fein President and gave the blessing for him to speak first.

"First of all, I would like to thank the people of the United States and primarily the Kennedy family for their gracious hospitality," Adams stated in his thick Irish accent. The delegations from both countries broke out in applause. "The Kennedys have never forgotten their ancestoral home land and we will never forget you."

The Prime Minister took his verbal queue. "Senator Kennedy," Stirling added looking over at the family patriarch. "Your family has also been a dear friend to Great Britain since the time your father served as Ambassador to the Court of St. James. Today, our debt to you grows even more. We came to Cape Cod burdened by ancient prejudices and we will leave with a new understanding of each other and a fresh and clear vision for the future. We have decided that it is time to offer Ireland back to its people. With the blessing of Irish President Bertie Ahern, Gerry Adams and I have agreed to put forth a referendum to the people of Northern Ireland."

Stirling looked to Adams who continued the announcement.

"In September of this year, Northern Ireland will decide its own future. Residents of the six counties will vote on whether to remain under British sovereignty, or to merge with the Irish Republic."

The announcement drew a round of applause from both delegations as their leaders stepped away from the lecterns and shook hands. The sound of flash bulbs could be heard over the clapping. Michael Logan pointed the camera at his long-time nemesis; his hands were moist with sweat. The killer was smiling as he shook Gerry Adams' hand. *I am Hell and Hell will come back for you one day.* The words echoed in Logan's fragile mind. His teeth clenched and his body was overcome with rage. How much longer could he stand in front of this man?

Where are you Viktor?

Russ Jacobsen saw it first. The Coast Guard Petty Officer had his binoculars pointing southeast when he noticed the small craft round the jetty and turn toward shore.

"Sir, we've got a vessel of unknown origin out by the breakwater," he radioed his captain. "It looks to be some kind of motorized rowboat with a single occupant on board."

"I see it also," replied the captain. "Boat's really getting hammered by the waves out there. He's probably having second thoughts about catching any blue fish today. Send two TPSB's (transportable port security boat) out there to meet him, let him know he's in a restricted area and escort him over to Sea Street Beach."

"Aye, aye."

Tarkov sat in the cab of his Toyota with his laptop computer open in front of him. The screen gave him a live feed from a tiny lipstick camera built into the sunglasses now being worn by the crash test dummy. Beads of salt water splashed across the camera lens making the live feed difficult to see. The Russian worked a small joystick on his keypad to steer the 14-foot boat by remote control. He had to get just a few yards closer.

The twin outboard engines churned in the water as Jacobsen thrust the 25-foot TPSB into high gear and sped toward the rowboat. Another Coast Guard boat followed immediately behind. Jacobsen grabbed a bullhorn out from under the steering wheel.

"This is the United States Coast Guard," he announced. "Stop right where you are. You are in a restricted area. Turn off your engine immediately."

There was no change in the speed or direction of the boat.

"I repeat; this is the United States Coast Guard. Turn off your engine."

There was still no response.

Jacobsen could hardly believe it. *Maybe this will work you stubborn pick.*

"Turn off your engine immediately, or you will be blown out of the water."

Rosary and Vincent jumped out of the Jaguar and took off in a full sprint down Scudder Avenue. Two state troopers gave chase with guns drawn.

"Stop!" they shouted in unison.

The men raised their hands above their heads but kept running.

"I'm a United States Secret Service Agent," Rosary screamed to the pursuing troopers. Rosary knew the phrase; *I'm a former United States Secret Service Agent* would not have the same effect. He and Vincent reached Irving Avenue before getting tackled by a swarm of security personnel.

"I'm Heath Rosary, Heath Rosary," he screamed from the bottom of the pile. "Former Special-Agent in charge of Boston."

He was pulled off the ground with two state troopers holding back his arms.

Vincent lay on the street with his face pressed against the pavement and his fingers folded around the back of his head. A burly state trooper knelt down on the small of his back.

Secret Service Agent Nick Franco saw what was happening and ran over to his former boss.

"He's clear, let him go," Franco ordered the state police officers.

"The one on the ground too, he's Irish police."

Rosary grabbed the agent by the collar of his sport coat.

"He's in there Nick! He's disguised as a cameraman!"

"Oh shit!" Franco replied putting his wrist microphone up to his lips.

"Agent Franco to Agent Tavano, over."

Tavano was standing at attention to the right of the principals. Her eyes were scanning the row of summerhouses directly across from the compound.

"Tavano here, go ahead Nick."

"Subject is here, I repeat subject is here."

Tavano's eyes were moving and now so were her feet.

"Do you have a location?" she asked calmly.

"Yes, subject is in the …"

The TPSB's surrounded the rowboat. The Coast Guard crews in both boats had their M16 rifles aimed at the fisherman in the long yellow coat. Petty Officer Jacobsen was now ten yards away from the vessel and got his first good look at the figure inside.

"Wait a minute, that's no man, it's a dummy," he shouted to his crew. "What the …"

The Kennedy compound was rocked by the sound of a deafening explosion. All heads turned toward Nantucket Sound as a large orange plume of fire and smoke filled the sky. That is, all heads but one. Michael Logan yanked off the battery and punched his hand through the back of the hollowed television camera. He pulled out his revolver and aimed it at Robert Stirling who stood a few yards away still startled by the explosion. At that moment, Mitch Handley focused his attention back on the press corps gathered behind the rope line. He noticed that one journalist was not paying attention to the explosion and then he noticed the weapon.

"Down!" Handley hollered as he ran toward his boss.

Logan aimed the revolver at Stirling's chest and fired. He heard screaming as the prime minister and the other man fell to the ground. The Dorcha waited to see which one of them would get up.

The gunfire set off a stampede of panic as delegation members and media scrambled for cover. Agent Tavano fought her way through the frenzied mob of people running away and moved toward the sound of the shot. Robert Stirling lay on the ground covered by his subordinate's body. The starched collar of Mitch Handley's white dress shirt was splattered with the man's own blood. The Dorcha ran forward to fire another round as Stirling rolled Handley's lifeless body off his own. "Gun!" Tavano yelled getting a clear view of the shooter for the first time. She brought her service weapon up and fired. Logan felt a sharp pain in his side as the bullet grazed his skin. He turned and fired back hitting the secret service agent in the abdomen. Tavano clutched her stomach and fell to the ground. Logan turned back toward the prime minister, but he was gone.

"Damn!" Logan yelled as he ran back toward the BBC satellite truck where Reporter Brian Leeds stood frozen; his eyes grew wider as Logan stepped closer. The Dorcha shoved him aside and moved toward the back of the truck. Kent Earle was the only photographer to catch the shootings on tape. He was still rolling when Logan made his escape.

"Kent, what the hell's going on?" Grace yelled into his earpiece. She had promised her viewers *History in Hyannisport,* but the live scene looked more like downtown Baghdad, people screaming and bodies on the ground.

"He's a photog!" Earle replied breathlessly. "The shooter is heading away from the compound."

Nick Franco's face turned pale upon hearing the news in his earpiece.

"Heath," he yelled over to his former boss. "Nikki's been hit!"

The three men ran toward the press gallery, Franco was out in front. Rosary saw another man running in the opposite direction out of the corner of his eye.

"That's him," he alerted Vincent. "He's headed for the golf course!"

Rosary reached down and tore the strap off the small gun attached to his ankle.

"Take it," he yelled to Vincent.

He then cut between two satellite trucks and gave chase. Vincent followed his friend.

As he ran, Vincent looked up and noticed a structure sitting at the top Hyannisport's highest point, Sunset Hill. It was a three-story fieldstone bell tower rising up from St. Andrew's Episcopal Church. *He's not heading to the golf course.*

Grace stood in the control room watching the live feed. She saw the shooter cut across the plush green lawn of a large clapboard house across the street from the compound. She noticed another man running after him. Grace only saw the back of his head, but she knew that her worst fears were about to be realized.

"Kent, who was that?" she asked already knowing the answer.

"Grace, I think it's Heath!"

Dear God.

The chiming of the bells in Logan's head blocked out the fluttering sound of chopper blades coming from the state police helicopter hovering above. *I'm coming Vincent! I'm coming!* He reached Irving Avenue and bolted across the street toward the stone steps leading to the church. Heath Rosary was fifty yards away and gaining fast. So far, Logan had not offered him a clear shot. *Sorry, Vincent but your brother's gonna pay for what he did to Nikki.*

Logan's head was swimming; images of Robert Stirling and Brother Tobias flashed through his fractured mind. Everything in his training told him to keep running and not enter the church where he could get trapped; yet something powerful drew him inside. He shot the steel lock off the heavy wooden door and entered the small building. The chapel was empty. St. Andrews was still a month away from opening for the summer season. Logan navigated his way through a row of pews toward another set of stone steps leading up to the bell tower. He was back in the dream. *Please don't hurt my brother.* Logan climbed the narrow, winding staircase. He was back inside Old Gomery. Michael Logan was thirteen-years-old again.

Rosary kicked open the door to the church and pointed his revolver inside. A soft light shone in from the stained glass mural of Jesus at the Sea of Galilee covering the wall behind the alter. He had no time to appreciate the artistry. He scanned the wooden pews and saw nothing. Suddenly he heard the faint sound of footsteps coming from above his head. He ran over to the stone staircase and made his way up slowly. The space was dark and cold. Rosary took each step carefully, his weapon held firmly in his grip. He reached the second floor and paused. He could hear the sound of heavy breathing coming from somewhere on the floor. At that moment, a hand came out of the darkness and chopped down on the back of his neck. Rosary cried out as he doubled over in pain. Another hand came around and slapped the revolver out of his grip. Rosary could hear the sound of metal hitting stone as the gun rolled down the steps. Relying only on instinct now, Rosary lunged into a front kick that caught Logan squarely in the chest. The Dorcha stumbled back against the wall. Rosary ran to retrieve his gun but was tackled at the top of the stairwell. Logan let out a savage growl as both men tumbled down the winding staircase. The Dorcha's powerful forearm was wrapped tightly under Rosary's chin. Logan bit down on the man's ear as both hit the floor. Rosary managed to roll away as Logan's head hit the stone floor hard. Heath jumped to his feet and kicked his attacker in the ribs. "That's for my friend you son of a bitch!"

The Dorcha winced as he clutched his side. "I won't let you do it, Brother Tobias!" he screamed out.

Rosary stepped back confused. "What the hell?"

Logan rolled over and pulled out the snub nosed revolver that had been tucked into his pants. He aimed the gun at Rosary's heart.

"You raped me you bastard. I won't let you get my brother."

Rosary stood with his back against the stone wall of the bell tower. It was becoming clear to him that Logan was having some sort of mental flashback, it was also clear to Heath Rosary that he was about to die.

"Michael, don't do it!" Vincent yelled climbing the staircase.

"Vincent, run! He can't hurt you now," Michael replied, the small gun now shaking in his hand.

"Please put the gun down, it's over. It's all over!" Vincent cried.

"It will be over when this devil goes back to hell."

Michael raised his gun and a shot rang out.

Rosary flinched but felt nothing. He opened his eyes, looked down and saw Michael lying in a pool of his own blood. He gazed over at Vincent who had

Rosary's throw away pistol in his hand. Vincent threw the weapon down and fell to the floor next to his brother.

"Oh God, what have I done? Michael, oh Michael!" he screamed while cradling his brother's head.

"Vincent, I found him." Michael smiled up at his twin. He coughed up an ounce of blood and closed his eyes.

Vincent wiped the warm liquid from his brother's lips and shook him gently.

"Stay with me brother, stay with me. Who? Who did you find?"

"The man ... who killed our father," Michael groaned. "There's a key wrapped around my neck. Take it Vincent. It will tell you everything."

The Dorcha's brown eyes fluttered as he was drew short breaths. His brother saw his life slipping away.

"Michael, please don't die," Vincent cried. "I've come all the way here to tell you something. You're going to be a father. You need to stay alive and see your son!"

The Dorcha smiled again and closed his eyes for one last time.

CHAPTER 42

"I'm glad your friend is going to be alright," Vincent told Rosary.

They sat on the hood of the silver Jaguar staring out at Nantucket Sound. There was a six pack of *Samuel Adams Summer Ale* sitting on the hood between them. The breeze was light and they watched a pair of seagulls dive into the calm sea searching for prey. Rosary took a sip of his beer. "The shot caught her right under her protective vest," he explained. "She lost a lot of blood but she'll pull through. Nikki Tavano's the toughest agent I ever worked with. She's not gonna let a bullet to the stomach keep her down." Rosary turned to Vincent. "What about you? You gonna be okay?"

Logan scratched his head and tried to come up with an answer. "I don't think I'll ever get the image out of my head." He started choking up. "I still can't believe I killed my own brother."

Rosary put his arm around his friend and let him cry.

They finished off the six-pack and climbed back into the car.

"What are you gonna do now?" Rosary asked.

"Stay here in the states until your government releases my brother's body. I'll take him back to Ireland and bury him next to our Da."

"What about the key?"

Neither had mentioned the key to investigators during three exhaustive debriefing sessions. Vincent pulled it out of his pocket. It was covered by a strip of tape that had the address to a *Mailbox Etc.* scribbled on it.

"My brother had gone quite mad there at the end," Vincent said holding up the key.

"But I should check it out. Who knows what could be inside."

"You want me to go with you?" Rosary asked.

"No, my friend. This is something that I have to do myself."

SAVANNAH, GEORGIA

"Mr. Forrest, you have a visitor sir," the maid called out in a slow, southern drawl.

"Damn Gladys, I'm not gonna open this house to another walking tour today," Todd Forrest replied as he pushed his wheel chair up to the door of his study and slammed it shut. Vincent Logan could hear the door slam from the front steps of the stately antebellum home on Monterey Square.

Gladys Chappelle rolled her eyes at the sound and smiled toward the visitor.

"What is your name again please?" she asked.

"Just tell Mister Forrest that Michael Logan sent me."

"Would you wait here one minute please?"

The woman disappeared inside the 18th century Federal style mansion. Logan stood out in the midday sun using a rolled up street map for a fan. The Georgia heat was oppressive, especially for an Irishman. He could hear the sound of a tire tread rolling across the polished wood floor inside. Todd Forrest appeared at the front door seconds later. The retired newsman saw his guest and could not believe his eyes. "Jesus, Michael Logan. You're supposed to be dead!"

"I'm sorry to have startled you Mister Forrest. I am not Michael Logan. I'm his twin brother Vincent."

Forrest placed his scarred right hand over his heart. "For a minute there, I'd thought I'd seen a ghost. Please come in Mister Logan."

Vincent followed the man through the parlor and into his study which was filled with potted plants to balance the color of the dark wood covering the walls. Todd Forrest spun his wheel chair around and locked the door behind them. "I thought you were just another tourist looking for the Mercer House," Forrest explained. "It's been off limits since the book got so popular. They can't poke around Jim Williams' old place, so they ask if they can see mine." Forrest had inherited the mansion next door to the home made famous by John Berendt's best selling book, *Midnight in the Garden of Good and Evil.* "Some times, I'll indulge the tourists if I'm bored. Other times, they scatter like rats at the mere sight at me."

Vincent looked out the window and away from his host.

Forrest rolled his wheel chair closer. "It's okay Mister Logan. Take a good look at me. I'm not ashamed of my appearance." His speech was slow and his breathing was labored.

Vincent's brown eyes shifted back to the man in the wheel chair. Forrest's legs had been amputated at the knees. Vincent counted only three fingers on the man's right hand; his left hand was just a nub. The face was the most disturbing feature. The forehead, cheeks and chin were all covered with thick scar tissue; the nose had been burned off.

"The Michael Logan I knew was not the madman he was made out to be in the press," Forrest told Vincent. "He was a killer, there is no denying that. But he lived by a certain code of honor." He wheeled over to his desk and used his one semi functioning hand to pour himself a glass of whiskey. "Would you like a drink, Mister Logan? The city of Savannah is known for its libations."

Vincent shook his head no.

The newsman took a small sip and continued his story. "After I lost my family, I stayed in the hospital for nearly a year and then a mental institution for another two. Your brother paid a visit to me once, and told me what he had done to the animals that killed my babies. Your brother was my avenging angel. His visit saved my life. I got better, came back to the states and took over my dear Aunt Vivian's estate." Drops of whiskey spilled down the man's chin as he finished his drink. "That's my story, now tell me yours."

Vincent pulled out a manila folder from under his arm. "Michael was my avenging angel also. I can never condone the life he led, but I can understand it. He had turned his back on the violence but something drew him back in. I now know what that something was. He died before justice could be done. I need your help to make sure that his death was not in vain."

C H A P T E R   43

LONDON

Brian Leeds held up a copy of the *Daily Mail* for the television camera.

"When we go live, I'd like you to start tight on the newspaper and then pull out to me," he politely asked his cameraman. After his brush with death on Cape Cod, Leeds had a new found respect for his colleagues behind the camera. In his earpiece, the reporter could hear the anchorman reading the lead to his story.

"Go Brian," the studio director told him in his ear.

"The headline says it all folks, the *Daily Mail* calls Robert Stirling *Mister Prime Sinister*. In a stunning turn of events, the man who was considered a leading candidate for the Nobel Peace Prize one month ago, is now public enemy number one here in Great Britain. The so-called *Forrest Report* has shaken the British government to its core. Robert Stirling has been recalled from his post after the release of secret documents revealing his involvement in the murder and torture of dozens of citizens in Northern Ireland and the Arab world. Among the victims, the father of Stirling's would be assassin, Michael Logan."

Leeds' producer back at the BBC studios leaned back in his chair and smiled. His senior correspondent was on a roll.

"I'm standing in front of Scotland Yard headquarters where just a few hours from now, Robert Stirling is expected to surrender on murder charges. The former prime minister vows a vigorous defense of the charges. Reporting live from London, I'm Brian Leeds, BBC News."

Robert Stirling sat behind his large mahogany desk in his private residence on the 50th floor of the Canada Tower. He checked his gold watch; his lawyer was due to arrive in twenty minutes to escort him to Scotland Yard. The attorney promised the ordeal would take no more than an hour and would not cut into his lunch plans at the Dorchester Hotel. For his defense, Stirling decided that he would take a page from the Americans. Wealthy Yanks flaunted their guilt and paid vast fortunes to insure their *not guilty* verdicts. Robert Stirling was one of the world's richest men; he would use every last euro to fight the charges.

He had been removed from his office at 10 Downing Street, but that was only a temporary setback in his mind. Who said there was no second act in politics? Stirling had no doubt that he could be a major political force again. For his surrender, he chose a $10,000 hand stitched Italian cut wool suit. It was the most expensive in his wardrobe. The suit was Stirling's way of saying; *fuck you* to the British police and the bloodthirsty media. He had been given the option of using an underground garage upon his arrival at Scotland Yard, but he declined. Robert Stirling wanted the public to see him with his head held high. *I was only following orders,* he thought. *If I go down, the British military will go down with me.*

Father O'Bannon peered out the small window of his sparse room. He could see a large crowd gathering across the street outside Scotland Yard headquarters. He ran his brittle fingers through his bristly hair and whispered a prayer and then stood up and returned to his bed where his vestments were laid out across the white cotton sheets. The items all bore thick creases from having been stored away for so long. He lifted the *alb* and placed his long arms through the sleeves of the dusty robe. "Make me white, O Lord, and cleanse my heart; that being made white in the Blood of the Lamb I deserve an eternal reward." O'Bannon reached down for the *amice* and placed the oblong hood on his head. "Place, O Lord on my head the helmet of salvation, that so I may resist the assaults of the Devil." The old priest made the sign of the cross and walked out of the room. He exited the boarding house, made his way across the street and disappeared into the sea of protesters awaiting Robert Stirling's arrival.

The limousine turned right off Victoria Street and then began speeding along Broadway. "Slow down, you fool," Stirling told the driver. "I want to enjoy this."

The former prime minister placed a Dunhill between his lips and pointed his sharp chin toward his lawyer, who then lit his cigarette. Stirling brought the smoke deep into his lungs and kept it there for a moment before blowing it back out toward the roof of the limousine.

"You appear to be very calm sir," the lawyer observed.

"Why shouldn't I be?" Stirling mused. "I'm paying you a fortune to clear me of these charges. Is there a reason that I should not have complete confidence in you?"

The attorney straightened his red tie. "No sir. I think we can mount a great defense and cause great embarrassment for the Crown."

Stirling smiled as he took another drag from his cigarette. "Absolutely delicious," he replied.

The woman seated to Stirling's right brushed his arm for attention. "Don't forget, you've got a sit-down interview with Brian Leeds from the BBC after lunch," she reminded him. Stirling rolled his eyes. "He's such an insufferable bore," he told her.

"That maybe sir, but it's all about getting *your* side of the story out," she replied. "After the Leeds interview, you've got CNN, the *Times*, and the publisher who's interested in your memoirs. They've already got a writer assigned to help you. He wrote that best seller about Churchill a few years back."

Churchill, he thought to himself. *I'm finally getting mentioned in the same breath with the great ones.* He had to admit however, it was not how he had envisioned his legend unfolding. *Fucking Michael Logan. I should have killed that boy in the grocery.* Still, there was no reason to doubt that he wouldn't have the last laugh in this great game.

Stirling gazed over to his new assistant. She had strawberry blond hair, porcelain skin and a nice bosom. She was much better on the eyes than the bloated Mitch Handley. He had to admit that he missed his old bulldog though. He had proved his loyalty right to the end. Still, his new assistant had her own attributes. He placed his hand on her thigh. She spread her legs slightly and invited him in. He moved his fingers under her skirt and inched his way up her silk stocking. She leaned over and nibbled on his ear lobe. The attorney seated opposite cleared his throat and looked away.

The shouts grew louder as the limousine got closer. The protesters were at a fever pitch as they pushed against the barricades in front of Scotland Yard. O'Bannon was getting knocked around as he made his way toward the front of the crowd. A police officer, who happened to be Catholic, saw the priest being jostled by the protesters and pulled him through. "You'll have to stay behind this barricade, Father," he warned. "Bless you my son," O'Bannon replied.

Stirling's lawyer stared out at the angry crowd from behind the protective glass of the limousine. "Are you sure that you want to get out *here*?" he asked nervously.

The former prime minister turned his tanned face up into a devilish grin. "As Shakespeare once wrote; All the world's a stage. And all the men and women merely players," he said. "Now let us go play our parts."

The long black vehicle pulled up to the curb and the attorney and assistant both stepped out. They were met by two police officers but their presence did not seem to calm the beautiful, young assistant. She was like a deer in the headlights. A chill ran down her spine as she stared out at the protesters whom were all spewing hateful words about her new boss and lover. *What am I doing here?* She asked herself. The assistant jumped as she felt a hand on her shoulder. "Easy now love," Stirling whispered in her ear as he stepped out of the limousine and onto the street. "Smile proudly for the cameras darling," he told her. "We've got nothing to be ashamed of."

O'Bannon swallowed hard as he watched Stirling engage the crowd. The accused killer smiled and waved defiantly to the protesters who all cursed him at the top of their lungs. Stirling and his small entourage continued down the line toward the spot where the old priest was standing. O'Bannon placed his right hand into his robe and retrieved a small holy card depicting the Archangel Michael with his long shining sword pointed toward the Devil who lay under his feet in a heap of flames. *Great Archangel Michael, defend us in battle. Be our defense against the wickedness and snares of the Devil. O Prince of the heavenly host, by the power of God, thrust into Hell the Adversary and all other evil spirits who prowl about the world for the ruin of souls.* After whispering the prayer, O'Bannon placed his left hand into his robe and reached for his gun.

The blond haired assistant followed Stirling around to the front of the limousine. The former prime minister paid no attention to the protesters now as he smiled proudly toward the television cameras. His assistant gripped his elbow tightly as she continued to gaze out at the angry crowd. They all looked alike to her; bearded and bespectacled students who spent their pathetic lives bouncing from one lost cause to the next. *This traveling circus will be someplace else tomorrow with new signs adorned with new hateful slogans,* she thought.

One protester wearing a tie-dye t-shirt and ponytail tried to lift his leg over the barricade. Three officers immediately intercepted the attempt, pushing the man back and tackling him to the ground. The crowd shifted its attention to the small melee while the priest stepped forward with sweaty palms and his finger on the trigger. The blonde saw the quivering arm reach out from the crowd. Her green eyes followed the arm down to the black barrel of a gun that was poking out from the end of the robe sleeve. Her eyes went wide as she released her hand from Stirling's elbow. He looked back at her curiously as she stepped away from him.

"What's the matter?" he asked.

She stood frozen and could not reply.

The priest squeezed the trigger and the gun went off. Robert Stirling's head snapped back and he fell to the ground.

"And I heard a loud voice in Heaven saying, now has come the salvation," O'Bannon screamed as he dropped the weapon at his feet. Another shot rang out and the priest gasped and stumbled forward over the wooden barricade. O'Bannon lay on the cold pavement clutching his bleeding chest as a swarm of police officers ran in his direction. The body of Robert Stirling lay just a few feet away. O'Bannon stared into the man's dead eyes and the priest's pale lips formed a smile. "And the great dragon was cast down," he whispered as he drifted off into darkness.

AUTHOR'S NOTE

Black Irish is a work of fiction that was influenced by facts. In an effort to bring authenticity to this story, I consulted dozens of sources including several important books. Much of the history of the Irish Republican Army and Bobby Sands was drawn from Tim Pat Coogan's valuable tome, *THE IRA,* and from David Beresford's *Ten Men Dead,* a blistering account of the tragic 1981 hunger strike.

If you would like more information on the United States Secret Service, the first book on your list should be *Standing next to History,* by former agent Joseph Petro.

Since this is merely a novel, many of the people and places come from my own imagination. For instance, you will not find a Catholic school for boys in the shadow of the Grey Abbey ruins. Any other mistakes that were unintentional are my fault alone.

I would like to acknowledge some very special people who helped make this project a reality. First, I'd like to thank my lovely wife Laura, who offered her love, patience and the keen insight I needed to keep the creative juices flowing. I'd also like to thank my beautiful daughters, Isabella and Mia for trying their best to play quietly while daddy worked. I'd like to thank my mother Diane Dodd, for being my biggest supporter and toughest critic. My thanks also go out to my brother Todd who offered sage advice along the way. And I offer my eternal gratitude to friends, Bob Stone, Tim White, Debbie Kim, Kasey Kaufman, Rob Gati and Frank Judge. All of whom read early drafts of this book and provided helpful tips and comments to improve the final product.

978-0-595-43080-2
0-595-43080-5

Printed in the United States
107020LV00004B/32/A